AN ALGONQUIN QUEST NOVEL

ALGONQUIN SPRING

Rick Revelle

DUNDURN
TORONTO

Project Editor: Jennifer McKnight
Editor: Allister Thompson
Design: Courtney Horner
Cover Design: Laura Boyle
Cover Image: TebNad/shutterstock.com
Printer: Webcom

Library and Archives Canada Cataloguing in Publication
Revelle, Rick, author
Algonquin spring : an Algonquin quest novel / Rick Revelle.

Issued in print and electronic formats.
ISBN 978-1-4597-3063-2 (pbk.).--ISBN 978-1-4597-3064-9 (pdf).--ISBN 978-1-4597-3065-6 (epub)

I. Title.

PS8635.E887A64 2015 jC813'.6 C2015-900543-4
C2015-900544-2

1 2 3 4 5 19 18 17 16 15

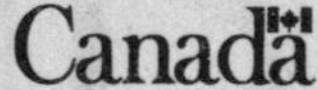

We acknowledge the support of the **Canada Council for the Arts** and the **Ontario Arts Council** for our publishing program. We also acknowledge the financial support of the **Government of Canada** through the **Canada Book Fund** and **Livres Canada Books**, and the **Government of Ontario** through the **Ontario Book Publishing Tax Credit** and the **Ontario Media Development Corporation**.

Care has been taken to trace the ownership of copyright material used in this book. The author and the publisher welcome any information enabling them to rectify any references or credits in subsequent editions.

J. Kirk Howard, President

The publisher is not responsible for websites or their content unless they are owned by the publisher.

Printed and bound in Canada.

Visit us at
Dundurn.com | @dundurnpress
Facebook.com/dundurnpress | Pinterest.com/dundurnpress

Dundurn
3 Church Street, Suite 500
Toronto, Ontario, Canada
M5E 1M2

Algonquin Spring *is an engaging read, holding my interest throughout. A hallmark of good historical fiction is accurate scholarship and to me this content demonstrated respect for cultural accuracy. The attempt to embed cultural teachings within a work that engages and entertains was, in my opinion, quite successful.*

WILLY BRUCE

Oshkaabewis

Aboriginal Veterans Autochtones

The modes of travel and the descriptions of the landscapes and vistas makes you want to go along for the ride. It gives the reader a glimpse of the appreciation of the lands that First Nations still occupy and interact with to this day, and shows how First Nations are still deeply intertwined with their lands through stories and adventures.

FRED MCGREGOR

Algonquin Storyteller and Pow Wow Emcee

As an Algonquin Traditional Elder, I can only commend you for your exceptional research and your writing creativity in bringing back our traditional orality to life again. My husband and I were amazed by your ability to bring to us as readers into a past that made us become spectators. We recognize that writing such a saga demands rigorous research of credible material and a cautious sense of reality in the fiction of your book.

ANNIE SMITH ST-GEORGES,

Traditional Algonquin Elder

ROBERT ST-GEORGES,

Métis Elder

Rick has provided a masterful description of survival, warfare, and relationships, both personal and tribal. His introduction of Glooscap, Crazy Crow, and others who connect with tribal legends and beliefs certainly tests the imagination. Once again, he has captured the culture of First Nations tribes in central Canada and the Maritimes.

Robert A. Thibeau

President, Aboriginal Veterans Autochtones

This book is very vivid and written with enough detail to make you believe you were there alongside the characters throughout the amazing journey. Written as a fiction novel, but enough research done to show a side of Aboriginal people that is never shown enough. What a wonderful book!

Silver Vautour–Wilmot

Member of the Listuguj Mi'gmaq Community

Undergrad at St. Mary's University

I found the story interesting. It actually brought me vividly back to a time in my people's past. I have often wondered what it must have been like before contact. I feel now I have been there.

Joe Wilmot

Mi'gmaq Language and Culture Coordinator

Listuguj Mi'gmaq Community

To the memory of
Shanawdithit, the last Beothuk, and
dedicated to my two Viking friends
Jørgen (the Dane) Jensen and
Edvard (the Norwegian) Strand.
Great friends and good Vikings.

AUTHOR'S NOTE

Life on Turtle Island in the late 1320s, when this story resumes, had yet to taste the horrors of the "European Invasion" that was only a short two hundred years away.

During the course of this book the reader is going to learn about an amazing jewel that very few Canadians know about, Anticosti Island (Natigòsteg, Forward Land in Mi'kmaq or Notiskuan, Where the Bears are Hunted, in Innu).

Anticosti Island is the largest island in the St. Lawrence River, the twentieth largest island in Canada and ninetieth largest in the world. It is one and a half times larger than Prince Edward Island. Before the Europeans came, the indigenous mammals there were the red fox, river otter, deer mouse, American otter, and black bear. There are no longer any American martins or black bears on the island. The introduction of white-tailed deer in 1896 was the start of the extinction of bear from the island as they competed for the same food. The deer population on the island is now over 160,000. Brook trout, Atlantic salmon, and American eel swim up the island's rivers, and grey and harbour seals inhabit the coastal regions.

The island is 7,900 square kilometres (3,050 square miles), with a population of 281 people (2006). The island receives three hundred centimeters (one hundred and twenty inches) of snow per year. Twenty-four rivers and streams drain the island, and there are two small lakes and a waterfall named Vauréal Falls that has a drop of 250 feet, which is 165 feet taller than Niagara Falls.

The reader will also read about the Beothuks of Newfoundland, an indigenous tribe that had made the island their home for eons. However, the coming of the Europeans was a death sentence for the Beothuk people. The last member of these island natives died in St. John's, Newfoundland, in June 1829. Her name was Shanawdithit. Along with her died the language of the Beothuk. As hard as I tried, I could not find enough of this ancient language to use it in this book. With the Algonquin, Mi'kmaq, Mohawk, and Norse languages I am able to introduce the reader to nouns in their vernacular. Sadly, I was not able to do this with the Beothuk language. I, as a writer and Native Canadian, consider this a tragedy beyond reproach. The Beothuk did not deserve to disappear from the annals of history like they did. This was such an immense atrocity and a sad and unnecessary ending to a human race that had lived in peace for all of its existence — until the coming of the Europeans.

...

I would like to thank my wife, Muriel, for helping with the editing and understanding my writing needs, and my son Andrew, who actually does read my books.

Todd Labrador, a Mi'kmaq boat maker from Nova Scotia, who gave me his time and knowledge.

Claudia Syllibi, from Truro, Nova Scotia.

Nikki Auten, a Mohawk linguistic.

As always, my Mohawk friend Ed Maracle, who is now becoming a great source of knowledge and information for me as a result of his efforts to learn about his ancestors and their language.

My friend Larry Porter, who has always been my go-to guy about all things East Coast and maritime, who I will write a book about if I live long enough.

William Arthur Allen, who knows everything about eels.

My special go-to person about hunting and fishing, Al Whitfield.

Above all, Anne Holley-Hime, who is living proof that behind any good author is a great editor!

Special thanks to my publishing editor, Allister Thompson, who had to put up with my firm stands on "Native Ways." In the end Allister did a wonderful job to make this a novel to be proud of.

As a writer, sometimes wonderful things just drop onto your lap during research, by luck or by chance. For me, finding the Listuguj Mi'gmaq Community website was one of those times. This talking dictionary of the spoken word for the Mi'kmaq language is a Canadian treasure. Any Native Nation that is thinking of preserving its language, I can only suggest you go to the site (http://www.mikmaqonline.org) and see what a wonderful job this community has done to conserve the language for their children and all who will follow in their footsteps eons from now.

I want to thank some special schoolchildren:

Janis Swaren's 2013 Grade 11 Native Voices class from QECVI, Kingston, Ontario.

Lindsay Scott's 2013/14 Grade 8 class from Fairfield Public School in Amherstview, Ontario.

Carolyn De Groot's extra special 2013/14 Grade 5/6 class from Perth Road Public School.

These pupils made me realize the power of the written word and amazed me with their understanding and exuberance for what I had written in my first book, *I Am Algonquin*.

Finally, I want the reader to realize that the Haudenosaunee, even though they might come across in this novel as the "bad guys," are not. They were no different from the Omàmiwinini, the Ouendat, the Mi'kmaq, or any of the other Nations talked about. They were just trying to survive in the same harsh environment as the others. The real problem was still two or three hundred years away.

The Haudenosaunee would become the most powerful military force east of the Mississippi River once the Prophet came and pulled the Five Nations together. The Haudenosaunee would hold this power until the might of the Anishinaabe (Ojibwa) came from the Lake Huron and Lake Superior areas in the 1600s and proved they were just as fierce and powerful.

West of the Mississippi at this time, a Nation called the Sahnish (Arikara) were the central power there. Sadly, though, in the late eighteenth century a smallpox epidemic wiped out 90 percent of the 30,000-strong tribe.

Before contact by the Europeans, there were hundreds of Nations in the Americas. A few of them were able to make alliances, but at times it could be a very harsh environment of regional warfare and subsistence.

This book takes place around 1330. During that era in Europe from 1315 to 1317, a great famine killed millions.

In May 1315, it started to rain. It did not stop anywhere in northern Europe until August. Next came the four coldest winters in a millennium. Two separate animal epidemics killed nearly 80 percent of northern Europe's livestock. Wars between Scotland and England, France and Flanders, and two rival claimants to the Holy Roman Empire destroyed all remaining farmland. After seven years, the combination of lost harvests, warfare, and pestilence would claim six million lives — one eighth of Europe's total population.

The Hundred Years War started in 1337. The Black Plague killed one third of the population of Europe from 1347 to 1351.

During that same time on Turtle Island, during what may have been as close to an "idyllic" era for the Native inhabitants as ever occurred in their past or future, there were no massive wars or pestilences. These horrors were still a couple hundred years in the future. Of course, there was starvation at times among tribes that may have come from crop failures and other problems, with the local animal population suffering generational dips in population. Disease was non-existent on a massive scale. Wars, well, they certainly did not ever encompass the continent like in Europe and Asia. There was always strife among neighbouring tribes, but never thousands of warriors marching across the countryside, burning, looting, pillaging, and murdering. During this time, in what would become Eastern Canada, an attacking force of four or five hundred would be a major undertaking in transportation and feeding. The most likely scenario would have seen a couple of hundred mobile warriors attacking an enemy to retake hunting grounds or for a mourning raid.

In the Americas, disease was unknown. Starvation, the elements, and regional warfare were the forces that took their toll on the people.

Pre-contact, there were 30 million Natives in South America and anywhere from two to 18 million in North America, depending on whose study you believe. By the seventeenth century, 50 percent had died from disease and warfare.

During the course of the book, you will notice that different nations of Natives converse among each other. The reader may question how they can do this if they talk different languages. For as long as Turtle Island has been here, different tribes have been able to express themselves through sign language and uttering the word(s) they are signing. Nations that have been allies for many years will start to understand each other's languages. When you read of different tribes talking to each other, picture them signing while they talk; it is the "universal language."

Finally, I would like to ask you, were the Native Americas discovered or conquered?

It had been six years since the battle at the Magwàizibò Sìbì (Iroquois River, now known as the Richelieu River) waterfall. Both the Haudenosaunee (Iroquois) and Omàmiwinini (Algonquin) had suffered irreplaceable losses. The Omàmiwinini had experienced huge losses of women, children, and warriors. The immediate family unit of Mahingan had lost a brother, Wàgosh, and his wife to the raid on the island (now Morrison Island) in the Kitcisìpi Sìbì (Ottawa River), which was the summer home of his Kitcisìpiriniwak tribe (People of the Great River), one of the eight Algonquin tribes of the Ottawa Valley.

Even though the Algonquins and their allies, the Ouendat (Huron), Nippissing, Wàbanaki (Abenaki), and Maliseet (Malècite), had defeated the Haudenosaunee at the waterfall, their own fatalities had caused great hardship among the tribes. Now, six years later, Mahingan, with his small family unit, is greeting a new spring on the lower part of the Kitcisìpi.

They had spent the winter on a riverbank on what is now the Rivière du Nord below a kishkàbikedjiwan (waterfall). Now near present-day Lachute, it was a day and a half by canoe from the Kitcisìpi (Ottawa River).

However, events that were taking place that spring 2,400 kilometers away, on what would become Newfoundland, would set in motion an adventure Mahingan's followers would recount in the glow of many fires for years to come.

1

WHO ARE THESE PEOPLE?

TALL MAN

"Shh, what is that?"

We stopped and listened to what sounded like a huge animal running through the underbrush, snapping small branches as it went. It was a bright and cold spring day, with large patches of snow that the sun had yet to reach in the depth of the woods. In the forest, sound seemed to travel in cascades when there was sharpness to the air, and whatever was running through the woods was blazing a trail of broken limbs, small trees, and making enough noise to announce its arrival akin to thunder and rain.

The community called me Tall Man. We identified ourselves as the Beothuk (the people). My name came naturally since I towered over my fellow tribesmen by a foot and a half. Standing over seven feet tall, I am an imposing figure, held in wonderment by all of the Beothuk.

Three companions and I had been hunting seals on the northwest part of our lands (present-day Newfoundland). The shore ice was starting to break up, but this did not hinder our ability to harpoon a couple of seals to take back to our winter village a day or so away.

The sounds were getting closer and we could make out the snorting of a caribou, plus what sounded like men yelling and dogs howling. Then, before we could react, the animal rushed out of a huge thicket in front of us, knocking over two of my travelling companions. Two arrows were sticking out of the animal's front withers, blood and phlegm spurted from its mouth, and a pack of five or six of what looked like wolves snapped at its legs, trying to hamstring it. As the animal neared me, I could see a look of total horror in its eyes. At that intense moment, a *whish, whish* sound passed my head. A spear embedded itself in the beast's neck, and with one dying bellow he spurted blood and saliva onto my face, took a few more steps, and fell with a sudden rush of air gusting from his body. The smell was horrendous, a mixture of rotting vegetation and gases.

Then, sudden silence. I had dropped my harpoon to wipe the assortment of stomach contents from my face. My two hunting companions that the beast had run over were slowly getting up; one was bleeding profusely from a neck wound that had occurred when the caribou sharply grazed him with his horn. Our fourth hunter was standing with his harpoon cocked back in a threatening manner.

Then, to our astonishment, three men unlike any we had seen before emerged from the thicket. Men with coloured hair, clothes the vividness of ripened berries, and weapons that were strange to us. One was holding what looked like a stick, but it gleamed in the sun. Another had a shaft with a sharp-looking grey shale head on it, but it was not shale. There we stood in a standoff over a dead caribou, one of our warriors slowly dying from a neck wound, me weaponless, and another on his hands and knees.

One of the strangers pointed at the animal and said a word I could not understand: "rheindyri," and then pointed at himself and said something else that gave me the impression he was saying the animal was his. Our companion with the harpoon was young and reckless, and I was concerned he was about to do something foolish that would result in sudden carnage. One of the yellow-haired men raised his weapon in anger, as if this unexpected meeting was wasting his time. Then he let out a bellow that caused my skin to rise.

At that precise moment, a harpoon sailed through the air and embedded itself in the man's neck, causing a sudden end to his yell and blood to spurt onto our friend on the ground.

Retribution was like summer lightning. The man with the sharp-looking weapon that gleamed in the sun took our young companion's throwing arm off with a mighty swing. I was just about to react when I heard an abrupt noise at my back, and a crushing blow to my head sent me into a world of darkness.

I do not know what woke me first, the bouncing that my body was enduring or the eye-burning stenches of urine, fish, and body odour of the men who were carrying me.

My head was throbbing and I was trying to resist, without much luck, losing consciousness. After awhile I was able to stay fully conscious.

Now I was able to understand the predicament that had befallen me and my fellow warriors. They had tied me up like a gutted animal on a stick, with my arms and legs bound by vines, and I was carried hanging from a stout sapling by two very smelly and strange-looking men.

I was able to look around and see only one other of my fellow tribesmen in the same predicament as myself. He was the eldest of our hunting party, one of the two men whom the wounded caribou had knocked down. His name was Whale Bone, a great hunter, but at this moment the fear in his eyes showed a weakness I had never seen in him before. Two men were carrying the slaughtered caribou in the same tied-up position as us. By the looks of things, this was not going to turn out well for my companion and me.

My hands and ankles were starting to chafe and bleed from the vines that bound them. The blood slowly dripped onto my skull and ran down my face, into my mouth. At least it was some liquid to moisten my lips, which were starting to dry out. My mouth was dry too, mostly because of the fear flowing through my body. I had a sudden urge to defecate and I did not know if I could resist the cramping of my intestines. I could not stand the pain, and with a sudden rush, my bowels emptied and spilled onto the ground, immediately causing the man at the end the stick to step into the excrement and slip. My last memory of that moment was a sudden foreign curse and my head hitting the ground, causing me to black out again.

It only seemed like I was out for a few minutes. This time, instead of my captors' smell awakening me, it was someone kicking me in the ribs, yelling "Skræling, Skræling," that woke me. The sudden pain and loud yelling caused me to sit up with a cold chill running through my body. My wrists and ankles were still raw and bleeding from being carried. With all four of my appendages still fastened, I was totally incapacitated and defenceless.

I opened my eyes and looked at my tormentor. The sun was setting behind him and the evening rays fell upon him, lighting his hair like a bonfire. His locks were a bright red, with facial hair to match. It was the colour of the red ochre that our people customarily painted themselves with.

Who were these people with the colours of the sun in their hair? They had hair on their faces, which I had never seen before on any of my kind. Their weapons were different from any I had ever encountered, and they were very efficient killers, from what I had seen in the forest.

My assailant untied me and gave me another kick in my ribs, and I got the hint he wanted me up. Whale Bone was standing behind me, whimpering and gagging. The poor man was going to die of fright before these strangers could do anything to him.

"Øysten," said Visäte, "why did you bring these men to our village? Look at them, they paint themselves in taufr (red ochre). They look like fools. These red men are of no use to us. Kill them!"

"We need them, Visäte, as þræls (slaves) to take over the oars for the two men we have lost in this forsaken land, Æirik the Elder who died after we arrived and Frømund, whom these Red Skrælings stuck with a harpoon. We probably would have killed the two of them but Floki sneaked up behind the giant there and rattled him in the head. Bior cut the arm off the youngest one, who bled out and died along with another of the weaklings who had been gored by the wounded rheindyri. The old one just curled up and started to puke his guts out. Not much sport in killing either of them in those circumstances."

"Well, feed them then, Øysten. We need them healthy for where we are going. We leave tomorrow for the island in the mists that my brother Edvard told us about when he came this route. It is essential that we catch enough lax (salmon) and obtain some björn (bear) meat for our journey home, plus the blessing of Óðinn (Odin) for our crossing. The sooner we leave this land, the easier I will feel. There has to be more of these red warriors and we cannot afford to lose any more of our men for naught. This land has nothing to offer except death and harsh elements."

I turned and looked at Whale Bone and said, "My friend, did you understand what these men were saying?"

"No, Tall Man, it was all just noise that I could not recognize," he replied.

"Strange, I could understand every word they said!" I replied.

Whale Bone looked at me oddly and his face twisted. "Tall Man, something out of the ordinary is happening; the Great Spirit may be preparing you for a journey. I hope he has plans for me also."

They gave us a strange vessel that was as hard as a rock. In it were a broth and chunks of caribou and our seal meat. We had not eaten in nearly a day. Whale Bone and I dipped our hands into the broth to grab the chunks of meat and just as quickly pulled them out. The broth was very hot and my fingers were throbbing. Whale Bone had popped a chunk of meat into his mouth and immediately spat it back out; he was gasping and spitting the hot residue out of his mouth.

Visäte turned to Øysten and said, "They don't even know enough to let the food cool down. How do you expect them to handle an oar? Kill them now and get it over with!"

2

THE ISLAND

EARLY THE NEXT MORNING, they took Whale Bone and me to a boat unlike any we had seen before. It was five to six times larger than one of our canoes and had eight sets of paddles on each side.

As we started to get aboard this vessel, we at once realized how many of the strange men there were. I counted over thirty, but I knew that I was missing some. They loaded weapons, shields, robes, and remnants of the caribou and seal onto the craft and then sat down on a wooden plank behind a huge paddle that protruded through a hole in the side of this huge boat.

Our captors led us toward the middle of the craft and put us behind one of these paddles. They then placed our hands on the wooden shaft.

As soon as we sat down, we could feel the boat start to move. About half the crew was pushing the craft out into the water, and as we felt it leaving the shore, the men who were pushing jumped into the vessel, accompanied by great shouts from all of the strangers.

"Øysten," said Visäte, "sigla (set sail) for the suður (south). Raise the sail and let us see how far the wind will take us today, saving the strength of our men. I want to reach this island of plenty in six days, if Njörðr (the God of sea and wind) looks kindly on us. When the wind dies, I want our men to be ready to row. With sixteen sets of oars and thirty-two men on them at all times, we will make good time. We have eight extra men, which will allow a break every four hours for the rowers. The Skrælings are to have no break for rowing. Keep them at their stations at all times. Feed them when the men eat, every six hours. They can rest when the wind blows. For now let the men relax and make sure they are fed and have water."

Whale Bone and I sat and held onto the wooden shaft, afraid to move. The damp ocean air made us shiver and the stench of the men around us made us gag. One of them brought us raw seal meat to eat and water. The men who were at the oars ate and then started to fall to sleep. We also noticed eight men lying between the two sets of oars, fast asleep. One who appeared to be the leader stood at the rear of the boat and seemed to steer it with a long-handled shaft. The boat glided through the water with no effort. It looked as if the only power that moved it was of a large piece of skin fastened to a tree without branches. The piece had striped colours running from top to bottom. When the wind blew, it made the skin bulge and propelled the boat along at a speed faster than our people could paddle a canoe. This continued for a long time until the sun started to drop toward the horizon. The skin lost its bulge and four of the strangers started to pull on ropes that dropped the skin lifeless. When finished, the leader yelled, "Rôdr (row)," and all of a sudden the men surrounding us started to pull on the large paddles. We looked around and the man who had kicked me in the ribs after my capture came up to us and yelled the same word.

I looked at Whale Bone and said, "Imitate what these strangers are doing."

After we did this for a long time, our hands started to bleed, so I tore off strips of my clothing, wrapped them tightly around my hands, and told Whale Bone to do the same. This absorbed the blood and eased the friction on our skin.

I watched the leader, who stood at the back of the boat with the long piece of wood in his hand. He seemed to steer the vessel using a piece of board floating in a bowl of water and looking from the bowl to the sun. During the night, he used the stars as a guide.

We were always in sight of land and as darkness began to fall, the leader, the one they called Visäte, started to manoeuvre the boat toward the land. We came ashore at the mouth of a small stream. Within minutes they had left the boat and had fires going and shelter made. One of them tied our legs together and tied our hands loosely to the wooden bench we had been sitting on. They then dropped the large skin down the length of the boat and threw some skins over us for warmth. This was to be our place for the night. There were no guards since we really had no place to go if we did decide to escape. Away from our island and in a land of people who were enemies of the Beothuk, we were safer with the strangers, so far.

Before long one of our captors brought us water and the same broth they had given us after our capture. This time we let it cool before attempting to eat.

Keeping close for body warmth, we both slept fitfully. At the first sign of morning, the outsiders came aboard and untied us. We just reversed the way we had sat the previous day and rowed out toward the open water. This big vessel could go forward or backward without turning the ship around. They accomplished this by switching our seating direction.

When the rising sun started to warm us, the winds came up. The strangers then raised the huge skin and lifted the big paddles. We were speeding along at a good pace when something happened that I had to see to believe. The paddles were almost three times the length of me, and now these strange men were using them to run races. With the crew holding the paddles straight out and keeping them firm, we watched as men took turns racing along the length of the boat on the shafts, turning and racing back, urged on by the cheering of their fellow warriors. As they ran along the length of the boat, I could see the paddles bend as they stepped on them. There were times when I was sure one of them would fall off into the ocean, but they always regained their balance and continued. After a while they became bored and started to run backwards, which was even more harrowing to watch. When they were going backward, to regain their balance they would flap their arms like a large bird. It definitely was amusing to watch them, and amazingly, during most of the afternoon, very few fell overboard.

After three nights of us staying on the boat tied up, they must have decided that they had came far enough away from our lands that they did not need to bind us on the vessel anymore. For the remainder of the trip we came ashore in the evening with them and slept by the fire. True, we were not going to try to escape just yet. We would pick our spot when we had a good chance of avoiding recapture and death at the hands of other enemies.

On the afternoon of the eighth sunrise, the boat approached a forested island. The strangers seemed to know where we were going and they kept the shoreline in sight until we came to the mouth of a river (the present-day Vauréal River). The boat went ashore and everyone stepped onto dry land. Whale Bone and I approached the river, stunned by what we observed. The water was teeming with fish. We now knew why these men came here. They would fill their boat with fish and head to their home. This was where we would have to make our escape. Our future with these strangers would take a turn for the worse, one way or another. We would have to bide our time. If we took flight here and hid, we knew that at least we would not starve to death. However, leaving this island and returning home would be nearly impossible. The alternative was definitely worse with our captors. I figured it would probably take five to eight suns to catch, cut up, smoke, and store these fish for what they needed for the voyage home. Enough time to plan our escape.

"Øysten," said Visäte, "our friend Edvard gave us excellent instructions to find this island and river. He was right when he said we would find the river teeming with fish, and with the help of Njörðr, we made it. Get the men to work along with those Skrælings, catching, cleaning, and smoking the lax. After six or seven days, we will send the Skrælings out with three or four men to hunt björn. This will give us enough food to get us home."

Whale Bone and I were both aching from having to row every day. Our hands were almost raw from the handles. We were able to find some dandelions and get enough juice from them to spread on our hands to help heal them. We would do this at the end of the day to enable the healing process while we slept.

For the next few days, we waded into the cold water and made fish weirs to trap the fish. Once the barrier was finished, the strangers took their spears, and standing in the river they impaled the fish and threw them onto the bank. It was our job to scale and gut and cut off the head and tail. The strangers had six dogs, which eagerly wolfed down all the fish guts, all the while snapping at the gulls that were also enjoying the feast, causing both sets of scavengers to be splattered with blood and entrails. After a while the growling of the dogs and screeching of the gulls dulled our senses.

The next step in the process was to cut the fish into strips, hanging them on racks made to suspend the fish over smoking fires. This dried the fish so it could be stored. After three days of this, our muscles were starting to ache from the constant scaling, gutting, and slicing. Our arm muscles were starting to twitch uncontrollably and then cramp. Our hands were becoming soft and wrinkly from working with the wet fish, causing our rowing wounds to reopen and bleed, mixing with the blood of the fish. To try to rid our bodies of the smell, we made sure to bathe every day, above where all the spearing was taking place. Grabbing handfuls of sand, we scrubbed our bloody bodies and clothes, rinsing sand, blood, and guts off by splashing ourselves with water. The days were not yet warm enough to please us, causing our bodies to chill after the experience each day, and so, as soon as we finished, we hurried to the fire to warm ourselves. The strangers, though, never seemed to clean themselves. Most of the time their smell made us gag. It was horrendous! Their breath was even worse — the smell of decaying meat, fish, and whatever else they had eaten. They also seemed to collect a lot of food in their beards, especially the fish eggs that they obtained by holding the fish up and squirting them out of the squirming body.

The strangers left Whale Bone and me alone, mostly. Occasionally one of us received a cuff to the head or a quick kick if they thought we were not putting enough effort into our duties. However, whenever I stood up straight they stepped back and showed me sudden respect because of my towering height. Whale Bone, on the other hand, was subject to more abuse. They seemed to take delight in tormenting him whenever the urge came upon them.

Food and water were plentiful, and they let us eat our fill of fish each day. The sea birds were starting to lay eggs and we were able to obtain some, a welcome break from fish. We also used the eggs to mix with the red clay to cover our bodies in red, a sacred colour to us, and it kept the stinging insects away.

Because we did most of the gutting of the fish that the strangers' dogs liked to eat, they took a fondness to Whale Bone and me and slept near us each night.

On the morning of the fifth day, I could see a group of the strangers talking, and one of them pointed at us.

"Hælgi, pick three men, a couple of the rakkis (dogs), and take the Skrælings also. We need a björn to finish our larder," said Visäte.

"Käre, Øpir, and Yngvar, bring the bleikr rakki (white dog) and blakkr rakki (black dog). Today we hunt björn! May Ullr (the God of skill and the hunt) guide us," declared Hælgi.

Whale Bone and I looked at each other; it seemed we were going into the forest to hunt. If there was to be any chance of escape at all, this would be our only opening. Once we got into that boat again, we were doomed. I was doubtful we could get close enough to anything to kill it. Any animal could smell these men coming from a long way off.

We kept to the banks of the river, totally ignoring the salmon swimming up it. My guess was that the men were after a bear, only because they had not headed into the forest. With this many fish, if there were bears around they would be gorging themselves after a winter's sleep. Hungry and irritable, they would not be an easy kill.

We accompanied the four strangers armed with bows, quivers of arrows, and spears. Two of them had a short-handled weapon like what had taken young Standing Man's arm off; the other had a longer version almost the length of his body. He carried if over his shoulder.

"Hælgi," asked Käre, "if we do not come across any björn, can we kill these Skrælings for sport?"

"Käre, I do not think that would be wise. You would have to answer to Visäte when we got back. The punishment would definitely outweigh the sport that you would have slaying these Red Men. He wants them as þrælls."

When the sun was higher, the small group stopped and two of the strangers waded into the river to spear fish, throwing them onto the bank at our feet. We still had the knives they had given us and we gutted the salmon while the other two prepared a fire. The men in the river stopped after about twelve fish and by the time we had them cleaned, the fire was going. They gave us each two sticks, on which we skewered the fish and thrust into the flames to cook. The dripping oils from the fish caused the fire to snap and rise. They had used cedar bows to help with the fire, and this caused an aromatic smell along with a smudge smoke. If there were any inhabitants on this island, this fire's smell and smoke would unquestionably warn them of our presence. These strangers were either stupid or had no fear for their safety because of their belief in their combative powers.

After eating we continued on, and toward evening I began to notice a reddening of the river's water. Within moments, the dogs started to growl.

"Øpir," said Hælgi, "go ahead and see what bothers the dogs."

The strangers had not noticed the colour of the river. I reached instantly for my knife sheath and felt a sense of protection. Something was about to happen and Whale Bone's and my immediate future would depend on the outcome.

Øpir came back with a look that told me whatever was ahead did not instill fear in him. He was smiling.

"Hælgi," said Øpir, "there are about six or seven Skrælings gutting a björn by the river. This is too easy. We will kill them and get our björn."

"Okay," said Hælgi. "Käre, you stay here with these two and Øpir, Yngvar, and I will handle what's up ahead."

The three strangers had just finished talking when the returning one screamed. I looked toward him and saw a knife protruding from his right leg. Then what looked like a child swinging a club at the man. The wounded man turned quickly and hit the little person with his shield with a bone-crunching sound. The recipient of the shield strike flew threw the air with blood flying from his head and landed in the river near the edge of the riverbank.

Almost immediately, several warriors came hurtling to our position. With the nearest stranger to me distracted by what was in front of us, I reached for my knife and rushed up behind him, plunging the knife into the side of his neck. Blood immediately spurted from the wound. He turned and with a look of amazement in his eyes opened his mouth to say something, but all that came out was a gush of vomit and blood.

Whale Bone grabbed one of man's weapons and rushed the nearest stranger. The man heard footsteps behind him and turned, swinging the short-handled club with the blade on it. He caught Whale Bone in the ribs and I heard his bones breaking before his screams. Whale Bone dropped to the ground, badly wounded. The stranger then turned to meet the oncoming rush of bodies. The screaming of men, barking of dogs, and smashing of bones were deafening.

I watched as one of the strangers hooked the leg of his attacker with the long axe-like weapon. He pulled the man off balance to him and then embedded a knife in the man's eye. I reached down and grabbed the remaining weapon of the man I had killed. It was similar to the one used on Whale Bone. Grasping it, I was about to enter the battle when I heard a loud moan. Looking in the direction of the sound, I saw what I had originally thought was a child floating away in the river current, but still alive. I immediately waded in and grabbed him by the scruff of the neck, dragging him ashore. He looked up at me thankfully and it was then I realized that he had all the features of an adult but not the size. His face was bloody and torn from where the shield had hit him.

Seeing he was all right for now, I looked up to where the clash was taking place. I was stunned! Never had I ever seen so much blood from anything except a hunting kill.

3

MI'KMAQ

BLOOD. THE RIVER AND ground were red with it. Two of the warriors that had been skinning the bear were battling with the last remaining stranger, taking turns striking the man with stone clubs. The man was on his knees and every strike caused his blood to fly into the air. One warrior hit him. Then he would turn to face him, and the other would strike. His right arm was broken and useless; in his left he held a weapon but could not strike because he was so weak. Finally, one of the antagonists was able to strike the stranger in the back of the head. His skull cracked open like an acorn and he fell forward.

The two young warriors stood motionless, covered with blood and gasping to catch their breath. When they quit panting, they inhaled and let out a cry, "Yo, yo, yo, yo." It echoed throughout the river valley.

I looked around. Whale Bone was dead, plus all the strangers and five of the native warriors. Some were missing heads, others arms. It was total mayhem.

The young men quickly realized I was a friend. They motioned to me to collect what weapons I needed. I removed a quiver of arrows and bow from one of the strangers, plus a shield and one of the weapons that was similar to our axes but much more lethal. I had watched two of my people be slain with this weapon and concluded that I could make it work for me. The stranger had carried this weapon most of the time in his hand, but he also had a leather belt with an open-ended piece attached that the shaft of the weapon fit into. I took it also.

The warriors looked at me, pointed to the bear, and said, "Mui'n."

I was able to understand some of their words with their sign. They wanted to finish skinning the bear. The animal was huge, and we set upon it with a nervous haste. It did not take long to separate the pelt from the meat. Then they took about two thirds of the animal, wrapped the meat in the pelt, tied it securely with vines, and went into the woods. There they walked to an old tree. One of the young men climbed up with a long vine. Once there, he tied one end to a branch and tossed the other end to the boy below. That one tied the bundle to it and his partner then hoisted it up. When it was firmly secured, the young warrior climbed down the tree and we went back to the river. There they retrieved the remaining meat and the front paws, wrapping it in a large deerskin.

They then motioned for me to help with the burial of their friends.

After I finished digging the graves with the two young warriors, I went and recovered the little person, who was still groggy, raised him onto my shoulders with his feet on either side of my neck, and followed the two warriors into the forest and toward my future fate.

We walked at a quick pace in total silence. The only noise came from the rustling of the trees, the sound of our moccasined feet, our breathing, and the dogs panting. I think the only reason these dogs followed me was because of the kindness Whale Bone and I had shown them during the fish cleaning. In the sky I would hear the occasional crow or jay. As we progressed deeper into the woods, following a warrior's trail, there appeared on the route more snow and ice that the sun had not yet been able to melt away, making the path very slippery. To keep from falling, I shuffled my feet on the glare ice and tried to keep my weight evenly distributed.

However, on a small downhill turn, my left foot shot upwards over my head. Weapons flew, and down I came with a resounding thud. I landed on my left forearm and elbow, causing my head to snap back, but I was able to control it and keep it from cracking against the solid core of ice underneath my falling body. Everyone stopped and turned to look. The spear that I was carrying was hanging in a small tree and upon contact with the ground, some of the arrows in my quiver exploded into the surrounding landscape. The sudden impact of me hitting the ground, causing an impulsive wrenching of my neck, gave me an instant headache. I looked up to see everyone standing in stunned silence and then they all started to laugh. I think really the most comical part of it was when the Little Person came back and offered his hand to pull me up. He had fallen from my shoulders and skidded back onto the path, bowling over the white dog, both of them landing in a yelping, yelling tangle. It took me a few minutes to pick up everything strewn around on the ground and in the trees. The Little Person motioned that he would walk for the time being, and grabbing the scruff of the white dog for balance, we continued on our way.

The sun began to drop below the tree line at about the same time as we were approaching a small stream. The two warriors motioned for us to stop. One of them started a fire. The other found a dead birch tree and made a cooking pot and cups with the bark, using pine gum to seal them with a vine strung through the pot for a handle.

He filled the pot with water, threw some cedar leaves into it, and hung it over the fire from a forked stick he had shoved into the ground. The other young man cut a big chunk of bear meat and put it on a spit. He then cut off another two strips and threw them to the dogs.

While they were doing this, I tended to the wounds of the little person. I dipped some moss into the boiling water and washed his wound. It was not deep, more of a huge scrape that had removed a lot of skin. The bleeding had stopped and I used the juice from some dandelions that I had picked and smeared it on the moss. Once I had covered the moss in the white juice, I dabbed it on the wound and then covered the wound with mud taken from the stream. This would help his wound to heal. I quickly made another boiling pot and threw some birch bark into it to boil. This tea would help my small friend's head to clear; I was quite sure it was pounding from the force of the shield that had struck him.

During the time I was tending to him, he asked me my name. My people call me Tall Man. He looked at me and smiled. Pointing at himself, he said his name, "Apistanéwj" (Marten).

While we ate, I learned the names of the two young warriors. They were cousins. The taller one called himself Matues (Porcupine) and the short stocky one was E's (Clam). They both still wore a covering of blood from the battle, but neither had any wounds. They said this was their first battle and the reason they survived unscathed was that as youngsters they had always practised fighting with the other children back to back, always watching out for each other and each forever ready to come quickly to the aid of the other. When it was for real, they said it worked and saved their lives.

E's told me that Apistanéwj was a Puglatm'j (A Little Person). On this island, they lived in caves near the big waterfall. They had survived on this island for all time and were the guardians. They were tricksters and good hunters. They tried to avoid battle because of their size. However, if cornered, they would fight with extreme ferocity and cunning.

The Mi'kmaq, which he and Matues were, sent their young warriors who were turning sixteen here for one purpose: to kill a mui'n and start their entrance into manhood. To get here they had to travel two to three days depending on wind, tides, and weather across the ocean from their home in Gespe'g. With them each year came one older matnaggewinu (warrior) plus the young matnaggewinu who had struck the first blow on the mui'n the preceding year. These men only came as guides for the crossing. They stayed with the canoes while the young warriors went into the island for the kill.

"There is one other person who had always come on the trip," Matues said. "We call her grandmother; she cooks and looks after everyone."

E's then said, "When the mui'n is killed we always give an offering to the Puglatm'j for allowing us to hunt in their territory. They always send one young matnaggewinu to hunt with us, which was Apistanéwj. We keep enough to eat for the trip back and the front paws to prove we made the kill. All the participants divide the claws up among themselves. Thus, only eight young men receive the honour of selection for this rite of passage. That way each warrior gets a claw. If the bear hasn't lost any, then the two that guided us also each get one."

"This hunt has presented many problems," said Matues. "We have lost six brothers and have battled the Eli'tuat (Men with Beards)."

"Some years," said Matues, "no one returns. The ocean crossing claims them. It is a quest that holds many dangers. There have also been years when the mui'n has killed warriors, but it is rare when the Eli'tuat are encountered."

"Yes, Matues," said E's, "they were problems that are over. However, we have a big one now: Apistanéwj. We cannot leave him here because his people do not come to this side of the island and he is too frail to go back on his own. Their warrior always stayed with the offering that would have hung in the same tree since the pact was made between our two Nations. The Puglatm'j would then come a couple days after we left to collect both their hunter and the meat. This time, though, we could not leave him in the shape he was. That was why we hung the skin and meat in that tree, as our people have always done. The Eli'tuat will search for their hunting party in another day or two. Leaving Apistanéwj there would have been too dangerous in this situation. The Puglatm'j will stay hidden. They are no match for the Eli'tuat."

"Tall Man," said E's, "you will have to take over the responsibility for Apistanéwj. It is forbidden for the Mi'kmaq to bring one back to Gespe'g. However, you were the one who saved him, carried him out, and tended his wounds, so now you are his guardian until such time that he returns to Natigòsteg (Forward Land). In essence, it is you bringing him back, not us."

We decided that there was no need for anyone to stay awake for a watch tonight. Anyone who woke during the night was to tend the fire. Looking over at the two dogs, I chuckled to myself. There, curled up between them and fast asleep, was the Little One. I had trouble sleeping, homesick for my village, and now I was responsible for Apistanéwj. What next?

4

WATER VOYAGE

ØYSTEN LOOKED TOWARD the forest from their makeshift shore camp.

"Visäte," he said, "it has been a day and a half and our hunters are not back. They have probably had a successful hunt and are struggling to get back with the meat. Take some men, find them, and help them get back to camp. I have had enough of this barren island and want to head for home."

"Okay, Øysten, we will go, lighten their load, and return soon."

Two days later the searchers came back.

"Øysten," exclaimed Visäte, "our men were in a battle. There were no survivors and whoever killed them took all their weapons. We buried them there but without weaponry for them to take to Valhalla. All we hope is that Óðinn will take pity on them and know that they died in battle, but had no control over their weapons stolen after their deaths. Øysten, I must tell you, though, the whole time we were there burying our dead I felt we were being watched."

"We leave now; this is a place of bad omens!"

Tall Man

I had awakened several times during the night to keep the fire going. Finally, the warmth of the flames relaxed me enough for sleep to arrive, and I drifted off into my dreams. It seemed like I was only asleep for a couple of minutes when I awoke to the smell of boiling cedar tea and bear meat. After rising, I went into the forest. Finding a tree that had fallen, I was able to sit down and overhang my backside, relieving myself. After using some moss and leaves to clean up, I returned to our small camp.

Everyone sat in silence drinking the hot brew to ward off the early morning chill. The bear meat was still very fresh, and whenever I took a bite, the juice dripped down my chin onto the ground, where the black dog licked up the minute drippings and then stood looking at me with great anticipation for more. I watched as Apistanéwj took a bite of his meat, chewed it, and reached into his mouth, taking a portion out and giving it to the white dog.

After everyone had eaten and drunk their fill, the two Mi'kmaq boys motioned for us to follow. It was still early spring and there was frost on the ground. Again, I would have to watch my footing and because of my height keep from hitting my head on low-slung branches. We maintained a quick pace, and Apistanéwj surprisingly was able to stay with us.

I realized that this trek to the opposite shore and the Mi'kmaq boats was bringing me to safety; however, I was travelling farther away from my birthplace and my people.

The trail became perilous from the iciness and the incline. The four of us had to make sure that we constantly shuffled our feet on the icy trail. Too much weight on a forward foot would cause us to lose our balance and possibly fall. We approached a small hill, and because of the hoarfrost, we had to walk along the side of the trail, where we could grasp the trees to keep our balance.

Apistanéwj had no trouble keeping up to us since the pace was very slow, and whenever he thought he was about to slip, he would grab on to one of the dogs. He had named them Na'gweg (Day) and Tepgig (Night) from the Mi'kmaq language.

At the crown of the hill, we stepped one by one back onto the footpath. E's was the last to near the crest, and being a little too anxious to stay up with us, he stepped too soon from the safety of the trees. He was not quite at the top, and when he made his move to the path, he started to slide backward down the hill. Trying to stop his momentum, he turned sideways, but all that accomplished was spreading his legs until they stretched out as far as they could go. We all stood wide-eyed, anticipating his next move. Afraid that if he fell he would end up where he began, E's steered himself in slow motion toward the side, until he was able to clasp a tree stopping his downward slide. E's had ended up halfway down the hill. He had never shown any sign of panic, just a big smirk when he finally saved himself from further embarrassment. He looked up at us and started to laugh, and we all joined in as he made his way up. This time he did not cross over until he was well clear of the ridge.

All he said was, "That was an odd feeling."

As we continued our walk, Apistanéwj astounded me by talking to me in my language. I asked him how he knew my tongue.

"Tall Man," he said, "my people know all and see all." With that, he started to tell me about himself and his family group, all this without having to use any sign language and with me understanding every word. Was this another sign from the Great Spirit?

"Tall Man," he said, "we have been here since the beginning of time. Our people came over from Mi'kmaq Land with the help of the Mi'kmaq animals. Migjigi (Turtle) and Giwnig (Otter) brought the men; the women were delivered on the wings of Gitpu (Eagle)."

"The Creator then asked my people to be the Guardians of the Island, to watch over Mui'n and only take from Mui'n enough of his fur and meat to stay warm and to survive.

"Wookwiss (Fox) and Apistanéwj (Marten) also came over on Migjigi's back. However, there was no room for Lentug (Deer) and Tia'm (Moose). Mui'n had come to the Island many years before on the back of Bootup (Whale).

"My people have always lived in the caves by the big waterfall. We became adept at fishing and hunting seals. We only hunted Mui'n in the fall when they were fat from summer foraging. We have never slain a Mui'n that had cubs with her.

"After the Mi'kmaq first came to our shores, we made a pact with them. We allowed them to slay one male every spring. They were able to keep half the meat and the front paws. The pelt and everything else came back to us. They were happy with the agreement since it gave them a safe haven for their young warriors to prove themselves.

"The Mi'kmaq, though, had earned this privilege and our respect because the first time that they came to the Island they stumbled upon a battle between my people and a band of Inuit. The Mi'kmaq took our side and drove off our attackers. They saved many Puglatm'j that day. The Inuit had come upon my great-grandfather and some hunters out in the open along one of the rivers as they were fishing. They had not posted any forward guards and the Inuit surprised them. The Mi'kmaq warriors came upon the battle shortly after it had begun. They were able to drive off the attackers, but not before my people had lost three warriors and one woman in battle.

"The Inuit had always come to Natigòsteg to hunt seals, but they had never before ventured inland to hunt or fish, so we had no reason to fear them. For our part we never showed ourselves to them, always watching them, keeping hidden from view.

"One spring the Inuit came to hunt seals. I was only eight or nine summers old, but I still vividly remember the carnage that transpired. I, with my father, brother, and a few warriors, were out hunting seals along the shoreline. One of the men ahead motioned for us to go into the forest as he was running back to us.

"Inuit," he said, "but there are also Innu and they are killing each other along the shore and on the ice floes.

"Tall Man, we kept to the woods, staying well out of sight. Our small number approached where the massacre was taking place. There were maybe a dozen Inuit but over twenty Innu and the Innu were holding the upper hand. I counted seven arrows in one Inuit and three spears in another. The Innu were hacking the Inuit with their clubs and goring them with their spears. When it was done the ice was blood red and the Innu were stripping the clothes off their enemies and then hacking off arms and legs and throwing the limbs into the ocean.

"With one of the captured Inuit, they stripped him and staked him on his back. Then the Innu took turns grabbing hot embers from a fire they had made for the upcoming torture they had planned. They put the coals on the man's testicles, eyes, into his mouth, up his nose, and on his chest. The Inuit never screamed or made a sound, but you knew he was in immense pain.

"We left then, not being able to watch any longer and with the memory of the torture etched into our minds. It was from that moment on we realized our people had to always be vigilant whenever we were near the shorelines of the island. However, this kept the Inuit away from the island for many years. Rarely did the Inuit or Innu come into the interior since there were no deer or moose, though when they did they kept to the river banks looking for feeding bears.

"The island receives huge amounts of snow and the summers are rainy, not the type of weather that encouraged either of the two tribes to settle on the island.

"The Puglatm'j totals no more than one hundred people, with only about thirty warriors. The rest are women and children. We were dispersed into three bands with an elder in each band responsible for all decisions and to settle any differences among the band.

"My father will be looking for the Mui'n offering and for me. When he cannot find me he will assume that I died in the battle, but being unable able to find my body will puzzle him, knowing that the Mi'kmaq have never taken one of us from the Island.

"I am convinced that if you had not pulled me from the river when you did, I would have drowned. I was going in and out of consciousness. Tall Man, I see in the future many adventures for us."

Matues turned and told us we would soon be at the campsite. We then came to a steep, ice-covered hill. Apistanéwj held onto the dogs and went down first. The sure-footed Eli'tuat dogs reached the bottom without incident. E's and Matues motioned for me to go ahead. I took two steps then realized I was in trouble. Stepping to the wrong side of the trail, I soon realized I was out of reach of a nearby tree to sustain my balance. With only the option of stepping to my left, I misjudged the distance, and before I could react I was sliding on my rump, hitting a projecting stone that then knocked me onto my back. Saved from tumbling over a large embankment by going crotch first into a large birch tree, my pain was sudden and intense. In the process I lost a chunk of skin from my rear end and upper back. This time there was no laughing, just gasps of relief that I had not gone over the chasm. Two falls on this trip so far and no broken bones — luck was with me.

Matues reached out with his spear and I able to grasp it and safely weave down the rest of the hill. Once I was there, Apistanéwj attended to my wounds. We watched as E's and Matues safely descended.

Our small group continued for the rest of the day with no further incidents. The fragrant smell of spring from the forest is one of the many joys of life. The newly budding trees gave off an aroma to announce that they had awakened from their long winter dormancy. Along with the warming of the daylight hours, there came a sense of security in the coming days. Next to this aromatic smell, I could now detect an odour of sea salt.

E's and Matues stopped in the trail ahead and turned to Apistanéwj and me, saying, "We are very close to our campsite. A tia'm (moose) call will warn our people we are coming. Because there are no tia'm on the island, this signal is always used here."

E's bellowed out the call and received one from the distance in return. In a few minutes we walked from the forest into a small clearing a stone's throw from the ocean. There beside a campfire were two warriors and an old woman. They stood as we entered their campsite. As Apistanéwj and I entered into view, their eyes bulged and they seemed to gasp for air. The elder one asked where the rest of the young men were and E's told him about the battle with the Eli'tuat. The man then looked at my small companion and me and said, "You lose six warriors and bring me back a Megwe'g Jenu (Red Giant) and a Puglatm'j?"

"Jilte'g (Scar), they helped us and contributed during the battle. The one we identify as Tall Man, that you call a Red Giant, killed one of the enemies with just a fishing knife, and the little one warned us of the attack and was the first to draw blood. They are warriors."

"Well, we have three boats and barely enough to man two of them. Now we are going to have to watch for the big Eli'tuat boat, as they will probably come through the channel on the way to their homelands. These two big dogs, are they for eating or are we to load them also?" asked Jilte'g. "If we run into any bad weather with four and a half men plus an old woman we will be lucky to survive. Grandmother and this dwarf will both have to take the place of young warriors. I think we would have better luck to try to walk back. Hopefully the Red Giant can take the place of five men."

Matues then turned to me and said, "Now that you have met Jilte'g, let me introduce you to the rest of our small group. This is Ta's'ji'jg (Little Bit) and Grandmother, who is also known as Nukumi. She is our provider and life teacher."

Nukumi looked at me and winked, making me smile. She then looked at Apistanéwj and the two dogs and stated, "I have been waiting for all of you for a long time. Come and eat."

I looked at my small friend and asked, "Any idea what that was all about?"

Apistanéwj answered, "No, not yet, Tall Man, although I have a feeling someone has chosen a path for us."

Nukumi then set about making us supper. She boiled a big birch container of cedar tea for us to drink and restore our energy. Then she wrapped clams and lobster in seaweed, cooking them over a fire pit. The food was delicious and we ate the seaweed along with the meat cooked inside it.

After we finished eating, Jilte'g rose and said, "I am going to go and see if I can hear the Sabawaelnu sing. Nukumi, I need some tmawei (tobacco) as an offering to keep them happy."

Nukumi reached into a pouch around her waist and gave him a small amount of what they called tmawei.

I looked at E's and asked, "What is a Sabawaelnu?"

"Tall Man," he replied, "they are Halfway People who are half human and half fish. They sing to elders and children, but when they stop it means there is a storm approaching. If you give them a small gift of tobacco, they will be your friends, although if you insult or slight them they will bring a storm upon you. Jilte'g needs to know when the good weather will be so that we can safely travel back home to Gespe'g. There are many stories of Mi'kmaq travellers that either did not consult the Sabawaelnu about the weather or insulted them. Either way, you risk your life."

Nukumi asked E's and Matues about the young warriors' burial, and they told her that they were able to bury them as custom dictated, in the sitting position. It was a battlefield burial, though. Matues said, "We had no skins to wrap them in, and even though we had access to two dogs, we did not think it right to kill them to send them on into the other world. The animals were unknown to our dead companions and they might not lead our brethren to the correct Spirit World. We were, though, able to bury their weapons with them."

"Boys," said Nukumi, "that was not a good burial; those warriors' spirits will inhabit that area for eternity."

The moon was visible before Jilte'g returned. He spoke not a word until after he sat and had some tea. "We leave at noon sky tomorrow. I will think about the boat assignments during my sleep tonight." He then finished his tea, lay down, and went to sleep.

The morning dawned with frost on the ground and a coolness to the salty sea air. Nukumi had hollowed out a tree stump, filled it with water, and then put heated rocks from the fire into the water. She then added sixty or seventy birds' eggs that she had foraged into this huge stump. After letting them boil in the water for a short time, she directed us to help ourselves, but we had to drop them in a container of cold water for a bit before eating them. After taking them out of the cold water, we peeled the shells off and ate the whites and yolk. Some of the eggs had had been fertilized, which was considered a delicacy. Nukumi took the remainder and placed them in a container for the sea voyage.

After eating, Jilte'g called us together and said, "We have seven people and two dogs to get back to our native soil. With the loss of the six young men, we will need luck to get back because we certainly do not have too much skill with this group."

Nukumi replied, "Jilte'g, do not worry; we have all we need with this group."

He looked at her and walked away muttering to himself.

Nukumi then directed us with different chores to prepare for the crossing. She asked us to fill all the water skins with fresh water and then to walk the beach, digging clams and harvesting seaweed.

Jilte'g, Apistanéwj, Grandmother, one of the imu'j (dogs), and I would be in a canoe together, leaving E's, Matues, Ta's'ji'jg, and the remaining imu'j. The three young warriors would have the bulk of the supplies to carry with them. We would also have a couple of fishing lines trailing the boats. Fresh fish, even uncooked, would always be welcome.

After a midmorning meal of fish stew and more tea, we loaded the canoes. The sea was very calm when the Jilte'g gave the word to leave. We pushed the large canoes out into the surf and started a rhythmic paddling, all the time hoping that the wind would come up strong enough to use the small sails that each canoe had. Their canoes were different from what my people used for the ocean. Our canoes had a raised middle section that kept the boat steady in rough waters and prevented water from washing into it. There was always a certain amount of bailing needed in harsh seas but our design kept it at a minimum.

The Mi'kmaq sea canoe that I was now in was over three times my body length and had a square-rigged sail made of skins that they were able to manoeuvre when there was wind.

The gulls followed us until we lost sight of land. In the far distance we could see a bootup blow his air hole. The Mi'kmaq liked to sing when they paddled to break the monotony. I listened to their voices, and calmness fell over me as they sung about their lands, families, and battles.

I took the time during the boredom of the paddling to take in the characteristics of the people with whom I was sharing this adventure. Matues and E's were still young warriors and had not yet shaved their heads with a scalp lock design. Their hair hung loose. They both were slender of build, with round faces. Both wore deerskin shirts and leggings.

Ta's'ji'jg had shaved both sides of his head and made his black hair stand up with gobs of bear grease that made it shine in the sunlight. Along the nape of his neck hung two eagle feathers wrapped with a strip of beaver fur around the quills. He was shorter than his two younger companions but more muscled. He also a round, unscarred face and wore a breechcloth with a sealskin shirt.

Nukumi was very fit. Her hair was starting to turn grey, but her face still had a look of youth — no wrinkles, and a permanent smile. She wore a white dress made from the skin of young seals.

Apistanéwj, though short, was heavily muscled in his arms and legs. His face was weather-beaten and his hair braided in one long plait down his back, with white gull feathers tied into the tress along the length. His clothes were of bearskin.

Jilte'g was every bit a warrior: head shaved at the front, with a long braid interspersed with turkey feathers. He had a scar that ran from the top of his right shoulder to his elbow and another on his forehead that looked like he had lost a chunk of skin, which was now just a red blotch. The scar on his arm stood out because of its whiteness. He had a snake's head tattoo where the scar ended at his elbow. Jilte'g was taller than the other three Mi'kmaq warriors and was heavily muscled. When he paddled, you could see the sinews and muscles in his arms and back expand and contract. He never tired and carried himself as a man who you did not want to provoke. Enemy no, ally yes.

We paddled until my arms felt like they were going to go numb. The wind came up at our backs in the late afternoon and since we could sail we were able to relax, eat, and drink.

The sails had been up for only a short while before Matues yelled and pointed toward the western horizon. It was just a speck but there was no mistaking the Eli'tuats' ship. We hastily dropped our sails and put our backs into paddling as hard as we could, hoping we could avoid detection. When we looked back to see if we had been spotted we were stunned at what our eyes beheld. At least twenty whales had positioned themselves between the Eli'tuat ship and us, blowing water from their spouts. They kept this up until dusk then disappeared, and when they did, we could see no sign of the ship. Bootup, my old friend, had caused enough of a diversion for us to escape discovery. I reached into my pouch and pulled out one of the few items I valued, my clay pipe. Standing up in the canoe, I threw it into the ocean and yelled, "Bootup, when you enjoy this pipe think of my gratitude for saving us!"

Little did I know that this would not be the last time Bootup would come to my aid or the last time that I would encounter the Eli'tuat.

As darkness started to fall, we brought the two boats alongside each other to eat and then we tethered them together with spruce rope. This would keep us from separating during the evening and enable us to take turns sleeping while only two in each boat paddled. If the wind came up they would use the sails and then only one person in each boat would have to stay awake to steer by the stars and moon. If the clouds came in, they would drop the sails and float until daylight.

I had never been on the water overnight. It was an eerie feeling floating in an immense open space, not seeing anything, with the only the sound of the breathing of my sleeping companions and the lapping of the water alongside the canoes. When you are on land, you know where you are and can listen to the night noises. The one advantage, though, to being on the sea is that there are no bugs.

The morning sun rose with an intense brightness aided by its reflection off the surrounding waters. Nukumi gave us all gobs of bear fat to smear on our bodies to prevent our skin from burning from the intense sunlight that reflected off the ocean. I still had a good layer left from the previous day, but I added more. Mixing with the layer of red ochre on my body, it made for excellent protection. For our eyes, we cut strips of leather from our leggings, made small eye slits, and then tied them around our heads. The last thing you wanted was to go blind from the sun. I had witnessed this before in my homeland. Sometimes the eyesight came back, but more often the victim remained blind.

It was comical to watch the two dogs, though. Each of them stood in the forward bow of their respective canoes, facing in the direction we were going, as if they were leading us to the safety of the distant shore.

The winds dropped down at midmorning and we had to paddle for the rest of the day. Then, just as we were tying our boats together for the night and preparing our meal, we could see lightning in the distance. Jilte'g said, "Do not worry; we will encounter only a light shower. The main part of the storm will pass to the west. Sabawaelnu guaranteed our safe passage."

True to his prediction, we suffered only a light misting for most of the night, just enough to make us uncomfortable and cold and to sufficiently soak the dogs, giving them that wet, pungent smell. The morning sun would definitely be welcome to help dry us out. The bear grease did make us a little waterproof, but the dampness of our clothes made us shiver and yearn for shelter and the warmth of a fire. It is very difficult to sleep when you are wet. We did keep active by bailing water because between the choppiness of the ocean and the rain, we received lots of water in the boats.

At dawn we ate and the sun's warming rays helped us to dry out and feel better. The wind was very weak so our weary arms had to paddle again. We were now into our third day on the water and I was beginning to wonder if we would ever see land again. My small friend looked very exhausted. I knew he was not used to this kind of physical labour for sustained amounts of time, but to his credit he did not complain or shirk his responsibilities. Even Jilte'g had to admire Apistanéwj's persistence.

Just after midday we started to notice gulls. This gave us a newfound burst of energy because these birds signalled that land was near. The closer we came to shore, the more birds that appeared, until finally we could sight land in the distance. Then I beheld an amazing sight!

5

MAHINGAN AND WINTER'S END

MY NAME IS MAHINGAN (Wolf). Our small family unit of nineteen people was spending the winter close to a waterfall. The members of the band that I was responsible for were as follows: my son, Anokì (Hunt), and I. My brother, Kàg (Porcupine), Kàg's wife, Kinebigokesì (Cricket), and their twin sons Makwa and Wàbek (both names meaning Bear). The twins Makwa and Wàbek had grown into fearless warriors and hunters under the training of their uncle, Mitigomij, who still managed to hunt and war within the limitations that his club foot permitted. The twins were his constant companions, and the feared Black Panther Makadewà Wàban (Black Dawn) was his relentless protector.

My sister, Wàbìsì (Swan), had survived the massacre at the village and had been saved along with Kinebigokesì at the Battle of the Falls. Her husband was the great warrior,

Mònz (Moose). Wàbìsì had changed the pronunciation of her name from Mànabìsì because of a dream she had had after the battle, wherein a swan came and spoke to her and called her by the name Wàbìsì.

There was our younger brother, Mitigomij (Red Oak), and his Black Panther, Makadewà Wàban (Black Dawn). The Haudenosaunee still feared Mitigomij and his panther as Shape Shifters. They thought that he was Michabo (the Great Hare) Trickster God, inventor of fishing. The panther was even more feared since the Haudenosaunee were positive the animal was Gichi-Anami'e-Bizhiw (the Fabulous Night Panther).

Also with our family unit were three vicious warriors, of whom two were women. They were Agwanìwon (Shawl Woman), Kìnà Odenan (Sharp Tongue), and their close friend Kànikwe (No Hair).

A Wàbanaki (Abenaki) warrior named Nigig (Otter), his wife Shangweshì (Mink), daughters Àwadòsiwag (Minnow), Ininàtig (Maple), and his mother Àbita (Half) had been with my family for five years now.

Finally, there were the two young Ouendat (Huron) warriors, Odìngwey (Face) and Kekek (Hawk).

With twelve warriors the encampment was well looked after. They all were good hunters and providers. The camp also had eleven dogs and my wolf Ishkodewan (Blaze) as pack animals, hunting dogs, and in time of starvation, food.

I had brought the group here in the fall. We had not wintered in our ancestral homeland area for six years now. It brought back too many memories of my wife, Wàbananang (Morning Star), carried away by the

Haudenosaunee that fateful summer six years ago. Before Wàbananang suffered capture, she managed to hide our son with two guardian dogs, saving him from suffering the same fate as her. Nevertheless, I still brought this group back to the summer meeting place each year to trade, hunt, and, on occasion, war against our enemies with the rest of the Omàmiwinini (Algonquin) Nation.

The area we now wintered in had a decent supply of game that we were able to hunt in the fall. Winter, though, was still a lean time. We were lucky if we had enough food every other day most of the time. The one game that we were able to access on an almost constant basis was fish. The power of the waterfall kept an open area that we were able to put a net in for a good part of the winter. Some days we caught enough to feed the village for a couple of meals that day; other times we were lucky if we could feed the women and children. The animoshs (dogs) were on their own a large amount of the time for food. If there was a good catch of fish or someone slew a deer or moose, the animosh ate well from the guts and bones.

Further down the watercourse toward the Kitcisìpi, we kept some nets near a bend in the river. We set the nets in the ice by chopping open a big hole and slipping in the net. We would then cut another hole nearby, passing the net along with a stick under the ice. We did this until the net stretched out its length. Cutting another large hole, we then staked both ends of the net to the ice to keep it from slipping into the holes.

The first morning of the Kòn Tibik-Kìzis (Snow Moon, February) dawned bright and cold with blue skies. The winter was still hanging on, causing the open water close to the falls to freeze over, making it difficult to fish in this area. We would now have to rely more on our nets downriver.

Mitigomij entered my shelter with a steaming bowl of kìgònz kabàsigan (fish stew) and a bowl of kìjik anìbìsh (cedar tea).

"Mahingan," he said, "I have heard a wàbidì (elk) in the woods above the falls. I could also hear the cracking noises when it walked. By the tracks I have seen and the height of the marks it is leaving on the azàd mitigs (aspen trees) after eating the bark and twigs, I can tell it is a young bull. The snow is still deep and I think we can run him down with the dogs before the pack of wolves that claims this territory decide they can run and corner him. A kill like this would almost take us to spring."

"Yes, brother, we could definitely use the meat. It would certainly save us from having to kill some of the dogs. The last wàwàshkeshi (deer) that we were able to kill was over a moon ago. Kìgònz (fish), wàbòz (rabbit), and pine (partridge) with the odd kàg (porcupine) from our snares keep us barely alive. A wàbidì kill would keep our people strong and our warriors would have the strength to go out again and hunt more game. This moon we have been fortunate. There has been food almost every other day.

"What do you think of letting the twins and the two Ouendats go out for this hunt?"

Mitigomij replied, "I would like the two warrior women and Kànikwe to go also. If there is any trouble with wolves, their experience will go a long way in making this hunt successful. They will need to take seven of the animoshs. The hunters will need that many animosh to chase down the wàbidì and to bring back the meat if they are triumphant in the hunt."

"What about you and the big cat?" I replied.

"I would just slow them down," answered Mitigomij. "However, I would like to take them to the escarpment and show them where to start the quest. They will have to use snowshoes, which I can manage, but again I would hold them up."

"By sending seven warriors out, the camp will be left with just five fighting men and the nets downriver need to be checked. I will take Anokì and a couple of animosh with me; it is time he learned to help more.

"Our only enemies at this time are the Hochelagans, Stadaconas, and the Haudenosaunee. The Hochelagans are our closest danger because we are near their hunting grounds. Mandàmin Animosh (Corn Dog) is always a concern. He and his band of warriors have created havoc all along the Big River and its feeder lakes. Ever since he escaped from the battle at the Island and I killed his friend Mishi-pijiw Odjìshiziwin (Panther Scar) at the falls on their river, Corn Dog has taken it upon himself to destroy everything in his path. One day he will gain the courage to come back to the land of the Omàmiwinini and we will settle what was left unfinished from the Island six years ago."

"Yes, brother, but Corn Dog has been gaining strength in numbers and may be a force too strong for our people to defeat."

"We will worry about that, Mitigomij, when the time comes, but right now you must get the hunting party together to leave as soon as possible."

We met with the seven warriors who would be going out on the hunt. I asked Kànikwe to lead the group and to take all responsibility for any decisions that should have to be made.

They left at midmorning with Mitigomij leading them up to the escarpment. Once he had taken them to the area where he had last heard the beast, they would continue without Mitigomij and try to pick up signs of the animal.

Wàbidì could travel long distances in a few days, but if they found good forage, water, and cover, they would stay in that vicinity overnight and eat. Then, in the morning, they would travel to find more of the same.

When we slaughter the animal, we have found they have four stomachs. We use their teeth for ornaments and their antlers for weapons. However, the bulls would not have any racks at this time of the year.

After watching the hunters disappear up over the hill, I approached Kàg and asked him to make sure to post a couple of people on watch while the hunters and I were gone. I then went and woke my son, giving him the rest of the fish stew to eat. Once he was finished, I told him to get his weapons, because he was leaving with me to check the nets downriver. Giving him the responsibility to gather up Pìsà Animosh (Small Dog) plus Ishkodewan and another dog was a step in his growing from a child to a young man who could take on responsibilities and make decisions. Even a small decision like picking a dog for a small hunting trip was a step in the right direction.

We left with the one remaining odàbànàk (toboggan) that was left by the hunting group. Anokì strapped one of the dogs to the sled and threw extra rope onto it in case our catch was large enough that we needed two dogs to pull it back. I was hoping for a good catch of odawàjameg (salmon), because if our hunters were not successful, this fish would be all that would separate my people from life or death by starvation.

During our journey we walked along the river, staying close to the shoreline, staying out of the wind. I could see the cold wind blowing snow across the ice. We protected our exposed skin from the wind and sun by smearing on bear grease.

The surrounding woods were quiet. Occasionally we would hear the sound of a tree limb snapping in the cold or a pikwàkogwewesì (blue jay) announcing our passing. The sound of our àgimag (snowshoes) made a crunching sound as we walked and the cold air made our breath look like steam as it left our lungs.

Anokì was full of questions, and he always wanted me to tell the story of how his mother hid him in the small cave with the two dogs during the attack on the village five summers ago. Both dogs that had guarded Anokì were now dead. The red one was killed by a bear a couple of years later and the white one died of old age. They were the parents of the small dog that was a constant companion to my wolf. Every time I told the tale, he asked the same questions. How old was he when he she hid him? Was his mother alive? Did he cry? How did I find him? I never tired of answering his questions; it always reminded me of how brave his mother was and it kept her in my heart these last six years.

I broke trail. Then came Anokì, followed by the dogs. My son and I both wore snowshoes. The boy was strong for his age and I watched to see if he would tire. If that happened, I would put him on the sled. We stopped just before the noon sun and ate some dried meat I had brought. We drank from a moose bladder, which I had brought to carry our fresh water. After our quick meal we continued on, arriving at the river bend soon after. As I stepped out from the shadow of the trees on the curve of the river, I saw something that froze me in my tracks. Quickly I backtracked and told my son to take Pìsà Animosh and the other dog into the tree line and stay very still. I kept Ishkodewan with me.

Once Mitigomij had sent the hunting party on their way toward the shàwanong (south), they gave the dogs their heads and let them run ahead, searching for scent. The warriors kept a quick pace on their snowshoes, following the dogs, which were bounding through the snow, taking turns leading as the one ahead would fall back when it tired. For short distances the dogs came upon crusty snow that enabled them to run along the top without breaking through. One of the dogs had cut his dewclaw and was leaving a path of blood. The wàbida's scent was old but the dogs were able to pick it up and now became even more high-spirited for the chase. The group came to an open spot blown clear of snow and was able to see where the wàbidì had grazed the previous day. There was scat on the ground and they could see where he had stripped the bark of the aspen trees and had lain down to rest in the cedars.

After running around chasing scent, the dogs found where the big animal had been, and off they went barking with anticipation. The warriors were now sweating and they could see steam rising off their bodies as they kept up the chase behind the dogs. Near midday, the dogs disappeared over a bald, rocky knoll and the men picked out the sound of dogs snarling and yelping in pain. The hunters crested the hill and came upon a bloody sight on the snow.

Mahingan

Motioning Ishkodewan to follow, I stepped out onto the river ice and watched three men hunched over one of the nets. They were trying to break open the ice hole with a rock to pull the net up. I was not close enough to them to recognize to what tribe they belonged. Raising my bow, I snapped off an arrow that landed close to them, immediately getting their attention. They rose up, and holding their hands high told me in broken Algonquin that they had no weapons and were at my mercy. I recognized them as young Susquehannock warriors.

"Please do not kill us! We are starving and have not eaten anything other than bark and clumps of meadow grass in the last five or six days."

As I approached them, I could not see any weapons other than the rock that they were using to try to break the ice hole. When I drew near them, I noticed that they were emaciated, pale, and weak.

Just after I arrived at where they stood, I took my axe and finished chopping the ice from the hole they been standing over. After breaking the ice there, I continued onto the next opening and broke it free as well. Now that we had the holes free of their ice covering, the four of us were able to pull the net up onto the river ice. We then went to the second net and proceeded to do the same. There were seventy-four fish trapped in the nets, enough to feed the village two or three more days and ourselves before we headed back. We had to work quickly before the nets froze. If they stiffened in the cold air, we would not be able to get them back into the holes again. The three boys and I prevailed and were able to get the netting back into the river.

Our people call this way of fishing shìbàskobidjige (set a net under ice).

I called for my son to come out of hiding. With his help, we loaded the fish onto the toboggan and moved toward the shore to start a fire and feed the famished young men. I was about to ask Anokì to collect wood when I noticed him go to the toboggan and grab something.

"Father, see what I was able to kill with my bow while waiting for you?"

He held up a wàbòz (rabbit) and smiled.

"Anokì," I replied, "I will get the wood. You butcher your game and we will have rabbit and fish for this meal. Good hunting, son! You will also be able to make yourself a pair of mitts with the fur."

Before I left, I gave one of the young warriors my knife to clean the fish. The tallest one produced a woman's skinning knife and the two immediately started. I gave the third boy some bone fish hooks and line that were in my pouch, along with my stone axe. Then I instructed him to break open a couple of holes and bait the hooks with fish guts, tie the lines to sticks, and secure the branch in the snow so they would not be dragged into the opening. I hoped that we would be able to catch more fish before leaving for the village.

Telling Anokì to help watch the lines after he was finished with the wàbòz, I set out to get wood. The last sound I heard as I walked into the woods was the yelping of the dogs and wolf as they fought over the fish guts.

Once back with my son and the others, it was not long before I had a roaring fire, the rabbit on a spit, and the fish roasting on sticks. As we waited for the food to cook, I melted some water and made kìjik anìbìsh. The boys told me that they still had their childhood names. Captured close to two years ago, they never had a chance to earn warrior names. In the Susquehannock language, they divulged their names. The taller one called himself Sischijro (Eat); the eldest one, who was more muscular than the other two, they called Oneega (Water); and the youngest went by the name Abgarijo (Dog).

Oneega did the talking and related that they fell into the hands of a band of Haudenosaunee while they were on a hunting trip with their father and uncles. The three of them were brothers, all under the age of seventeen summers.

"We were camped in the midsummer beside a small stream and were around the fire, eating. Being deep into our own hunting grounds, we did not fear intruders, so we had no guard out. They struck quickly and silently. Many arrows thudded into the adults and then they were set upon with clubs and unmercifully hacked to pieces and thrown into the fire. My brothers and I never had a chance to help; we were pushed face first into the ground and held there, all the time listening to the sickening thuds of our relatives' mutilations.

"They jerked us roughly to our feet and prodded us at spear point into the woods just as our attackers finished their gruesome work with the fire. The attackers then ran us through the forest all night. Branches were slapping us in the face, shoulders, and chest. I was bleeding from scrapes and cuts, as were my brothers. Just as daylight approached, we stopped. They gave us each a handful of corn and allowed us to drink from a stream. I counted fourteen warriors, each one painted and only a breechcloth and moccasins for clothing. After a short while they started out again on the run. I presumed they wanted to get as far from our lands as quickly as possible. The Susquehannock and Haudenosaunee have been enemies forever and our people have always held their own when it comes to warfare with them. Many warriors from both sides have died defending their respective hunting grounds. They knew that if our people came across them, they would suffer terrible retribution. By midday, we met up with the main group of about forty warriors and some women and children. They presented us to the leader and he just looked at us and nodded. We understood the Haudenosaunee language, since it is very close to ours, and were able to comprehend the man as he talked to me and my brothers.

"'You will help the women with all camp duties. Attempted escape will bring death.'

"He talked in a very low voice, but you knew he commanded respect.

"'My Algonquin enemies call me Mandàmin Animosh (Corn Dog); to my people I am known as Ò:nenhste Erhar. To the three of you I am the only person who stands between you living or dying. Never forget that!'"

After listening to Oneega talk, I was curious. "How did you learn our language?"

He replied, "After we were captured we had to help the women cook, collect firewood, help tan animal hides, and whatever else they needed. Once in a while they took us on hunting trips but only as slaves to carry back the game. They were constantly raiding for the rest of the summer but always would leave enough men to guard us. Being so far from home and never knowing where we were, escape was always out of the question. During this time we became acquainted with an Algonquin woman and her young daughter. She had long black hair and attractive facial features. She taught us her language while we worked beside her. This woman, though, was a mystery. No one bothered her, ever. One day as we were out collecting wood with a woman from Corn Dog's group, we were able to obtain information about the Algonquin woman. Corn Dog had acquired her in a trade with another member of his tribe. The woman told us that when the Algonquin's daughter was about two years old, one of Corn Dog's wives, whose daughter had drowned, decided that she was going to take the Algonquin's daughter for her own. The Algonquin woman always carries a skinning knife and a stone club. They said that when Corn Dog's wife grabbed the young girl to take possession of her, the Algonquin struck quickly and violently. The Haudenosaunee women was dead before she hit the ground, her throat slashed and head bashed in."

"What did Corn Dog do?" I asked.

"Nothing. That is what made her even more of a mystery to the people. However, the Haudenosaunee women never bothered her again. The woman also told me that one of Corn Dog's men tried to have his way with her one night. She sliced his cheek open from below his eye to his chin. I have seen this man. The scar is horrific. She has a heart of a warrior and fears no one! Beautiful, smart, and dangerous, with a wonderful singing voice. She is always singing while she works and forever smiling. Her daughter is her world. After the incident with the warrior, the woman who related the story to me said that Corn Dog gave explicit orders she was not to be touched or harmed, that he had future plans for her that involved an old enemy."

"Oneega, what were this Algonquin woman's name and the age of her daughter?" I inquired.

"Her daughter was about a summer younger than your son. Her name is Wàbananang (Morning Star) and her daughter's name is Pangì Mahingan (Little Wolf)."

Kànìkwe

As the band of Algonquin hunters reached the top of the hill, a cascade of sounds greeted them. They could hear dogs snarling and yelping in pain, and the echoing screams of men in the pitch of battle.

Being the designated leader, I, Kànìkwe (No Hair), was the first to direct my eyes to the encounter below. It was taking place in a small clearing surrounded by aspen and birch in a valley about fifty feet further down from our present position. In the basin was a ball of bleeding, yelping, and shrieking animoshs and men, along with a bellowing, grunting wàbidì who, by this point, was fighting off a couple packs of animoshs and five hunters. The beast had a spear and some arrows protruding from his body. The front of his chest was red with the blood that was seeping from the spear wound. Dogs were charging the wàbidì and fighting among themselves as he vainly attempted to defend his life by striking at them with his massive head and hooves.

Because it was early spring, his antlers had not yet fully grown back. However, he still was able to use what he had grown as a lethal defence. The hunters were striking our dogs with spears and clubs and stabbing at the wàbidì with their weapons. I watched as one of the huntsmen strung an arrow and aimed in the direction of our largest dog. It embedded up to the feathers into the dog's neck. The animal went down and pawed at the shaft, trying to remove it. The man then walked up to him and clubbed the creature to death.

Agwanìwon and Kìnà Odenan looked at me and nodded, but before they were able to take the initiative and lead the charge into the bloody valley, the two Ouendats burst from the hill yelling their war charge with the rest of us behind them. Once we were three quarters down the hill, the hunter who had killed one of our dogs hastily released an arrow at our charging group, catching the lead Ouendat, Odìngwey, in the left shoulder. The young man lost his footing and fell face first directly onto the protruding shaft. As he fell, we could hear the shaft snap and his scream of pain as the arrow went deeper into his body. The remaining five Algonquins and the Ouendat, Kekek, met the mass of dogs, hunters, and dying wàbidì head on. The two women, who were always terrifying foes, reached the hunter with the bow and as Kìnà Odenan clubbed him on a kneecap, Agwanìwon shoved her spear into his open, screaming mouth. The blade, covered with grey matter, exited out the back of his head.

I became engaged in hand-to-hand struggle with a man at least six-inches taller then myself. We both had knifes and were each drawing blood with every thrust, slicing shirts and the skin beneath. Neither of us had yet inflicted a deep wound since our heavy clothing provided a certain amount of protection, keeping the wounds superficial. I grasped the club that I kept in my waistband, and as my foe made another thrust, I stepped aside and hit him flush in the face. Blood spattered all the way up my arm and I could hear the sound of breaking bone and his gasping for air. The warrior dropped to one knee and I buried my knife into his neck, with only the handle preventing the weapon from going any deeper. He turned and looked at me, spat out some teeth, smiled, and dropped on his side with a gush of air leaving his body. I reached down and cut off the ear nearest to me, putting it into the pouch where I carried the rest of my vanquished opponents' ears. I then returned my attention to the sounds of the battle around me.

I watched helplessly as the young warrior Kekek rushed an enemy with his lance. The hunter still had a large animosh on a rope. Upon Kekek rushing him, he released the animal. The beast grabbed Kekek by the right arm and I could hear him scream. He dropped his weapon and went for his knife with his free hand. The animosh was mangling Kekek's arm and his muzzle became covered with the Ouendat's blood.

I tried to pull away from the fighting dogs around me and get to my young friend's defence, but before I got to him, I watched as the hunter jammed his spear into Kekek's neck. The enemy looked in my direction and called the animosh, and they both ran off toward the deep woods. Kekek lay in a pool of blood, reddening the snow around him, with the spear protruding from his neck and his arm mangled and bloodied. Dying in a land far from his birthplace, Kekek departed this life fighting to keep his adopted friends from starving.

With the skirmish close to being over, I turned my attention to the sounds of an encounter to the rear of my position. The twins, Makwa and Wàbek, were having trouble with the last two remaining hunters. The boys were barely holding their own against the older, more experienced foes. Wàbek stumbled to the ground on one knee after taking a blow to the midsection from his opponent's club. Next, I heard a war cry and watched as two more of the enemy came out of the trees toward our position. They were quickly closing ground between themselves, the twins, and their antagonists. Hastily I rushed to the boys' aid, grabbing a discarded spear. Then, just as I reached the conflict, there was a sharp sound like a tree limb snapping on a cold winter's day. The man who stood over Wàbek suddenly was missing half of his forehead. He looked at me in amazement, put his hand to his head, and with chunks of skin and bone oozing from his fingers, took two steps toward me. He opened his mouth to say something and dropped at my feet, face first. At that moment everyone on the battlefield heard the blood-curdling scream of a panther. One of the charging warriors from the wooded area turned in mid-stride to see where the sound was coming from and as he did Makadewà Wàban hit him with the full force of his body on the dead run. Man and beast rolled on the ground with the panther rising from the tumbling collision with the man's throat locked into his jaws. The victim's eyes were bulging and blood was spurting from his nose and ears. With one shake of his massive head the man flew clear and the panther stood there with blood dripping from a huge piece of his casualty's throat.

The second man, who was battling with the twins, received two rapidly fired arrows in the base of his neck that came with such force that one protruded out through his throat and the other went through his body and impaled itself in a birch tree directly in front of the dying man.

The last remaining rival turned heel and yelled, "It is the Shape Shifters, Michabo and Gichi-Anami'e-Bizhiw!"

The women, the twins, and I all stood in amazement. Even the dogs fell silent. Where just a moment ago the battlefield had been a hornet's nest of sounds and activity, it was now deathly quiet. Five dead enemies and our Ouendat ally, Kekek, also slain. Four lifeless animoshs and a bleeding, bellowing wàbidì floundering around on the ground. I turned and motioned to Makwa and Wàbek to put the dying animal out of his misery.

I directed my attention to the top of the hill as a lone figure started to descend. It was joined by the big panther and they continued down together toward the carnage. There was no mistaking the limp. It was Mitigomij. The man always appeared when least expected. How he managed was a mystery to all. Maybe the Haudenosaunee were right — perhaps he and the panther were the Trickster Hare and the Fabulous Night Panther and were Shape Shifters. All I did know, though, was that he was dedicated to the twins and the panther to him. Mitigomij and the cat always brought death and destruction with them when there was a battle.

"Kànìkwe," whispered Mitigomij, "I will treat Odìngwey's wound. I will need to build a fire to heat my knife and cut the arrow out of his shoulder. The warrior women can hold him down while I treat him. He will not scream out but he may thrash around as the pain intensifies. I have asin odjìbik (stone root) and àmò-sizibàkwad (honey) to treat his wound. Once that is done, I will take him back with me."

"Mitigomij," I warned, "you know the hunters were Hochelagans and Haudenosaunee?"

"Yes," he replied. "Corn Dog is up to something. This is probably only one of many small hunting groups he has sent out as his warriors are on the move. Now I am sure he has a different quarry in mind. Mark my words. Our people are very close to his final plan. Kànìkwe, get the twins started on butchering the wàbidì and animoshs. The meat of these animals will sustain our people for a while and give strength for our hunters to go out on the hunt again. With the loss of Kekek and the inability of Odìngwey to aid in the return, everyone will have to carry extra. It seems some of the intruder's animoshs have stayed with our pack. Feed them well and they will help our animals carry the meat back to the village.

"Agwanìwon and Kìnà Odenan, come. I need your help!"

6

THE FEAST AND GUHN ACHGOOK (SNOW SNAKE)

Mahingan

After eating, we reset the nets with the help of the three young Susquehannocks. Anokì loaded the odàbànàk (toboggan) with the fish that we had taken from the nets plus another small amount that we had caught with the lines.

We would not reach the camp before nightfall so we set about and collected some green sapling branches, birch bark, and the bark of a dead elm. Using some vines, we fastened the elm bark to the sapling and sealed the joints with heated pine gum. Then, taking some dry leaves that were still on branches and dead pine needles, we rolled the birch bark up tightly. We stuffed all this into the opening of the elm bark. These would be our torches once darkness fell. Making enough that the four adults would each have a spare, we piled all on the odàbànàk with the fish.

As we walked, I asked the boys how they came to end up half-starved at this river.

They told me that after their capture, the three of them travelled northeast with Corn Dog and his people. He was constantly raiding and building up his group with young Haudenosaunee warriors who were leaving their villages to join him. Some of the captive men that his warriors had not tortured to death were made to run the gauntlet. Corn Dog had two ways for captives to run the gauntlet. One was solo and the other was when they led the victims through with a rope tied around their neck. These poor captives led through by the rope had no chance of survival and they on the most part were old men and old women, and sometimes young children. Struck repeatedly, the sufferers made their way through the double lines, and then, bloodied and dying, they were tossed into the fires. Corn Dog's people would cheer as the victims screamed in pain. The younger men were sent through the gauntlet solo. If they made it to the end mostly intact, they became worthy of being an adopted warrior of Corn Dog's Haudenosaunee. Young women he gave to his warriors as wives or slaves.

"Did you boys run the gauntlet?" I asked.

"No," answered Oneega. "We often wondered why torture or the gauntlet was never imposed on us. We were told by a couple of the women that the reason we had not been killed or used for sport was our ages; we were not children and neither were we yet warriors. Because we were Susquehannock, Corn Dog figured we would grow into great fighters and did not want to break our spirit. He would have a family or families adopt us and train the three of us as members of his warrior elite. Mahingan, he is building a massive warrior group and resources; he wants to control everything along the Big River!"

"Brother," added Sischijro, "you forgot to tell Mahingan about Corn Dog's brutal friend!"

"Yes! This man is scary, fierce, and huge. The tallest man I have ever seen. He raids constantly and brings many captives back to camp. As Corn Dog's closest friend, the man is involved in all decision-making. The women told us he comes from the east and is a Mi'kmaq. They call him Winpe."

"Corn Dog's captives have been mainly from the Wàbanaki (Abenaki), 'Lenepi (Delaware), Me'hiken (Mahican), and Pênâ-kuk (Pennacook) tribes. His warriors had now grown in numbers to close to one hundred and fifty and nearly one hundred women. Most of the women and approximately fifty of the men were captives from the four tribes. It took a lot of hunting to keep this group fed. Often Corn Dog had five or six groups of eight men out hunting. Only he and Winpe led raids. At no time were they both out on an attack; one of them always remained in camp to organize movement and hunting parties. When we escaped, they were planning to go into the land of the Wolastoqiyik (Maliseet) and Mi'kmaq to raid. After that he said there would be a revenge raid and he would go after control of the river your people call Kitcisìpi."

Sischijro continued, "We had been with them almost three moons when they started to let us go out with the hunting parties, but we always had to return our weapons when we arrived at the main camp. Wàbananang told us they made us do this because we were Susquehannock, mortal enemies of the Haudenosaunee. The Susquehannock had always chosen death over adoption into the Haudenosaunee tribe. Because we were young and had not reached warrior age with our people, Corn Dog hoped he could change that history. The Haudenosaunee were never able to defeat us in a major battle. Corn Dog knew this and wanted warriors like those of our nation. Nevertheless, he was going to make sure we were loyal before we were taken into their society of warriors."

He added, "Wàbananang was very guarded in her trust. She knew Corn Dog had a purpose for her. In spite of this, she did not want to push too far for the sake of her daughter. She said Corn Dog was going to build up his force a lot larger than it presently was before he would attempt to go up the Kitcisìpi again. He knew that he could count on some of his own people to join him; still, he wanted a massive force of warriors before asking his own nation to join the force he was gathering. The defeat from six summers ago still weighed heavy on his fellow tribesmen.

"She also told us that Winpe would be crossing the river to meet with the Hochelagans and Stadaconas to convince their people to join them as they raided the eastern tribes. Corn Dog's followers would then leave our camp and travel to the Haudenosaunee River, where they were to obtain canoes that they had cached. Morning Star told us that along this route we would find our best chance to escape. She spared us an extra skinning knife that she had obtained. Our best chance of escape was when the hunters came back with a big amount of game. They always gorged themselves and slept soundly after a huge feast and celebration dance. Telling us to eat well and to steal food for the journey, she said that with only a knife our chances were slim of obtaining much to eat until we met up with her people.

"Mahingan, Wàbananang saved our lives. In spite of this, we became lost and on the wrong side of the river. We stumbled north through the woods until we found a waterway. Thinking we were on the Kitcisìpi, we started upriver. Our food had run out five days before and we were becoming weak. Morning Star said that if we met any Algonquins we were to ask for a chief named Mahingan, the one who was missing half an ear taken by a Nipissing warrior in battle."

"Well, you found me, and the woman who helped you is my wife. The Haudenosaunee captured her six summers ago. The battle weakened the Algonquin Nation and our allies enough that we could not follow our enemy any further. We rescued some of the captives; the rest the enemy murdered on the battlefield or carried off when they retreated.

"The three of you are welcome to stay with us as long as you want. I have a brother, Mitigomij, who will train you in the way of the warrior. With his training and your heritage, I am positive that you all will be a force to contend with."

We were probably three quarters of the way from the encampment when the sun fell below the tree line and we lit the torches. Anokì was having a great time, following me and taking turns leading the dogs, pulling the odàbànàk and riding on the sled when he tired. The light from the torches amply highlighted the path Anokì, the animosh, and I had made this morning. By the time the moon had risen, we were within shouting distance of the camp. Making the sound of a wàwonesì (whip-poor-will),

I announced our entrance. We made this sound because our people in the camp knew this bird was gone for the winter and that our enemies would not use the signal of an absent bird. It was not long before my brother Kàg and the Wàbanaki Nigig came to greet us.

"Mahingan," Kàg exclaimed, "we were worried when we caught sight of four torches approaching. I see you have friends?"

"Kàg and Nigig, this is Sischijro, Oneega, and Abgarijo, three Susquehannock brothers with a very interesting story to tell."

"Brother," answered Kàg, "I am sure it will make for a good campfire tale. Just before we noticed your torches and heard your call, Mitigomij arrived back in camp with a wounded Odìngwey. There was a problem. We have to head out and give aid to the returning hunting party. Kekek has died in battle and I will fill you in on everything else that happened during our journey to meet Kànìkwe and the others."

"These boys need rest and food. They will stay with the camp while we continue on," I replied.

Kàg, his wife Kinebigokesì, Mònz, and my sister Wàbìsì, as well as the Wàbanaki, Nigig, his wife Shangweshì, and myself, my wolf, and a couple of other dogs set out to assist the hunting party with their return.

Kànìkwe

After Mitigomij and the women tended Odìngwey's wound, the two warriors and the panther headed back to the village. I told them to be vigilant on the return trip since there remained three enemy warriors out in the forest who might return with others to take back the elk or to wreak vengeance. These warriors had to belong to a hunting party for a bigger group. Three of the dead were Hochelagan and the others Haudenosaunee. It was mix I did not like and a sign that Corn Dog was likely travelling down the big river raiding, and in the meantime having success bringing the Hochelagans into his party.

After Mitigomij left, I asked the two women to take turns with a couple of animosh patrolling the forest around us. I could only spare one of them at a time while the rest of us butchered the dead animosh and wàbidì. It would take us most of what remained of the day to do this bloody work. There was also the task of burying Kekek, which we proceeded to do before anything else. I did not like travelling at night, although we had to make an exception at this time. There was danger nearby and the sooner we left this area, the better the chance all of us should survive and make it back to camp.

After butchering the animals, we loaded the odàbànàks with as much of the meat as the five us could pull. We let the dogs eat their fill from the carcass of the wàbidì, and then we packed the pelts from the dead animoshs with meat and loaded the packs onto the dogs' backs. Wanting to keep the wàbida's pelt intact, we made a travois for our biggest dog to pull. With eleven dogs, we were able to handle most of the kill. Whatever meat we were unable to take with us the women wrapped with vines and hung in some trees until we could come back for it. The rest we left for the wolves and ravens. Agwanìwon led the procession and then we spaced three dogs between the twins, Kìnà Odenan, and me. It made for better control over the dogs and spaced us adequately for protection and vigilance. Before we left we made torches to light our way in the darkness. Only Agwanìwon and I carried them. We needed the middle three to have their hands free to manage the dogs and defend our group in case of sudden attack. Walking through the night was slow going. After walking for what seemed a long time, we crested a small hill and in the distance could see lights. Shawl Woman stopped the procession and called me up.

"What do you think she said?"

"Hopefully it is Kàg, Mònz, and their wives. We will know in a moment."

I then made the sound of the wàwonesì. It echoed through the valley. Because the wàwonesì had not yet come back to our forest, it was a safe call. No answer and we would know that we were not among friends.

The call came back immediately and everyone knew that we would soon have help to relieve our aching backs.

When our two parties merged, Mahingan was leading them.

He embraced me and said, "Good work, Kànìkwe. You have saved our people from a great hunger. I have come back to our camp with more then fish. I came upon three young Susquehannock boys, news that my wife is alive, and that she has a daughter with her."

"Mahingan," I replied, "my heart is happy for you!"

"Thank you, brother. I love this woman very much and our time together was too short. I wait for the day when we will be reunited."

"While we are still close to the kill, let's double back with the extra odàbànàks you brought and pick up the remainder of the meat that we hung in some trees," I suggested.

Nigig, Mònz, Kàg, Mahingan, and I grabbed some extra torches and took the dogs they brought, including Mahingan's huge wolf, and struck out back for the meat we had stored in the trees.

"Kànìkwe," Mahingan warned, "the three young men also told me other news."

His voice had an ominous tone.

"The Susquehannock boys told me they had been captured by Corn Dog, and Morning Star helped them to escape. They also told me that Corn Dog is building a huge force of warriors and is heading for the land of the Mi'kmaq this spring. When he is done with them the Algonquins are the next target."

"Mahingan, did Mitigomij tell you who we battled with?"

"Yes, he did. Corn Dog must have a lot of mouths to feed if he is sending hunting parties out this far."

"Mahingan, when Corn Dog does attack, the Algonquin will not die easy!" I exclaimed.

"Spoken like a true warrior, my friend! When we get back, we will feast and have the women smoke the meat. Then our small group must strike out earlier than usual for our summer encampment. We will send out runners to call in all the family units to meet us there. Once the families start to come in, we need to send emissaries out to ask for help from the Ouendat and Nipissing," he replied.

"If we are in Corn Dog's plans, he will have his battle," I added.

We reached the meat at dawn without incident. Wolves and ravens were feasting on the carcass and they paid us no heed. We had tied our dogs and Mahingan's wolf up in the trees above the valley. The last thing we wanted to do was break up a fight between a pack of wolves and our dogs. Once loaded, we headed for home and were able to make good time. The trail was well broken now because of the activity during the past couple of days and we arrived at the camp just before the sun reached its highest point.

As we entered the site, Makwa and Wàbek came running toward us.

"Father and Uncles, Mitigomij and the women have decided that we are going to have a huge feast and then he said that he would lead the women and children in defeating the warriors at a game of Guhn Achgook (Snow Snake). The women have been preparing the meal and the rest of us have been working on the track all morning and have added water to it to make it slippery. It is very long and well packed and will be ready for tomorrow. Tonight, while we eat and dance, Mitigomij said he will make the snakes."

As soon as they said all that this, they turned and ran back. The four of us looked at each other and laughed.

That night, everyone filled their bellies with fish, elk, and dog meat. The twins and the three Susquehannock boys banged on the big drum until no one remained dancing.

The next morning Mitigomij awakened us all by going from lodge to lodge calling us to the morning meal. While we ate, he told us who would be on the teams.

"I have decided that the women, Kinebigokesì, Wàbìsì, Agwanìwon, Kìnà Odenan, Shangweshì, Àwadòsiwag, Ininàtig, Àbita, plus the three Susquehannock boys, Sischijro, Oneega, and Abgarijo, will be on my team. On Anokì's team will be all the male warriors, Mahingan, Mònz, Kàg, Kànikwe, Nigig, Makwa, Wàbek, and Odìngwey, who can use his good arm to throw. Each thrower can have two deaths. After the second death, they will be out of the game. Anokì and I will mark at each end with an upright spear to indicate the distance the second thrower has to get past to defeat his opponent. Since my team has eleven players and Anokì only has nine, counting himself, I will not throw but he will. In addition, once Anokì's team suffers its first two deaths, they can come back in to play for two more losses, which will even up the sides. Six of my players will stay on the end closest to the falls and the other five will come to the far end. Anokì will decide whom he wants to place where. Decide your lineup to throw, and it must stay that way. When you finish your throw, you go to the back of the line and move up to play your next opponent when the line comes to you again. Each player has one toss per turn and only one foul (a stick leaving the track) per turn. We will play the best of three total games. Losers must, for the next two days, prepare the evening meal and collect firewood and water for the meals."

"One more thing," Mitigomij added, "the dogs will be let loose to warn us of any danger, and those who are eliminated early must take it upon themselves to go on watch around the area. We start after our meal and will not eat again until there is a losing team to arrange the evening meal."

The throwing spears that Mitigomij had made were as long as our tallest person and each weighted with small stones on the leading end. Each person had their own distinct way of throwing the sticks. Some ran great distances to gain momentum; others relied on arm strength to propel the staff down the track. There were some very good throws, and twice during the first round Kàg threw his shaft all the way down and off the end. This was quite an accomplishment because the trough was very long and level. Anoki's team won the first match with four players remaining. The second round, it looked like his team was going to win handily again. However, Nigig's daughter, Ininàtig (Maple), who was tall and slender, had mastered throwing the stick by running very fast up to the opening and a tremendous release. We had three throwers remaining, all with two lives, Kàg, Mahingan, and amazingly the Ouendat Odìngwey, who seemed to be making a very fast recovery from the wound that Mitigomij had been ministering. Ininàtig defeated them all, accompanied by a huge cheering section from her team. There was much laughter and competitiveness from both sides, as well as many side bets between the competitors.

The final game started, and what advantage the warrior team held up until now slowly began to wane. The women and the Susquehannock boys were catching on and quickly gaining an advantage in the final matchups. The sun was starting to set, casting a reddening glow on the snow and highlighting the track in a cascade of light. The final two competitors, each with only one life left, lined up at the waterfall end. The twin, Wàbek, was throwing against Nigig's other daughter, Àwadòsiwag (Minnow). Àwadòsiwag threw first, and it was very good. Mitigomij and Anokì marked it. Just before Wàbek threw, Minnow walked up to him and planted a kiss on his cheek. Flustered, he threw his first throw off the track. Gaining his composure, he retrieved the stick, and crouching down to gain momentum, he rushed to the opening. With his moccasined feet crunching the snow underneath and with a huge grunting sound expelled from his lungs, as well as his face reddening, he propelled the stick with all his might toward the opening.

7

GESPE'G (LAND'S END)

TALL MAN

"Grandmother, this is amazing!" I said.

There before us stood a huge rock with three arches carved into it and thousands of birds nesting on its summit. Then, to the west, an island with even more jipji'js (birds.) The sheer amount of birds made the island look snow-covered!

Grandmother then turned and spoke to me. "Tall Man, we will go to the island and collect eggs to take back to the village. Everyone will carry a leather sack and cover the collected eggs with layers of moss and grass to keep them from breaking. We will collect enough for our village to have a feast when we return to them."

Once we stepped ashore, the two dogs immediately began to bark and chase the birds, which made it easy for us to rob the nests. When these birds lose the single egg that they have in the nest, they will lay another within the breeding season, enabling both of our species to continue, us by avoiding starvation, the birds by nesting again.

Everywhere I stepped there were bird droppings, eventually turning my moccasins white. By the time of the noon sun, we had collected all the eggs we could carry in the leather bags Grandmother had given us. When we returned to the boats, she had a fire going with a chunk of bear meat on a spit and tea boiling in a vessel. We called the dogs in because we were getting tired of their constant barking, and as long as the birds remained in the air, they would splatter us with their droppings. I reached into my hair, and when I drew my hand back I could see it was white with feces.

"The only predators on the island are wowkwiss (fox)," E's told me, "and they are well fed, Tall Man."

We decided that we would spend the night on the island, proceed in the morning to the Gespe'g shore, and continue inland to their village.

Right after we finished eating, Matues developed a toothache. He rocked back and forth on his haunches, gripping the side of his face with both hands.

Nukumi approached him and said, "Matues, chew on these willow leaves and inner bark for a while and your toothache will disappear. If it still bothers you after trying this, I will take my knife and a rock and knock it out."

She then turned, winked at me with a smile, and went back to her fur bed.

Trying to find a place to lie where there was not any bird excrement was a futile endeavour. Furthermore, the constantly screeching birds made my ears ring. For entertainment, we sat by the fire and watched the birds dive from tremendous heights into the ocean waters for fish. Very rarely did a bird come to the surface without a fish in its beak. After the sunset, the colony became quiet and I fell asleep.

The night was chilly and we had to keep the fire tended. I woke once during the night to relieve myself and found Ta's'ji'jg up tending the fire and eating eggs. I could see him in the glow of the fire with yolk running down his chin, feeding the dogs the shells. Matues was sound asleep, which told me Nukumi's toothache remedy had worked.

Coming back to the fire, I sat beside him and asked about his people.

He answered, "We call ourselves the L'nu'k, which means 'The People.' Others call us Mi'kmaq, the friendly people. In the winter, we live inland and hunt tia'm and lentug (moose and deer). Once the snow leaves, the young men leave for the Island of the Bears and the rest of our people prepare to move to the coast. When the young hunters come home, everyone feasts on bear meat and spring moose. After the celebration, we leave for the shore to fish, hunt seal, and collect eggs. The women spend the summer drying fish and making sealskin clothing. We also trade with our cousins to the southeast and raid our enemies."

I shared some eggs with him and talked some more about his people and mine. The stories that intrigued me the most were the ones about raiding and battles with enemies of the Mi'kmaq. Ta's'ji'jg had a hard time understanding that our people were not warlike and that we really had no enemies. I told him that during my lifetime, we had one bloody encounter with a group of people that call themselves Inuit, but it was not a common occurrence. Our two peoples very rarely came in contact, and when we did, it was usually in the spring while we both were hunting seals, and most times it would be from a distance.

After we shared our stories, I went back to my sleeping spot beside Apistanéwj and the two dogs, Na'gweg and Tepgig. Just before I fell asleep, I thought that the Mi'kmaq really were no different from the Beothuk. Were all peoples the same?

"Rise up," cried Grandmother to the camp, "we will eat and then embark for our lands." She looked at me and smiled. "Tall Man, our adventures are just beginning!"

Nukumi had me puzzled because she seemed to know my future. I must admit, though, whenever I was around her I sensed a great calm.

After eating, we hurriedly loaded the canoes trying to leave before disturbing the island's birds. We had had enough of their bowel movements showering us. E's told me that it would take most of the day to get to Gespe'g. He added that our small group would hug the shoreline for safety. Once we reached the peninsula, it would take us another couple of days to reach the winter village.

The voyage along the coast was uneventful and the shoreline was heavily wooded and misty, not unlike my homeland. We entered a deep bay after leaving the three-arched rock and did not leave the area until the noon sun. Rounding a peninsula, we came upon a seal rookery and speared a half dozen of the animals. Jilte'g stated that we would put ashore in a sheltered bay where they had camped before. There we would skin the seals and camp for the night. The two dogs, Na'gweg and Tepgig, amazed me with their seaworthiness when they were in the boats. They were usually doing one of two things, standing at the prow of their respective vessel or sleeping. The pair became Apistanéwj's guardians, always following him around and sleeping with him between them at night. They were also very fond of Grandmother, who spoiled them with food. When I put a pack on them, they never put up a fuss, nor did they strain under the load. Both of them had amazing stamina, and even though they had yet to prove it, I had no doubt they were vigilant and protective camp dogs.

The sun was partway down to the horizon when we reached the small sheltered bay. Dragging the seals from the canoes, we were not long in skinning and dressing them, with the two dogs feasting on the guts. We boiled the seal fat, and once the oil floated to the surface Grandmother dipped it out and put it in moose bladders. In the future, this precious liquid would be of use to the Mi'kmaq for food flavouring and hair and body oil. That night we gorged on seal meat and Grandmother's boiled cedar tea. Apistanéwj, who was a very descriptive storyteller, kept us in suspense with his narratives. The night air was damp and the smell of the salt water hung heavily in the air, but the fire cast warmth that made me drowsy, and my newfound friends made me feel welcome and safe. The stars were bright in the sky and the moon looked like you could reach out and touch it. I looked to see where Apistanéwj and the dogs were sleeping and nestled up to Tepgig for extra warmth against the dampness of the night. Sleep came quickly.

Our group rose early, loaded the canoes, and struck out for the last leg of our journey. In the future there would be more people to meet and things to see. I had become very close to the friends that I had acquired since my escape from the Eli'tuat. Grandmother in particular seemed to know something about me and what lay ahead for us all. I could not figure her out; she was harmless but mysterious.

The only breaks in the forests were where a river flowed into the sea or where there had been a forest fire, which had burned up to the edge of the land and was halted by the ocean. Occasionally we saw seals and once a pod of whales in the distance. The wind was calm on the ocean that day, forcing us to paddle.

With two hours of sunlight left, Jilte'g motioned for us to go ashore. He had us pull the canoes onshore, turn them upside down, and cover them with brush.

"We will be going inland tomorrow to our winter village. Tonight we will stay in one of our summer wikuoms (wigwam)," he explained.

Our small party of six men, one woman, and two large dogs proceeded into the woods and after a short time came upon a deserted summer village. Some of the wikuoms were in need of repair but we found two side by side that would serve our needs that night. Nukumi, who had a fire going in no time, turned to Matues and said, "I want to serve matuesuei (porcupine meat) tonight, so you have been elected to get me one. Take the big one with you. Leave the dogs here, because I do not want to be pulling quills out of their mouths tonight."

"Grandmother, I am here to serve you!" he replied.

"Come, Tall Man. I will teach you something!" exclaimed Matues.

We walked through the woods along a game path. Matues said, "The matues (porcupine) is plentiful in our homeland and considered a delicacy. Nukumi will boil it and it tastes a lot like apji'jgmuj (black duck). You have to be careful when you skin it because it is covered in quills."

Matues continued to tell me about how they used this animal.

"The women of our village dye the quills and use them to decorate our clothing and make small baskets. Nukumi will gladly cook this creature in exchange for its pelt of barbs."

Suddenly Matues stopped and pointed to a tree. There I laid eyes on one of the strangest creatures I have ever seen. Pointy, stiff, white-tipped hairs covered this seemingly docile animal.

Matues loosened an arrow and the animal fell out of the sapling with a thud. Quickly he turned the animal over with a stick and skinned it. He handed me the pelt. I carefully ran my left hand over it. It was very pointy.

"Matues, from where I come from we have no such animal as this; it is very strange indeed."

We made it back to camp before sunset and gave Nukumi the matues. She was very pleased and quickly took the pelt, wrapping it in a skin.

The meat was delicious, a little oily but very tasty. It did taste like duck. The seven of us made short work of the animal; Grandmother had also cooked some seal, so we were able to fill our bellies.

After we finished eating Apistanéwj motioned to the two dogs to stay in the shelter with grandmother, and the men went to the adjacent one for the evening. Once we had a fire going, the place became very comfortable and I fell asleep in no time.

At daybreak, Ta's'ji'jg woke Apistanéwj and me.

"Bring your weapons," he said. "We are going hunting for apli'kmuj (rabbit). Little one, bring your dogs!"

Apistanéwj made a clicking sound with his tongue and immediately the two dogs were at his side.

With the dogs leading the way, we left the encampment and travelled south. It was not long before they started to scare up the apli'kmuj that we had come for. The three of us kept busy shooting the zig-zagging creatures. It was a constant barrage of the two dogs barking and these furry little animals running amok. By the time everything had settled down, our arrows had found their marks fourteen times. Taking some vines, we tethered their legs together and slung them over our shoulders for the trip back. Along the way, we stopped and picked some leeks. Grandmother would throw these into the water along with the meat.

After arriving back at the camp, everyone helped in the skinning of the animals. Making an incision along the legs of the rabbit, I put my fingers in between the skin and the meat and pulled the pelt upwards toward the head. With this done, I cut the skin at the neck and pulled it off the body. Then, after cutting off the head, I gutted the rabbit and threw the head and innards to the dogs. We also kept the claws of the rabbit and gave them to Grandmother; she would use them for necklaces and decorations on shirts.

Nukumi put the meat and leeks into the boiling bark container and soon we were eating. What we did not finish she wrapped in grass and moss and put in a sack to eat on the trail.

With our bellies full, we quickly put packs on the dogs, struck camp, and headed for the Mi'kmaq village. The forest canopy was dense but the sunlight was able to streak through and in spots made it look like beams of light were showing us the way. The smells of the forest decay mingled with the aromas of new spring growth. It seemed like Gisu'lg (the Creator) was showing us only a small part of what he was capable of doing with just the sun and our surroundings. The smells, sights, and the sounds of the birds made the setting almost magical, everything coming together just for us.

We had to veer north to avoid a river that was too high to ford this early in the spring. E's mentioned that on the Mi'kmaqs' return trip to their summer lodges near the ocean they came to this river to catch tagawan (salmon) as the fish returned from the sea to spawn.

It was not long, though, before the glmuej (mosquitoes) started to feast on our bare skin. I stopped and applied more of the red ochre on my body and covered my little friend Apistanéwj with it. The Mi'kmaqs stopped and picked some ferns that were growing along the trail. They crushed them and then rubbed them on their skin. Two different methods, but both successful in keeping the small biters away from our exposed bodies. E's took some of the fern and rubbed the two dogs' muzzles. Now all of us had protection.

Occasionally we came upon a meadow that a forest fire had created. In one of these areas we scared a couple of deer into the protection of the forest. Another time one of the clearings had a small stream babbling through it. Stopping here, we lay down on the ground and drank our fill, then filled up our water bladders. Taking our time, we rested and finished off the rabbit and enjoyed the warmth of the sun.

Jilte'g was not a man who said a lot, but when we were rising to leave this spot, he said, "We are not far from our winter village. If we see another deer, we will try to slay it for the coming feast. I want more than bear and seal meat to herald our return. E's, take the red one that calls himself Tall Man and the dogs with you. Keep your eyes open for lentug (deer). If you see one, take the shot and set the dogs on it to run it until it drops. The rest of us will continue on to the camp area our people have always used when preparing to enter the village. We will wait for you there."

E's turned to me and said, "Let's go. We will try to get ahead of the rest and then walk as silently as possible. There is another clearing ahead. If we are to be successful, that is where we might find our prey."

Soundlessly, we left the main group and let the dogs take the lead. Walking as noiselessly as possible and only using hand signals, we found a game trail that cut across our trail. E's signalled for me to follow, and we diverted from the main trail. It was not long before he stopped and picked something up from the trail. After handling it and smelling the object, he handed it to me. It was the warm dung of a lentug. Our quarry was close by.

E's handed me a piece of rope and we leashed both dogs. We did not want them to scare our prey before we got off a shot. E's whispered that there was a clearing ahead and a small spring-fed pond where the lentug would probably be drinking.

I am still amazed at how well trained and obedient these two dogs were. Once we put the leather leads on them they waited for our command.

With E's leading, we continued through the forest. The smell of the pine trees emitted an aroma that made me homesick with memories of days past. I thought of my dead friends from that ill-fated hunting trip and my friends and family from my village. They probably were wondering why we never returned and what our fate had been.

A hand on my shoulder roused me from my thoughts. We were on the edge of a clearing. E's pointed through the trees and I glimpsed five lentugs at the small pond. We were safely upwind from them and undetectable for the time being. Squatting down, E's whispered that two of the does had fawns with them. We would target the one that did not; shooting the mother of a nursing fawn would doom the young newborn to death by starvation. We took only what was needed without upsetting the balance of nature any more than necessary.

We each strung an arrow into our bows and slowly rose. I drew the bow back until the feathers touched my cheek. Together we loosened our taut bow sinews. I watched as my arrow travelled across the pond and struck the target with a thud. E's arrow hit its mark the same instant as mine. We had struck where the neck met her chest. The animal dropped to one knee then as quickly rose up and ran. The other two does and their fawns ran in separate directions into the forest cover.

Now it was time for the dogs to do their part. We let the two dogs loose from the small tree where we had tethered them, and they were quick to get the trail. Our plan was to try to keep up following the blood trail. The dogs' job was to run the deer until it bled out. I hoped the animal would die swiftly. In her panic, the doe crashed through the nearest avenue of escape, a thicket of thorns and tangled undergrowth. It was not long before our uncovered hands and legs were bleeding from the barbs. This did not hinder our dogs since their long hair deflected most of the spiny prickles. We could see clumps of dog and lentug hair on the thorny bush. Finally, we entered a forested area where we could make better time. The doe was leaving great blotches of blood and we could hear the dogs in the near distance. We soon realized that they were no longer moving because their barking was getting closer as we closed the gap. Running at full sprint, we rounded a small rock outcrop and almost ran into the tangle of animals. We found the lentug caught up in a deadfall, her eyes glazed over and the front of her chest covered with blood. The dogs stood over her, barking. I called them off and reached for my knife. I slit her throat to finish the kill, and E's and I gave thanks to Gisu'lg for giving us the skill to take one of his creatures. E's sprinkled some tobacco around the dead animal as a gift to the Creator while I started to gut the animal. E's then made a fire so we could eat before we left for the prearranged meeting place where the others were waiting for us.

I cut out the heart and shared it with E's. He took the ribs and hung them over the fire for our meal. By the time I finished with the animal, our food would be ready. There was enough daylight left for us to reach the gathering place once we had finished. I threw the intestines and other guts to the dogs. They had earned their feast. They ravenously ate what I threw to them. As I continued my work on the animal, I looked over at E's. He was popping chunks of bloody meat into his mouth. He returned my look with a huge smile reddened by the impromptu meal. We would use everything from this animal. Nothing would go to waste. Bones for weapons and tools, the hide for clothes, the stomach to carry water, the brain to tan the hide, and the sinew for bowstrings — everything had its use.

After eating the ribs, we cut a small sapling about eight feet long and tied the lentug's legs to it. We then boosted the animal onto our shoulders and, with the dogs in the lead, headed out. Being a foot and a half taller than E's, I let him take the front, hoping that the slanting of the poles forward would be a better option for him.

8

THE LAND OF THE MI'KMAQ

WE REACHED THE APPOINTED meeting place just before dusk. With everyone working on the carcass, we had it cut up in no time. In addition to the venison, we also had the seal and bear meat. The whole group, including the dogs, now would be loaded down for the remainder of the journey. Enough hopefully for the feast ahead to mourn the dead warriors left behind. After we butchered the animal the flies became thick on the meat so we built up our fire, making it smoke by placing it under a lean-to of branches and bark.

Like the Beothuk, the Mi'kmaq spent their summers by the sea, for the fish, lobster, and clams. Sea breezes kept the flies and mosquitoes away.

During the night, the temperature dropped to near freezing and we awoke to a frost and no flies. Jilte'g said we would reach the village by noon. Quickly eating our morning meal, we broke camp and headed west. The sun rose brightly in a cloudless sky as we set out for the final leg of the journey. We followed a well-worn path that the Mi'kmaq had used for years to make their way to the ocean from their winter camps. With Ta's'ji'jg leading the way and Apistanéwj keeping pace by holding onto the dogs, our small group made good time.

I could smell the village before we came upon it. My nostrils picked up the aromas of midday fires and cooking meals. As we approached the community, a pack of camp dogs ran out to defend their terrain. The alpha male was a long-legged, wolf-like creature that postured and barked at us. Seeing the two dogs with us, he approached them and issued a challenge. Without even a returning growl or bark, the black dog broke away from Apistanéwj's grasp and leaped upon the challenging male. He gripped the challenger by the nape of his neck and violently shook him, as if he were nothing more than a small rabbit. With a mighty twist of his head, he tossed the Mi'kmaq dog into the air. The dog hit the ground with a yelp and rolled three or four times. He quickly regained his stance and composure, took one more look at Tepgig, and sulked back to the village. The big dog then returned to Apistanéwj's side. Jilte'g and the other Mi'kmaqs at first stood in awe, and then they all started to laugh. E's was laughing so hard that he dropped to one knee and tears were flowing from his eyes.

Matues exclaimed, "I have never seen anything like that before. That camp dog is not used to a challenge returned! That was a blow to his ego!"

Walking into the village, we passed a group of young children taking part in a game with long sticks that had leather netting on the end, playing with a ball of leather. It seemed very rough and a few of the children were bleeding from various parts of their bodies. Nevertheless, they were all shouting, laughing, and having a good time. The constant clatter of the sticks told me they were playing this game for keeps.

As we passed the playing field, the rest of the village soon became aware our presence and ran out to meet us. One thing that was common among most of the men, women, and young children was the redness of their eyes. The cause of this was spending most of their time during the winter inside their birch-enclosed, smoky wikuoms. My people suffered the same ailment. We, like the Mi'kmaq, used the centres of the mountain maple's small twigs to make a poultice to treat the smoke-irritated eyes. Both tribes also burned the stems of the willow and used the ashes to treat the redness. Anything to ease the watering and itching of our eyes was a welcome relief.

One young boy walked up to me and looked up with his mouth hanging open. He turned to one of his friends and said in his language, "This man is as tall as a tree, and look at the strange shield and weapon hanging from his waist!" Then, taking one more look at me, he smiled and quickly ran away. I laughed to myself. The strange weapon he had talked about would have been the axe that I had taken from the dead Eli'tuat. I had almost forgotten about it. It seemed such a part of me now. E's had taken a shield plus one of the weapons that the strangers had used to hack off arms and heads.

Matues had been content to take control of a spear and as many arrows as he could carry in his quiver. Some of the men gathered around E's as he handled the weapon, asking him what it was.

I interjected, telling them the Eli'tuat in their language called the weapon a "sverð." They looked at me, shook their heads, and walked away talking amongst themselves.

I realized that I had talked to them in the language of the Eli'tuat. Where were these powers coming from?

E's said, "They have never seen a weapon as heavy as this. It does take strength to swing it, but from my first-hand experience watching the strangers fight with them, they can cause horrendous wounds."

The village was scattered along a small, quick-flowing, and very clear stream about seven feet wide. There would be no problem walking across the waterway since it was only a couple of feet deep. However, the inhabitants of the village had built a narrow bridge of wood over which they could come and go from each side. At a quick glance, I counted a little over twenty shelters giving refuge to over a hundred people. There were a few young women tending cooking vessels and carrying wood for the fires.

The rest of the village was gathering around Jilte'g. An elder they called Magisgonat (Big Nose) stepped forward and said, "You know the rules. You are to never bring any of the Island People from their lands!"

From behind Magisgonat strode a heavily muscled warrior who carried the authority of a chief. "Where are our young boys that left on this journey under your protection?"

Then, looking directly at me he said, “I am Gaqtugwan Musigisg (Thunder Sky), chief of the Gespe'gewa'gi (Last Land). Who is this giant?”

“Gaqtugwan Musigisg,” replied E’s, “there was trouble with the Eli’tuat, with losses on both sides. The Little One suffered a head wound and this giant saved his life during the altercation. Captured by the Eli’tuat in his homeland, they brought him to the Island as a prisoner. “

E’s continued telling the story of the island battle. After he related how the young warriors fell, a group of women started weeping uncontrollably. They were the mothers, sisters, and grandmothers of the dead boys. The sound of their sorrow was heartwrenching. The Mi’kmaq women would cry until they could not produce any more tears. The grieving helped them cope with the loss of their sons.

Over the wailing of the grief-stricken females, E’s continued his story. Many of the people surrounded Apistanéwj, touching him and staring at him. They all had heard stories about these people but none had actually seen them in person. The young children ran up to him, giggled, and then ran away. They were more in awe of him than the adults.

After a while they turned their attention to me. The parents stood back and looked while the young ones ran around me, touching me and squealing in delight. The antics of the children had a calming affect on the rest of the people, and soon they were all smiling and offering food and water to Apistanéwj and me.

The Elder Magisgonat asked my name, and Jilte'g replied, “Tall Man.”

Magisgonat shook his head and said, “No! That is not his name. It is Glooscap!”

As soon as he uttered that word, the entire village stopped what it was doing. Even the mourning women went silent. They all stood and stared. Then a deafening rallying cry arose that echoed throughout the village. They began to chant the name “Glooscap” repeatedly. Men, women, and children ran up and touched me. I looked around and caught Nukumi’s eye. She was smiling and clapping. Apistanéwj was leaning up against the dogs with a big grin. Who was I that these people were so in awe of me? Grandmother and Apistanéwj seemed to know. It looked as if I had a lot to learn about who the Mi’kmaq thought I was. Things were definitely going to get interesting!

The beating of the drums stirred me from my thoughts. Ah, a celebration and a new chapter in my life was about to unfold.

9

KANIEN'KEHÁ:KA (MOHAWK): (PEOPLE OF THE FLINT)

CORN DOG'S PEOPLE CAME from the south during a period of global warming pre-1300s. They were able to plant the Three Sisters in the fertile land near present-day Lake Ontario and the Mohawk Valley and erected palisades of trees to protect the villages of longhouses. Since they were constantly at war with neighbouring tribes, protection of the village was paramount. They cleared vast acreage by burning off the forests and planting corn, squash, and beans to feed the inhabitants. At this time in history, the League of Iroquois was still 150 to 200 years in the future. The Kanien'kehá:ka survived and grew by capturing their enemies and adopting them into the tribe.

This is where we now find Corn Dog and his people, raiding along what are now the St. Lawrence and Ottawa Rivers. The Algonquin called him Mandàmin Animosh; to his people he was Ó:newhste Erhar. Surviving the raid into

Algonquin Lands those six long years ago and barely escaping with his life, he and the remnants of his raiding party had stumbled through the unfamiliar lands of their enemies. Living off the land, they were able to make their way back to the village of his people near Caniaderi Guarunte (Door of the Country, present-day Lake Champlain). There they found out that his friend Panther Scar had lost his life at the Battle of the Waterfall on the Magwàizibò Sìbì, slain by the war chief of the Omàmiwinini, Mahingan. Since that day he had a burning rage in his heart to avenge the death of his friend. He also had the bait he needed to draw out the war chief of the Algonquins, his she-cat of a wife he had obtained in a trade with her captor. She was going to be the inducement to enable his vengeance. He would have both Mahingan and his shape-changing brother's heads on a stake in front of his longhouse this year.

Corn Dog was very tempted to turn around and send a force to destroy Mahingan in his winter lodgings after learning of the encounter with his hunting party. However, he knew that it would be risky at this time of year and he needed more warriors. He had to stay focused on the task. Destroying the allies of the Algonquins in the east would weaken the Bark Eaters when the final battle occurred. Meanwhile, he would receive much-needed support from his allies the Stadaconas and the Hochelagans, both foes of the Bark Eaters.

The Hochelagans had suffered defeat at the hands of Mahingan's people the same summer as Panther Scar's death. Now he needed his people to stay and rest up in their winter village. In the spring they would ask the Hochelagan warriors to continue with them to the Stadacona Nation, where the plan was to cross the Kaniatarowanenneh (Big Waterway). Once on the other side they would raid the Mi'kmaq Nation and then the Wàbanaki, putting his warriors between the Innu and Maliseet people, leaving the Bark Eaters with no readily available allies on the east. After accomplishing these planned strikes, he would have the strength of the Hochelagans and Stadaconas, putting an end to the Algonquin danger to his people forevermore.

Once he had won this war, he could go to his Clan Mother and the rest of his people with the heads of his enemies. This should prove to them his leadership qualities, enabling him to unite all the peoples of the valley. After this accomplishment, none of their enemies would be able to withstand the dominance of the Kanien'kehá:ka warriors.

After raiding for most of the fall, he had his people fortify a winter village where the Haudenosaunee River leaves the Caniaderi Guarunte (Lake Champlain). Here they would stay until the ennisko:wa moon (much lateness moon of March). They would be safe here during kohsera'kène (winter). With lots of corn captured from their raids and an abundance of game nearby, they would survive. Then they would visit their friends the Hochelagans and Stadaconas to obtain their help in his plan. As soon as the bite of winter left them and the sun provided warmth during the day, he made the decision to leave.

Corn Dog

Entering Hochelagan land, we encountered a small hunting party of their people. Two of them left the next day to announce our coming to the village. The remainder joined forces with a group of our warriors and continued with their quest for fresh meat. These were the group of men that had encountered the Bark Eaters while hunting, suffering the loss of five warriors.

Winpe wanted at that time to take men and hunt down the enemy who had slain our people. Again, as much as I hated the Bark Eaters, this was not yet the time. The summer would bring our revenge.

Winpe sent two other hunting parties out after the return of the tattered group that had suffered at the hands of the Bark Eaters. The rest of us continued on our way. We were running out of food and my men were starting to question a trek like this in the spring. I told them it was essential that we made contact with the Hochelagans to convince them to join our revenge raids.

Hungry stomachs, though, do not listen well. As hungry as they were, they never dropped off the pace. All of my followers were young and the women with us were youthful and strong. The few children who travelled with the women caused no problems since their mothers made sure they kept pace.

Mahingan's wife was diligent in her chores, and both her and her child asked for nothing other than what we gave them. I suspected that she had a hand in the escape of the three young Susquehannock boys, but I could not prove it. I kept my suspicions to myself. This woman would prove too valuable later on, and I did not need Winpe or any of my other warriors to throw her into the fire for her perceived offence.

During the day, the warriors that were on the flanks were able to kill a dozen squirrels and three porcupines.

There would be fresh meat over the fires, but feeding over two hundred people on the move was a constant worry.

I have seen starvation among my people many times through the years. The Kionhekwa (Three Sisters) that we planted every year, ò:nenhste (corn), ohsahèta (beans), and onon'onhsera (squash) were the staple of the Kanien'kehá:ka diet. The practice was always to plant enough to get the people through to the next spring when hunting became better and the new season brought plants to eat. One year there was a severe drought, and the tsyòkawe (crow), atiron (raccoon), and the ohskennonton (deer) population overran our fields of corn and beans, devouring them, leaving only our squash. We were barely able to save enough seed for the following year. That winter, when all the animals were asleep in the woods, the ohskennonton (deer) and the ska'nyonhsa (moose) became elusive, causing hunger pangs among the people.

Because of the lack of food during the chill of that season, many in our tribe suffered and died. The children who survived suffered a growth setback that seemed to take years to recover from. There was much sorrow during that period of cold. Along with the weakness brought on by the lack of food, some of our people started bleeding from their gums and losing their teeth. Our shamans went out into the woods and cut several baskets full of needles from the ohnehta'kowa (pine tree) and the yonen'tòren (white cedar tree). They boiled them in separate vessels. From the pine they scooped out the needles, which left an enriching tea. The cedar tea had a scum on its surface, which they skimmed off. Everyone, with and without aliments, was given the teas to drink for the rest of the winter. These teas saved many lives.

That was twelve winters ago. After that, the Clan Mothers made a decision that in the future should avert any threat to the tribe in the times of drought or other crop crisis. They also came up with a plan to keep the animals away. During the spring, while the some of the older warriors went out to hunt, the mothers put all the remaining warriors and young boys to work to claim more land from the forest. The wood they saved for warmth and the cooking fires. The burning of the brush helped keep the biting insects at bay and produced wood ash that the women collected in turn for use in the making of corn soup and fertilizer. Using crude axes, it would take them until planting time to get all the extra land cleared. The women this year wanted to plant enough of the corn and beans to last two years. This, they concluded, should keep the people from starving if once again they had a crop failure or another drought in future.

When planting the corn, the women made a small hill where the seed went. The squash seed they planted beside the hill. Their leaves would help keep the weeds down. Once the corn stalk appeared, they planted the beans on the hill. The stalk provided the needed climbing trunk for the bean plant. In turn, the women knew from the lessons taught to them from their mothers that the beans supplied natural nourishment for the corn and squash.

Now the women added one more job for the young boys of the village. They had purposely instructed the men that when clearing the extra area, they were to leave small areas of three to four trees standing. Within this small grove of trees, they were to build platforms. For the areas that had previously been cleared over the years, the women tasked the warriors with taking tree posts of twelve to fourteen feet and firmly planting them in the ground, again adding platforms to these as they previously did in the tree groves.

Once this was completed, the women called together all the young boys.

"From this day forward until you become a Haudenosaunee warrior, your jobs are to protect the Three Sisters once they start to produce on the vine. Blankets to wave and drums to beat when the crows come to feed will be your weapons on the platforms. In addition, you will patrol the grounds with bow and arrow day and night to slay raccoons and deer that come to feed in our fields. The older boys will decide the rotation. All must contribute. The animals that you slay are yours to do with as you will. The survival of your families depends on how well you protect our food in the fields!"

Since that day our people have flourished. Our Clan Mothers shared their knowledge with our neighbours to the west of us. The Shotinontowane'hàka (Seneca Nation) and the Ononta'kehàka (Onondaga Nation) were at times allies and at other times bitter enemies of the Kanien'kehá:ka. Many times during the years of our ancestors, they would try to bring about a peace among the three tribes. However, for one reason or another the calm would be short-lived and they would again war amongst themselves. When there was harmony among our peoples, all our enemies feared us because of the strength of our numbers.

The hunters that Winpe had sent out in the next couple of days were able to come back to camp with a small doe, some squirrels, and rabbits. That night, at least, our bellies received a bit of nourishment. Continuing on the next morning, we came upon a party of Hochelagans that was seeking us out to bring to their village.

The Hochelagans and Stadaconas had always been allies of the Kanien'kehá:ka. They had survived along the Kaniatarowanenneh (St. Lawrence River) since our Father's Fathers. The two nations had a diet consisting mostly of onenhste (corn) and kèntsyonk (fish). Their enemies were the Mi'kmaq, Omàmiwinini (Algonquin), Innu, Maliseet, and Wàbanaki Nations — tribes that we too were constantly at war with.

Once we arrived at the village, the old chief we called Tsyatak Erhar (Seven Dogs) came and greeted us. "Corn Dog we do not have much food, but we will share. Tonight during the evening fire we will talk."

That night Seven Dogs and I sat beside the fire with some of our warriors. After eating what meagre offerings they could spare us, the old chief addressed all that sat in council. "What do the Haudenosaunee need that brings them to our lands in the early spring?"

I replied, "Seven Dogs, we have many common enemies, most powerful among them the Bark Eaters to your west and the Mi'kmaq to the east. I have been amassing a force to defeat the Bark Eaters, but I need your help. Knowing that the Mi'kmaq are always a threat to you and the Stadaconas, I am proposing that we join forces and raid them. In return, after destroying the Mi'kmaqs, your people and the Stadaconas will help us defeat the Bark Eaters."

The old man sat and never said a word. The pipe that he was smoking was emitting a huge puff, almost completely obscuring his head. After what seemed an endless pause, he spoke.

"Corn Dog, I like your plan, but at the moment my people are near starvation. Soon it will be spring and the bears will come out of their dens from their long sleep; the deer and the moose will appear from the deep woods, and the river will open up for my people to fish and hunt geese. We will then become strong. We have still not recovered from the loss of the warriors that went into the land of the Algonquins six summers ago. Only three men made it back, and all of them were without their fingers. Of them, there is just one still alive. He-Who-Walks now has to rely on his sons to provide for him. He cannot hunt for his family anymore. Yes, we will help you, but not until the ohiari:wa moon (ripening time moon of June). Then you can bring your warriors back and we will walk the path of war with you. Until then my people need to gain back their strength from the long winter."

I looked at Winpe and saw the disappointment on his face. We now had to return to the village and hope that some of the young men from our village who had stayed behind would join us when we returned.

"I accept your offer, Seven Dogs. My people will rest up for two days and then we will leave for home. The ohiari:wa moon will bring us back."

After my answer, more of their scanty food supply appeared, along with tobacco, and we spent the rest of the evening telling stories about past raids and hunts.

In the morning I was awakened by a young girl screaming, "Wegimindj, wegimindj!" (mother) in the Algonquin language. Stepping out of the lodge, I could see two Hochelagan warriors five lodges away dragging a woman by her arms as she struggled to escape. As soon as I saw the young daughter trailing behind I knew this was going to end badly for someone, most likely the two warriors. They approached Seven Dogs' longhouse and called to him. The old chief came outside to view the spectacle that was taking place in front of him. By this time a crowd had gathered and Winpe had started to step forward toward the woman. I held out my arm and stopped him.

The tallest warrior spoke. "Seven Dogs, I have found an enemy of the Hochelagans in our midst; this woman is an Algonquin. We want her to burn in our fires."

However, before Seven Dogs could speak or I could say she was a slave of our people, what I feared most happened. Wàbananang turned and bit the smaller man on the bicep of the arm clutching her, taking a chunk out of his skin the size of a child's fist. Spitting out the chunk of meat in the midst of the man's screams of agony, she swiftly reached inside her shirt with her free hand and drew out her skinning knife. The warrior still holding the woman's other arm turned to face her and at that moment she plunged her knife into his lower jaw at such an angle that it came out of his screaming mouth. With blood dripping from her mouth and running down her knife hand, she seized the last screaming warrior's knife from the leather sheath hanging around his neck. Then, turning to the kneeling warrior she had just bit, she buried that knife to the hilt into his cheek, exiting the other side. She then jerked the knife forward toward the front of his mouth, tearing off the front of his face. She calmly reached down and pulled her skinning knife from the jaw of her other captor, wiped it on his leggings, and placed it back in its original spot inside her shirt. Turning to her daughter, she called her name and the young girl wrapped her hands around her mother's waist.

All this happened in two or three heartbeats. The woman was that ruthless and decisive in her actions. The onlookers that had arrived to see the origins of all the noise stood in mute silence. Never had they seen such sudden and brutal violence from a woman.

I raised my hand in a signal to Winpe. He stepped forward and returned with Wàbananang and her daughter, Pangì Mahingan, bringing them to my side.

Seven Dogs turned to me with a look of shock and said, "If this woman is any indication of the strength of the Algonquin warriors, I want to feast on their bodies to gain this power! She has taken two warriors from my force. Neither of these men, if they survive, will be capable of hunting or warring. They will have to help the women of our village from now on. What do you offer in return? Her life?"

"Seven Dogs," I replied, "I cannot give you her for the fires; I need this woman for my future plans. However, I will give you five of my warriors to help you with your hunting. Then, when we come back during the ohiari:wa moon, I will lead you and your people to a successful war with our enemies, where you will have many captives for slaves or adoptions and others for the fires."

"Corn Dog," he warned, "your life depends on the success of this summer revenge war. Now get her out of my sight and give me ten warriors until your return!"

10

WÀBANAKI LAND

AFTER SELECTING TEN warriors to stay with the Hochelagans, I asked Winpe to gather our people to leave. We were down to one hundred and thirty-seven warriors, plus around a hundred captive women and young boys and a few young children.

Now we had to trek back to our village and try to convince the Clan Mother to let me go to war with our young braves. I hoped that the captives I was bringing into the encampment to replace dead and departed people of our tribe would lead to a favourable decision.

"Winpe, we will need two hunting parties out at all times plus scouts ahead of us and a rear guard. Have the women carry the loads; let the camp erhar (dogs) run loose to be our eyes and ears. The hunters also will need three or four erhars to track for them! We have a dangerous journey ahead and we must be attentive; our lives depend on it.

We were able to avoid our enemies during the trip to the Hochelagan Lands, but may not be so easy on the return trip. We have to be alert once we reach the Magwàizibò Sìbì (Iroquois River, now known as the Richelieu River). Our enemies will be rising from their winter slumbers and will be hunting along both the Kaniatarowanenneh and Magwàizibò Sìbì Rivers. The sooner that we can travel clear of this area, the safer we will be."

Thinking back, it was not really a wasted trip, except for the woman's coldblooded violence that caused me the short-term loss of ten warriors. I knew, though, that if I had a hundred warriors as heartless as her in battle I could defeat all my enemies with ease. The trip back to our village would be a lot easier now that I knew the Hochelagans and their allies the Stadaconas would join us during the ohiari:wa moon for our raid into the Land of the L'nu'k (The People, Mi'kmaq) We were in the late part of the ennisko:wa moon (much lateness March). Our journey home to my village of Ossernenon would take seven to ten days, depending on how fast we could keep our people going and, of course, fed.

Keeping over two hundred people on the move and nourished was a major undertaking. I instructed Winpe to have three hunting parties out every morning, plus an advanced scouting group and a rear guard. If caught in an ambush, it would be devastating.

We put our canoes into the Kaniatarowanenneh and made our way across. Evading floating chunks of ice, the only sound was the swish of the paddles. Everyone was silent, thinking about the journey before us. When we reached the other shore, the men cached the canoes for our return. The women hastily gutted the fish they had caught with hooks and lines on the trip over. The snarling and fighting of the dogs over the fish guts drowned out all the other sounds we made while organizing for the next leg of our passage.

Now that it was warming, the captive women and maybe some of the adopted warriors would be tempted to escape. My men would have to be attentive to that possibility. The loss of the Susquehannock brothers was still bothering me. I had no reason to suspect them escaping so far from their homeland.

Before we started down the warrior's trail that would lead us to Ossernenon, I announced, "If any captives decide to escape, remember this: you will feel the wrath of my warrior's clubs. Then you will be fed to the dogs. There will be no mercy. If our rear guards come upon anyone that cannot keep up with the group, they have orders to club them and leave them on the side of the trail for the wolves and bears. We will travel from morning's first light to the disappearance of the sun in the evening. There must be silence on the trail at all times. Children must be kept quiet or we will silence them. The women will be responsible for keeping fires going and food ready after we make camp. The children are responsible for keeping the fires tended. All will share in what food we have. Weakness, sickness, and not keeping up will be your downfall."

Once the women had the fish readied to take with us, we started for home. For such a large amount of people, there was very little sound, except for the whisper of clothes rubbing against bodies and encroaching brush along the trail. With very little snow remaining in the woods, the warriors leading the column did not have to wear snowshoes to break trail for those who followed. This helped make the walking very easy and enabled the group to keep up a good pace. The forward scouting units' responsibilities were to be on the lookout for enemies and to clear the trail of deadfalls.

The path gave up the sound of the crunch of frozen mud, leaves, and melting snow. The forest that we were walking through blocked the view of the sun most of the time. Walking was easy. The ground below made for soft walking among the blanket of needles in the absence of snow cover. The tall pine forests kept out the sun's rays, preventing undergrowth from surviving without the sun's light. Other times, when walking through hardwood stands, the leaf cover was not as extensive and our shadows grew long from the sun penetrating the canopy. Now, because the sun was reaching the forest floor, there was undergrowth to negotiate. Other times we came upon spaces where fire had ravaged the area and walking became a little easier among the meadows that could now grow after being exposed to the unhindered sunlight. Always, though, there was a trail. Warriors had come through this area since our 'Nihas (Fathers') time to hunt and war.

Shelters to protect us from the elements were not often necessary. There were areas on the trail where the pine forests' canopy and needle-covered ground made bedding down for the night very comfortable. Sometimes there would be caves or large rock overhangs that sufficed for the evening. Occasionally we would come upon shelters that previous groups had made and, with some repair, would suffice for that night.

The first night, though, we did raise shelters, and for that reason we made an early camp. The younger warriors prepared the shelters by cutting down small saplings. Depending on the clearing they had to work with, they erected two posts at each end, three if there was room to make a shelter wider than twelve feet. The third post would go in the middle to prevent sagging. Another sapling would run along the top of the post width. From there they attached the brace poles toward the back on a slant for the roof and support. They then attached more saplings across the back width from the slanted support posts. Here the young men would lay cedar boughs or elm bark to make a roof and cedar boughs on the ground for bedding. The saplings were tied together with vines. Depending on the size, these shelters could hold eight to twelve inhabitants. If it was not raining, many people would still sleep outside the shelter near the fire. The young warriors were very adept at erecting these covers and could get them done by the time the women had prepared the evening meal.

None of our hunting groups were back yet; nevertheless, some of the younger boys had killed six kwa'yenha (rabbit) with their crude bows and arrows. Along with some frozen berries found along the trail, wild onions, and some corn that we had, the women prepared a stew. If the hunting parties came back empty-handed, we would have to slay one or two of the dogs for a more significant meal than this stew.

Winpe approached me just at dusk. "Corn Dog, one of our hunting groups has not yet returned. They were the forward party that went out. The other two are back with an ohskennonton (deer) and a wahkwari'tahònsti (black bear), but no sign of the one in question."

I replied, "They probably were further than they thought from the main group and have decided to find a site for the night. I am sure our scouts will find them heading back to us in the morning. Since we now have some venison and bear, there is something more substantial than the rabbit stew."

The first day produced neither escape attempts nor any stragglers. As long as our hunting parties were successful, there would be no weakness from hunger. If we could keep up this pace, we would make Ossernenon in eight days.

We woke up in the morning to a light drizzle, making everyone, dogs included, wet and miserable. The trees blocked the direct rain, but whenever someone brushed a branch, water would trickle down on the person behind. To stay away from a drenching, the group became more strung out as they were spacing themselves from the walker ahead of them.

Toward midmorning, our scouting party came running toward us.

"O:newwhste Erhar, we have found our hunting party," said Tsihsterkeri (Owl). "They are off the main trail past that rock bluff ahead near a stream. All are dead!"

Turning to one of the older men, Karònya Kayènkwire (Sky Arrow), I told him to keep the group on the trail.

Turning to Winpe, I said, "Select a dozen warriors to follow with us!"

Motioning to Owl and his scouts to lead the way, we silently followed. Upon reaching the small stream, we came upon an okwàho (wolf) pack of nine animals and a gaunt-looking boar bear ravishing the bodies. The wolves were easily scared off at the sight of us, but the bear was not going to give up this meal so readily. He rose up on his hind legs over the body that he was devouring. In that instant, several arrows pierced his heart. Spurting blood from the wounds and his mouth, he made one mighty bellow producing a torrent of blood, mucus, and spittle, swatted at the arrows, then dropped stone dead.

Upon inspection of our men, we noticed that they all had suffered fatal wounds that would indicate they never saw their attackers. They had probably stopped to drink from the stream and had been attacked while quenching their thirst. One of the five had arrow wounds in his chest, and his face had been smashed in by a club, indicating he had turned to face the enemy. The hunters' three dogs had also come under the axe of the enemy. The wolves had made short work of their carcasses before moving on to the warriors. There were signs also that they had slain a deer to bring back to camp. The combatants had taken scalps, ears, and fingers from the bodies.

Turning to the five scouts, I said, "Find their trail! We will follow as soon as we are done here."

They soundlessly disappeared into the forest.

Turning to the rest, I said, "Try to bury our fallen warriors as deep as possible, and then pile rocks on their graves to keep the animals from the bodies. At the same time, butcher the bear and take as much meat as you can reasonably carry for food for the trail we are about to take. Kahònsti Sorak (Black Duck), I am going to ask you to select one man to help take the remainder of the meat back to the column and tell Sky Arrow to keep the people going. We will meet up in a couple of days."

Turning to Winpe, I said, "How many do you think were involved in this?"

"By the look of the signs left behind it was a party of twenty to twenty-five, half women and children. Probably a Wàbanaki family unit that is moving toward a main spring camp. It was just bad luck for our hunting party that this group stumbled onto them and took advantage of the circumstance presented to them. They would not suspect that the hunting party was part of a larger group. They almost certainly think the hunters were this far north looking for game, killing and caching until they had enough to return."

"Winpe, we have to find and dispose of this band before they reach their destination. If that happens someone might figure out our hunters were not foraging for a village but for a large party on the move," I warned.

"Black Duck, when you get back tell the Algonquin woman she is responsible for all the women. If anything happens, her daughter will suffer for it," I exclaimed. "There are to be no hunting parties to go out. They are to hunt by chance and must survive for the next two or three days on what they now have. Double the strength of the both the scouting parties and rear guard, and put out flankers. The Wàbanaki are on the move back to spring camps; we cannot afford any more accidental encounters."

It did not take long for the burials and the harvesting of the bear. Winpe and I led the remaining ten warriors at a trot to catch up to our scouts. This trail had less wear than the one we had been travelling on. Our scouts were blazing as they travelled, setting an easy trail to follow.

Just after the noon sun, two of them met us on the trail. Stopping for a moment, the men ate the raw bear meat, some corn, and drank from their water gourds.

"Corn Dog, we have found them. They are close ahead by a small waterfall, filling their water gourds and skins. The women have a small fire going and they are roasting the deer that they took from our hunters. There is only one guard at the top of the waterfall where the trail goes, plus one other on the back trail. No one is at all vigilant. The two guards are smoking and watching the camp. We counted twelve women, seven children, and nine warriors. They are too at ease to think there is anyone on their back trail. There are a few dogs so we must strike quickly before they give the alarm."

"Winpe," I said, "you will take the three scouts that are up ahead, with three other warriors, and eliminate the scout above the falls. Block off any retreat. Capture any women and children and kill the warriors. I'll take the remaining nine and attack from the front."

Swiftly, I led the men to where the other three scouts were. Winpe's warriors then melted into the shadows of the forest. When we arrived near the encampment, we could see the back of the rear guard with smoke rising in wisps above his head. I motioned to one of my warriors who had stopped a fair distance behind us. He rattled two deer horns together, making it sound like two bucks were jousting in the near forest. The guard turned his head, smiled, and stood up. He entered the forest, stringing his bow, hoping for a shot at one of the two preoccupied bucks that he thought he was hearing. As soon as he entered the shadows of the forest, one of my men drove his spear into the nape of his neck, paralyzing him, and as the man dropped to his knees the warrior slit his throat, scalped him, and cut off his head.

Leaving the dead man's body on the forest floor in a pool of blood for forest denizens to devour, we silently continued. Looking across to the top of the falls, we noticed the other guard had also disappeared. Now was the time to strike.

Tossing the head of the slain Wàbanaki down the hill into the campsite of the enemy, we emitted a blood-curdling war cry and charged into the encampment. The inhabitants looked up in stunned silence; we were upon them before they realized the danger that was about to beset their camp. I watched as one young warrior grabbed his wife and ran toward the trail above. He reached the top, where he received a smash to the face from a war club. Bone and blood flew into the air, and he tumbled backward down the hill, flipping and landing face first in the stream, bloodying the water around him. His young wife was bound to a tree. The other six warriors and some women stood their ground. I was the first to reach the camp and was met by a warrior with half of his head shaved. He had a stone axe in his hand and tried to swing it at me as he rose. With my war club in one hand and my knife in the other I swung the club as hard as I could, catching the man on his chin. I could hear his jaw break as he let out a scream of pain. The blow staggered him and he fell to one knee, but rising quickly, he staggered toward me, spitting blood on the ground. His eyes glazed as I drove my knife into his heart. He died in that instant, covering me with his blood. Cutting his heart out to eat, I now gained his strength.

Covered with blood, I looked around. The water was blood-red and the rocks had turned the colour of the onekwenhtara tsi'tenha (red bird) of the forest. The battle was over in a very short time. We captured only one warrior. We would take him back to our main camp for the gauntlet and the stake. He should supply us with future pleasure. Two women had died defending their men and families. The other ten and the children would become Kanien'kehá:ka, adopted by families who previously had suffered the loss of family members. Our attack was sudden and quick, but we did suffer a loss. One of our warriors had taken an arrow in the throat from a quick-reacting Wàbanaki. Two others had suffered wounds that we treated with our healing herbs.

We buried our fallen warrior. The bodies of the enemy were stripped, mutilated, skinned, and then threw into the fires. Tonight we would stay and rest here. Sunrise would find us on the trail to rejoin our people. With all the captives I had to present to the village residents, surely this should prove to the Clan Mothers that I was a strong war chief, and they would release the warriors to me!

11

BREAKING WINTER CAMP

MAHINGAN

After the kiss from Àwadòsiwag, Wàbek had thrown his first toss off the chute. Now, with all his might he had tossed his final stick. All the contestants were yelling, with Anokì's team frantically cheering for the projectile to stay on course. Mitigomij's players shouted encouragement for the staff to stop or fly off the slide. The staff was nearing the spot where Àwadòsiwag's stick had stopped, when it hit a crack in the channel and flew end-for-end away from the game area. The men stood in mute silence, the women and Susquehannock boys starting laughing. All the commotion caused the camp dogs to bark and growl. Soon everyone was laughing and slapping each other on the back. The men had cook and collect firewood for the next two days. It was all in fun and a welcome relief from the rigours that the winter had brought us.

The early spring sun was starting to melt the snow, and in a week or two the ice would start to leave the Kitcisìpi. Once that began, our people would leave for the summer hunting grounds and join up with the other families that had wintered in their areas.

As soon as we were all together, the Family Leaders decided on our plan of action against Corn Dog. My thinking was that he would surely attack us once he finished raiding and gathering his allies from the Hochelagans and Stadaconas. His band of warriors would cut us off from our eastern allies, in addition to attacking and weakening them. Could I count again on the Nipissing and Ouendat Nations to aid us? Our Nation would survive or die with the events that could befall us in the coming summer and fall.

Our people should not confront this threat blindly. We had to find out where Corn Dog was. Our allies who lived along the Magotogoek Sìbì (the Path that Walks, present-day St. Lawrence River) would not be able to help us with this problem. We would have to find where he was and follow his movements. To do this I had to split up our small family unit and undertake a very dangerous mission. My Nation's survival would depend on locating Corn Dog and planning on how to handle his advancement against us. Stealth and bravery would rule the moment.

"Mitigomij, call the people together. It is essential we talk to them about the gathering threat that the Haudenosaunee are trying to bring down on our heads."

After the meeting, we all decided that we would go to Asinabka (place of glare rock, now present-day Chaudière Falls). There we would spear name (sturgeon) and ogà (walleye) during their spring run. With our supply of pimizì (eel) completely eaten during the winter, we desperately needed the nourishment that this fish would provide.

That day we took the wìgwàs-chìmàn (birch bark canoes) out from their winter storage to prepare for the journey back down the river to the Kitcisìpi Sìbì and then to our summer camp.

We were now twenty-one people with the addition of the three Susquehannock boys and the loss of Kekek. We had seven canoes to carry all our possessions, dogs, and ourselves. There would be at least two capable paddlers in each boat. Everyone had to contribute on the water and on the onigam (portage), even Anokì.

Nigig was helping me uncover one of the canoes when he said, "Mahingan, I want to tell you something my mother, Àbita, saw while collecting firewood."

"Go ahead," I answered.

"It was right after the hunters had left to hunt the wàbidì, where they had the encounter with the Hochelagan hunting party. Àbita said she was out collecting firewood and upon tiring she sat down on a rock to rest. After a few moments she heard footsteps to her left. She sat very still. In a small clearing she watched as Mitigomij removed all his clothes and weapons. He laid his clothes on the ground, put his weapons on them, and rolled them up inside the clothing. Taking the roll, he tied it to Makadewà Wàban's back. Your brother then reached his hands to the sky and said something Àbita could not hear. After he said these words, a blinding flash of light struck the exact spot where Mitigomij stood. Once Àbita's eyes readjusted, to her amazement a wàbòz had appeared in the spot Mitigomij had been. The wàbòz then sped off with the panther following. Mahingan, she swore what she saw was true!"

"Nigig, I need to ask you to talk to your mother and request that she keeps to herself what she experienced. In addition, I must trust you to do the same."

"Mahingan, then is it true what the Haudenosaunee say, that your brother and the big cat are Shape Shifters? Are they Michabo and Gichi-Anami'e-Bizhiw?"

"It seems so, my friend, it seems so," I replied. "Nigig, this secret is yours, Àbita's, and mine. We have a very powerful ally in my brother and Makadewà Wàban, something that the Haudenosaunee fear beyond all else. It explains how he can move from place to place with such speed. It seems that his powers are increasing and he has found the way to control it to his benefit. Are he and the cat immortal? That I do not know. I recognize that he is a powerful warrior and the cat is a deadly killer. Nevertheless, he is my brother and his secret stays with the three of us, till death."

"You have my word as a Wàbanaki warrior, Mahingan. Àbita and I will never divulge what we know. Death will take us before we give up this information!"

"I trust you. Mitigomij cannot find out from us that we know. The mystery is safe."

I knew the time would come when I would have to reveal to Mitigomij what I knew about him, but for now his secret was safe.

We continued with the job at hand. Once we had uncovered and lined up all the boats, the people inspected them for small tears. They repaired the canoes by scraping pine resin off the trees and heating it, then spreading it on the slit. Once cooled it would seal and waterproof the split.

That night was the last evening we spent at the winter camp. You could sense the excitement of the community as we readied for the move. There would be ample food after reaching Asinabka, and then after that they would renew old friendships when all the family units arrived at the summer site. That morning found us travelling up the Kitcisìpi Sìbì; it would take three or four days against the current to arrive at our destination.

The first day everyone was keen, even though the winter had made our paddling muscles soft. The canoes were well loaded with three people to each boat, along with a couple of dogs. My boat had my nephew, Makwa, and Anokì, who was now sound asleep between his constant guardians Pìsà Animosh and my wolf Ishkodewan. The wolf had grown into an immense, imposing animal. He was all black except for the white blaze on his face and totally dedicated to my son and myself. The camp dogs looked to him for leadership, and none had ever challenged him. I had seen him take down a full-grown wàwàshkeshi on the dead run several times. He could carry twice the pack weight that the other dogs could. He defended me when we were involved in the mìgàdinàn (war) at the waterfalls. Still, Ishkodewan had yet to prove he was as lethal a killer of men as the big cat that followed Mitigomij. The small dog was his constant companion and had the heart of a bear. I had never seen this small dog back off from danger.

We camped that night beside a set of rapids that we had to onigam (portage.) Everyone tired easily on this first day of paddling since last fall. It did not take long to prepare the shelters for the night. We were able to repair some of the cover that previous travellers had erected and construct a few new ones. Then the women started fires and prepared food. The people were not long for sleep once they had eaten. Mitigomij and I took the first watch and tended the fires. We would switch with someone else once we tired, and then that pair would do the same when sleep started to overcome them. During the course of the night, probably five or six teams would take their turns.

Before dawn, the last watch woke everyone. While the meal was prepared, the boats were loaded. After dousing the fires, we set out on the river to continue toward our destination. I gave the task of fishing to Anokì and Àbita, the youngest and the eldest, while the others paddled. They worked diligently at this chore and were quite successful.

Black rain clouds started to form at midday, forcing us to shore. We hurriedly pulled the boats into the tree line a good distance from the river then turned them over to protect our belongings. The women hurried off to collect as much firewood as they could before the skies opened up, and we rushed to get a large shelter erected instead of several smaller ones. A larger cover would enable us to work faster because we would only need to construct two ends instead of ten or twelve. This refuge would also need bark on the roof to keep out the rain. The men worked swiftly, and just as a light rain started, they finished. Soon we had two fires going and a fish stew with some spring plants the women were able to forage. The haven soon became crowded with all the people and dogs, but all were warm and dry. My nose was definitely sensitive to the fish cooking, the body odour, and the smell of the wet dogs. That soon waned, though, as my nostrils became inured to the surrounding intermingling stenches.

With the skies now opening up and the thunder and lightning causing the dogs to cower and whine, Nokomis (Mother Earth) was putting on a show. I looked out onto the river to see the rain producing numerous splashes on the water. The driving rain was not as powerful as a waterway but still possessed enough energy to force my people to shelter.

It was while I watched the rain that I remembered last fall's pimizì harvest. It was the first one that the twins, Makwa and Wàbek, had actually participated in since coming of age. With everyone huddled around the fires, I thought this would be a worthy story to pass a little time and relate how the eel was such a vital part of our sustenance.

For the Omàmiwinini people, the pimizì supplies us with more fat and life-sustaining meat than any other awsìnz (animal) in the woods or kìgònz (fish) in the water. The late summer and early fall migration that they take is essential to our well-being. The Algonquin people always gathered at Asinabka to harvest this staple of their diet.

Last fall, as we travelled down the Kitcisìpi Sìbì, we stopped there to harvest the eel. Usually there were two men to each boat; one steered the canoe to where the eels were and the other speared the prey. The spear that we used was different from a fish spear. The men would each cut some six- to eight-foot saplings, and then take three deer prongs, which they barbed. The creator of the spear fastened the tines to the bottom of the shaft, spaced evenly apart. The barbs were essential because the eels would wiggle off an ordinary fish spear.

Because this was the twins' first eel hunt, we allowed them to be in the first boat to go out below the rapids. The creatures were abundant, churning and frothing the water. Wàbek was in the bow with the spear and Makwa manoeuvred the boat. The rest of us stood on the shore with smiles on our faces. The boys had forgotten to take rocks to kill these slippery denizens of the river. To kill them you had to place their head on a stone and smash it with another rock. All of us on shore knew what was going to take place next with the writhing snake-like creature in the bottom of the boat. After a few missed opportunities, Wàbek soon got the knack of spearing. However, pulling them off the barbs was another matter. The boys' hands would slide away from the slimy bodies when they attempted to remove them. Finally, Makwa cut a piece of leather from his leggings, wrapped it around his hand and then, and only then, was he was able to tug the eel off the spear.

Now the fun was going to start: the boat was starting to fill with squirming eels that were still very much alive. True, they were speared, but not maimed. In a short while both of the boys started to yell. Wàbek had eels wrapped around his legs and working their way up his body. Makwa, who had sat most of the time to steer the canoe, now had eels on his lap, arms, and some were draped around his neck and shoulders. Standing up, he vainly tried to brush the twisting mess of slimy pimizì from his body. By this time everyone on shore was laughing and shouting at the boys to come to ground. When finally they beached the canoe, the eels were spilling over the side of the vessel, wrapping around the paddle and the boys. The twins rolled on the ground to try to dislodge their visitors. After much laughter and carrying on, we gathered up as many of the eels as we could. The boys by this time had regained their composure and were chuckling along with the rest of us.

It was their father, Kàg, who started the hooting and snickering again when he approached the boys and said, "You might need these the next time!" And he handed them two rocks.

Retelling this story brought back memories and renewed laughter. Makwa and Wàbek enjoyed the story and the teasing all over again, laughing until the tears rolled down their cheeks. The resulting laughter woke Ishkodewan and the dogs. Thinking something was approaching our encampment, they all stood at the edge of the shelter looking out, trying to figure out why we were making so much noise.

That fall day, after everyone had regained their composure, the men launched their canoes into the river and continued with the spearing. We spent two days there stocking up with all that we could carry. Winters are the starvation season and the community would need all the nourishment it could transport.

To skin the eels we forced a stick into the gills and through the head. To keep the eel's body still while skinning it (even in death they still squirmed) we rested it on a forked branch forced into the ground. Using a leather grip so the eel did not slip, we were able to remove the skin, which we used to make clothes, pakìgino-makizinan (moccasins), and bags. Eel skin lasts longer than leather and is softer to wear. The women then smoked the pimizì over fires and stored them in bark baskets.

We cooked the fresh eel by shoving a stick through the length of its body then roasting it on a spit over the fires. Pimizì is a delicacy enjoyed by all.

With the harvest over, we buried the heart, liver, and heads of some of the eels to thank Kije-Manidò (the Great Spirit) for the successful hunt. This dweller of the river got us through most of the pibòn (winter).

The pimizì never turned up in abundant numbers until the late summer during their migration to the ocean. Occasionally during the summer we would catch an eel on a migiskan (hook), in an asab (net), or while spearing fish.

But only in the fall did they congregate in the numbers that enabled us to spear them in huge quantities.

The rain never let up until late into the day. With little daylight left, we made the decision to stay the night. In the meantime, a couple of hunting groups ventured out to seek whatever they could find for a meal. Just before dusk, they came back with an interesting mixture for the evening stew: amik (beaver) and a nika (goose). The women skinned the amik, saving the pelt to tan later. They cut the tail off the body to be roasted; it definitely was not bound for the stew vessel. The nika's feathers were taken off and given to the young people for decoration. The bird's innards they put into the stew and the carcass on a spit to roast alongside the amik's tail. Everyone had a portion of the stew and the ones that wanted amik or nika used a piece of bark to hold the hot meat. Tonight all went to sleep on a full stomach. Tomorrow would be another day.

That morning all that we had left to sustain us was tea. My hope was that Àbita and Anokì would be able to catch a few kìgònz for a midday meal.

One canoe had three strong paddlers compared with the others, and this vessel led our small group through the waterway. They were able to scout far ahead and find the best landing places to go around rapids and ensure our safety. Every person who travelled this river used these portages. Sometimes during the spring, the movement of the melting river ice would crush shorelines, moving rocks and trees. Storms would bring weak trees crashing to the ground, blocking access to the pathways around the rapids. When the lead canoe found obstacles like this, those paddlers' job was to clear away the debris or to find another exit from the river to skirt the white waters. The lead canoe contained three fierce warriors, Agwanìwon, Kìnà Odenan, and Kànikwe, the two women and their hairless friend.

Agwanìwon and Kìnà Odenan were nìj manidò (two spirits) (lesbians). They were vicious in battle, proving themselves repeatedly. The two women were also healers and looked after the elderly and orphans. Dedicated at all costs to the well-being of the Omàmiwinini community, they were among the first to volunteer for hunting or war parties.

Kànikwe was not nìj manidò. He was a close friend to the two women, owing his life to them. When they were young girls, they found him in a swamp bleeding from a severe head wound, completely covered with honey. He had raided a beehive for the precious healing power of the honey to cover the injury. Taking him back to their village, they cared for him until he healed. To this day, he was devoted to them. Kànikwe had no hair and a deeply scarred head. He painted his skull black and his own scalp hung from his war axe.

These three were our eyes and ears, leading us to safety each day. Mitigomij, who was by far the strongest paddler, always had one of the twins in his boat. On this trip, it was Wàbek, along with a dog. Always at the rear of the line when we were in the water, he guarded us from any surprises. His cat Makadewà Wàban never travelled in a canoe unless necessary. He patrolled the shore beside us, never letting Mitigomij out of his sight.

Anokì tired today of his fishing just before midday. He had caught five fish and they were lying on the bottom of the boat, a couple still flopping around my feet. He was not long in curling up to Ishkodewan. The big wolf turned his head and licked the boy's face. Anokì giggled then laid his head on the chest of the animal and fell fast asleep.

The sun was reaching its midday height when we rounded a bend in the river. Kànikwe was waving everyone in. There were rapids ahead so we had to go ashore and skirt around them. Kànikwe was all smiles. The women and he had come upon a wàwàshkeshi swimming across in front of them just before they had landed. They had been able to kill it and pull the animal into the canoe. The women had the big buck, which was just starting to grow its spring antlers back, hanging from a tree, gutting it. The dogs were feasting on the entrails. I whistled for the wolf and he came running to share in the bounty. In times of starvation, the dogs might not have been able to share in this reward, but today they did. This meat would keep us fed for days. Along with the fish Anokì and Àbita were catching, we would have enough to eat for the rest of the trip until we got to Asinabka.

The rapids roared loudly. We decided that once the women finished with the deer, we would eat and continue. In the meantime, we had to bring the canoes ashore and carry them above the rapids. It was at this time I realized that I had not seen Anokì since I left the boat. When I had whistled for Ishkodewan, the boy must have woken up. Where was he? I looked toward the river, hearing my name called. There was Anokì, tumbling down the rapids, yelling my name.

"ANOKÌ!" I screamed above the roar of the river.

12

THE BLOODIED LAND

TALL MAN/GLOOSCAP

After the cheering had stopped, I turned to E's and asked, "Why were they calling me this name — Glooscap?"

"Because," he answered, "you are a hero and protector to our people. Our elders have said that a giant of a man, along with two dogs and a little person, will appear and keep us from harm. All the animals are your friends. Nukumi told us that you would be coming, but Magisgonat had to lay eyes on you and confirm her prophecy. Now that he has confirmed what Nukumi foretold, you are one of us. The L'nu'k people now feel safe!"

I stood there, my head reeling. Just a short while ago I was a Beothuk warrior on an island far from this place. Now I was a mythical guardian to a people I previously never knew existed. Now I knew that the Great Spirit had planned a path for me, which I would trust him to lead me through.

From that moment on, the L'nu'k let Apistanéwj and I have the run of the village. We constantly practised our marksmanship with our weapons. I was starting to get the feel of the axe that I had taken from the dead Eli'tuat. It was a formidable weapon. I took a sharpened bone and drilled a hole into the handle, threading a leather strip through it. By wrapping this leather around my wrist during battle, I should be able to avoid dropping or losing it.

The people of the village and I watched curiously as E's and Matues noisily sparred with the two large-handled weapons with sharp blades that they had claimed from the fallen bearded men at the battle of the island river. They were constantly sharpening the edges with leather and flint. Unlike the bone knives that we all used, these weapons had a cutting edge on both sides. Just touching their edges would draw blood.

One thing that I noticed in my walks around the camp was that unlike my people, who used wood to make runners for our winter sleds, these people used a large bone.

"Matues," I asked, "where do you find such a large bone to put on your sleds?"

"Tia'm gives us his ribs after we take his life. They work very well in the snow."

I thought this tia'm must be a huge animal to have a rib like this. The caribou from my land are not as large as this beast!

The village that we were staying in was the winter residence, maybe forty to fifty inhabitants and only about a dozen warriors. They were starting to prepare for their annual migration back to the coast. There they would join up with other small bands for protection during the summer and fall and harvest the creatures from the sea. Matues told me that during this time on the coast there was an abundance of food to harvest from the surrounding lands and waters. Seals, clams, eggs, birds, lobsters, and fish. However, now, during the last few days of winter, food was scarce. The women were using animal hooves, bones, roots, and last season's acorns to make stews. Soon they would have to kill a few of the dogs to survive. Setting out on the trip to the coast in this weak condition from the lack of meat would result in death for the weak and young. Already an older woman and a young child had succumbed to the hunger pangs that were starting to take hold of the village.

The hunting parties that had been going out lately were only able to snare small animals. The larger animals were now able to manoeuvre in the woods because of the disappearing snow. These animals were now further afield from the camp. The distance now involved seeking game, and the constant shortage of food among the people affected their hunting abilities. The L'nu'k called this time of the year the moon of Penamuikús (birds lay eggs moon, April).

That evening, Gaqtugwan Musigisg called Nukumi, the elders, and the warriors to council. "I have decided that we have to send a hunting party farther afield for fresh meat. They will have to go to the valley. Now that the weather is getting warmer, the mui'n will be coming out of hibernation. They will be weak, hungry, and seeking out food. There will be no summer fat on them, but it is still meat and we need it to make our way to the coast. I have chosen Glooscap, Apistanéwj, E's, Matues,

Ta's'ji'jg, and Jilte'g to be the ones for the hunt. Take the two big dogs with you, along with three of our camp dogs. The dogs of our visitors look like they can handle a mui'n. There will be no women going with you this time. We need all of them to stay here and prepare for the journey to the coast. The dogs will be able to pack most of the meat. What they cannot carry the six of you can."

Jilte'g then spoke. "This will leave you with only eight warriors to protect the community, Gaqtugwan Musigisg."

"It is too early in the siggw (spring) for the Haudenosaunee to be raiding this far east of their river, and the Stadaconas are too lazy to come over their river," he replied.

E's spoke up and said, "What about the Broken Talkers (Maliseet)? They cannot be trusted. One year they are our allies and the next they are attacking us and taking captives to trade with the Stadaconas and Haudenosaunee to save their own necks!"

The chief answered, "It is also too early in the spring for them to leave the warmth of their huts. We will be all right. I expect Migjigi (Turtle) and his group to be here in the next while to join up with us for the trek to the sea."

"We will leave at sunrise," said Jilte'g. "I hope you are right about Migjigi. I have a bad feeling about this!"

He looked at Nukumi, and all she said was, "Persevere; look to Glooscap in time of peril."

Who do these people think I am? I said to myself.

The next morning we walked into the morning mist after the six of us had eaten a meagre meal of cedar tea, a handful of boiled atu'tuej (squirrel), and the hoof of an unknown animal. The smell of the food, though, did not deter me from eating. The last few days I could feel my stomach shrink from the lack of food. The weakness had not yet spread to my legs. I can remember once when I was a young man, and it had been a winter of heavy snow. Food was scarce. I became very weak from the lack of food, I could not move my legs well, and I had trouble thinking and talking. The only thing that saved my family and village that year was that one of the elders thought it was his time to die, and he went into the woods to pass on to the afterlife. There he found the rotting carcass of a caribou that the wolves had killed and fed on. He came back to our shelters and gathered the men that still had strength to follow him to the spot. When they arrived, the wolves had returned. The story that was passed on since that day was of a battle between man and beast for these decaying remains. My people were more determined than the pack that day. They brought home the meat of the caribou and two wolves that they had killed. The elder? He died in his sleep years later. His name was Man Who Liked the Summer: my grandfather.

Matues made a framed carrier of two poles woven with leather with a deerskin thrown on it for the dogs Tepgig and Na'gweg to take turns pulling. If Apistanéwj tired, he could ride on this carrier. Matues and E's put their newfound weapons and shields on it so that they would not have to carry them. I also put my shield on the carrier.

We left at a brisk pace with the little one holding on to Tepgig and keeping up with us. We topped the rise overlooking the village; Jilte'g stopped and looked back, bowed his head, and then led us on.

Walking beside E's, I asked him how Jilte'g received the scar on his arm.

"One fall day, when he was a young, unproven warrior, Jilte'g left to go on a hunt by himself. He took neither a dog nor another hunter with him. The animals had started to go into their winter dens, and the ones that did not sleep were going deeper into the forest. I remember the day because it was unusually warm for the fall, with a brilliant blue sky. The sun highlighted the colour of the turning leaves to a brilliancy that rivalled a sunlit rainbow!

"After two days in the woods, all he had to show for his efforts was the skin, feathers, and meat of two apli'kmuj that he was eating to survive. He was determined not to leave the woodland empty-handed, but he would have to turn back for home soon. He was roaming too far afield. The morning of the third day, he woke to a blanket of snow covering the lean-to he had erected. The storm was intensifying and he knew he had to find a better shelter or he would freeze to death. Quickly he gathered up his weapons and fur blanket to find a better refuge. Nearly blinded from the driving snow, he crawled into an enclosure made by a large tree blown over by a big wind. The derooting of the tree had made a huge enclosure underneath the base. Crawling into the dark hole out of the storm saved his life.

"As he laid out his fur robe to ride out the storm, he had a sense he was not alone. As his eyes were adjusting to the darkness of the hole, his nostrils picked up a smell that made him freeze and break out into a clammy sweat. Mui'n! He slowly felt for his bone knife. The space was small — not a place where he wanted to die! He remained perfectly still. Outside was a white death and inside a black one. He knew that the bear would have only been in the den for a few days. The animal probably was not all the way into its sleep. Then his eyes became accustomed to the dimness of the dank hole. He could see the bear's nose moving. The animal would not be able to stand up or move quickly, but neither could he.

"Then there was a roar in the small enclosure that almost deafened him. He could see the huge paw reaching for him, and it raked his right shoulder all the way down to his elbow. The pain was numbing. He switched the knife to his left hand. The bear, after striking out at him, dropped its head. Jilte'g then took this opportunity to bury the knife into the animal's neck just below the skull. Another roar, and he stabbed again. The bear groaned and it was then he took the head of his war club in both hands and smashed the beast's skull. There was scarcely any room for him to elevate the weapon and strike down on the animal; nevertheless, he was able to bring down the club enough times to finish off the beast. Then silence.

"His head throbbed from the roar of the creature in the close confines of the hole. He was covered in blood, his and the bear's, and drenched in sweat. He was going into shock and had to get the bleeding stopped. Cutting a piece of leather from his clothing, he tied it above his bicep, then, taking a stick, he tightened the strip until the bleeding stopped. With his arm pounding and his heart racing, he crawled out of the hole. His blood reddened the new snow as he searched for what he needed to save his life. Finding a basswood tree, he sliced off chunks of bark to dress the wound. Then he cut some cedar branches. Taking his club, he pounded the cedar until he had a paste. He returned to the hole and cut the sinew away from the creature's two front legs. Finding some dry wood around the fallen tree, he started a fire and took his water vessel, threw some snow in, and added cedar and pine needles for a tea. Then, taking a bone needle he had, he used the sinew to sew his wound shut. The pain was excruciating. After that, he smeared the cedar paste on the gash and wrapped the basswood bark around his arm, tying it with leather strips cut from his shirt.

"He was gone for almost twenty suns. Everyone thought that he had died in the forest. Then one day toward evening the camp dogs started to bark. There he was, dragging a makeshift sled and pulling the bear carcass. He told us that he had almost passed to the other side. Running a fever, he would pass out and then come to long enough to boil tea and eat a chunk of raw bear meat. Sometimes he would stay alert long enough to keep the fire going and roast some meat. The fever finally broke and he was able to prepare for the journey home. The stench of the decomposing bear in the enclosed darkness had become nauseating. After making it back to the village, he dropped from exhaustion. Nukumi kept watch over him and brought him back to health. He is a warrior that everyone admires. The scar, a reminder of his bravery, and the tattoo of the snakehead, warn his enemies that he is quick and deadly in battle. Jilte'g always says the only thing that saved him in that hole was that the bear could not stand up to use its back legs for the strength it needed to overpower him."

E's then looked at me and said, "This is Jilte'g's warrior story and this is why myself and other warriors follow him. He has proven himself as a leader of men. We as warriors only follow a leader who will lead us wisely and get us home safely."

Looking ahead to Jilte'g as he led our group, I thought that this man I would follow into battle. The chief Gaqtugwan Musigisg had such confidence in him that he trusted him with his only son, Ta's'ji'jg, on this hunt.

The snow was starting to vanish from the landscape. There still were small patches on the northern sides of exposed hills and rocks, but other than that, the spring sun was working its magic. The biting insects had yet to appear, much to our joy.

Our group kept up a good brisk walk until the first stop, which was at a small stream to drink and fill our water bags and vessels. Jilte'g called E's to him and then the young warrior left swiftly up the trail.

Matues turned to me and said, "Jilte'g is sending him ahead for a reason. He wants him to scout out an area where there might be an ap'tapegijit (turkey) roost. We need food by tonight or else we will have to make a camp and hunt until we find something for ourselves. That would waste valuable time needed to hunt the mui'n and return to the village with its meat. Every day is precious to keep our people from starving."

The water from the stream was cold and refreshing but did not take the place of the food needed to sustain our strength.

Before we took to the trail, Jilte'g instructed us to leash the dogs. Normally they let them run free to flush out game. Tethering them kept the dogs from foraging ahead of us and scattering any ap'tapegijit. The sun was starting to disappear below the trees, dispersing shafts of brilliant sunlight through the forest, when E's rejoined our group.

"There is a flock of turkeys ahead and they are starting to fly up into the trees to roost," he said. "If we wait to just before dusk they will all be perched and we will be able to get a chance of shooting them down before they scatter."

We sat and waited, no one saying a word. Everyone except E's had a leashed dog. I had Na'gweg and passed the time stroking the big animal's neck.

Jilte'g rose, approached Apistanéwj, and handed him his leashed dog. He motioned for the rest of us to do the same.

E's silently led the group toward the roost. We arrived just at the hint of dusk. E's pointed up into the trees, where I could see the outlines of the birds. Everyone strung an arrow and stuck one or two more into the ground. The hope was that we should be able to get off a couple of shots before the birds took flight. Matues said they could not fly far like most birds, but they were quick in the air and would go far enough to get out of danger.

Jilte'g gave the signal and all five of us shot our arrows. I was able to get three arrows off before my targets vanished in a series of clucks and flapping sounds. We were able to collect eleven birds. Not bad, only about four misses. There would be bragging and teasing once everyone identified their arrows in the dead creatures.

I gave out a whistle that brought Apistanéwj and the dogs to us. He unleashed them and the three camp dogs rushed ahead. His two companions stayed with him.

He strode into our camp with a big smile on his face. In his hand he had an ap'tapegijit.

"I could hear all the clucking and flapping and then this bird dropped right in front of me," he exclaimed. "I do not know who was more taken aback by the sudden turn of events, me or the bird! Using my club, I cut the creature's astonishment short with a strike to the head, dropping it dead at my feet! Everything happened so quickly that the dogs never even barked, just gave a couple of small growls that never really amounted to anything."

Everyone stood and looked at him, and then we all broke out laughing. Each person grabbed a bird and started removing the feathers. I was able to decorate my shield and axe with feathers and Apistanéwj completely covered the frame that the two dogs pulled for him. All had enough feathers to do what they wanted. Even the dogs had plumes braided into their manes.

While we cleaned the birds, we asked Apistanéwj to start the fires and make some spits to roast our meal. We threw the guts and heads to the dogs; later they would get the bones after we had eaten the meat from them.

We cooked three of the turkeys for our meal; the others we smoked to keep from spoiling on the trail. After smoking them over the fire that night, we would cut them up in the morning and distribute the meat amongst everyone.

The sun had already set as I sat crouched by the fire, enjoying the aroma of the food as it cooked. The fat from the birds dripped into the fire, making a sizzle and shooting flames up. Cutting a huge piece of the meat off, I set it on a piece of bark to eat. Sitting down, I leaned up against Na'gweg for a backrest. He let out a grunt but never moved. With his belly full, all the dog had on his mind was sleep. Placing my water pouch on the ground within reach, I took a bite. The juice from the meat ran down my chin, and wiping it off with my hand I licked the moisture and felt a sudden sensation of homesickness. Looking up at the starry night, I wondered how my people were coping so far away. Did they even wonder if I were alive? No, by now they would have given up hope.

While we had been waiting for the birds to cook, Ta's'ji'jg, Matues, and I erected a couple of lean-tos for shelter. After eating, we eagerly retired to these makeshift covers, and using the dogs and our fur covers for warmth, sleep came swiftly.

I awoke to the early morning sounds of E's expelling a bountiful amount of stored-up gas. I do not know what bothered me more, the smell or the constant noise. E's made such a stench and racket that Na'gweg, who had been resting beside me, jumped up, snorted, growled, and vigorously shook his body to get rid of the stink before he hastily left the close confines of the shelter. Once the dog left, Apistanéwj, who had been nestled into the big dog's backside, got a sample of the full aroma of last night's turkey dinner. He gagged and stammered something about a decomposing whale. The shelter cleared with E's going into the woods to rid the source of this smell from his body and the rest of us to go in the opposite direction to empty our bladders.

We had a fire going and tea brewing by the time E's came out of the woods. As he approached the blaze, Na'gweg took one look at him, growled, and moved to the edge of the forest. Having a mouth full of warm tea when this exchange took place, I had to spit it out in a fit of laughter.

"E's, that is a sure sign of disgust when even a dog cannot stand your smell!" I remarked.

Immediately, everyone else broke out in fits of laughter and E's face turned red as he filled up his vessel with the cedar tea.

Jilte'g added, "I am sure that wherever you relieved yourself, it will guarantee that no wild animals will grace that spot for the rest of the summer. The smell of death will scare them off!"

More laughter ensued. E's ignored us. He stood up from his crouch, turned and walked away, but not before letting out a loud fart that brought tears to all our eyes.

"E's," Jilte'g shouted, "you will serve as rear guard today. I want to experience the smells of the forest without any contribution from you."

The day began with everyone in high spirits at the expense of E's.

We gave the dogs their heads for the morning. If there were bears around, we needed advance warning from the animals for our safety.

Everyone ate on the trail as we walked. The turkey meat did not need to be cooked once it had been smoked. The Mi'kmaq warriors did not tire easily, and I could walk all day without rest. The little one jumped onto the carrier that the big dogs pulled for him when he tired.

Ta's'ji'jg had earned the position of advance scout since the demotion of E's to the rear. It was mid-afternoon when he came back toward us.

"Apistanéwj," he said, "leash the dogs for now. There is a mui'n ahead at the edge of a small clearing. He is watching a lentug give birth. As soon as the lentug'ji'j (fawn) is born, the bear will make his kill."

The Mi'kmaq try to avoid killing a doe that has a fawn. Only in times of starvation will they even consider doing that. Their people were close to malnourishment now, but the bear was giving them an alternate choice. A bear would supply just as much meat, but also at this time of year the fur would be heavier and make an excellent robe. A deer usually has twins or triplets, but once the bear saw the first-born, he would charge to make the kill. Once this happened we would release the dogs and start yelling. That would bring the bear about to meet the danger approaching him from behind. During the confusion, the doe and fawn would make their escape. A fawn can walk immediately after birth; it would not be as agile as its mother but would be able to follow her to the safety of the woods. There she would continue giving birth to the others.

The mui'n's circumstances had now changed from gtantegewinu (hunter) to hunted. Na'gweg and Tepgig were quickly closing the gap between the bear and themselves, with the three Mi'kmaq dogs closely behind. The black beast stood on his rear legs to meet the advancing danger. Tepgig made a charge and barely avoided a huge, swinging paw from the roaring boar. At that moment the other four dogs hit the mui'n's unprotected side at full force. The sudden weight of four charging dogs caused a forced roll of snarling canines and a very agitated mui'n. The bear came up swinging and caught a Mi'kmaq imu'j square in the face with a massive front foot, flipping the dog end over end. Before the other dogs could regain their footing, the bear sped off for the nearest tall pine tree. With a gigantic leap, he propelled himself seven or eight feet up the wooden sanctuary. Snapping branches and roaring loudly, he rapidly ascended. By now we had reached the base of the tree, along with five very worked-up dogs, one of whom was bleeding from its mouth, and every time it barked, bloody spit spewed on everyone around.

With the bear now cornered up the tree, the six of us started shooting arrows up at him. The animal had made it halfway up the tree and was now resting and panting on a large limb. The chase had terrified the beast and now it was defecating from the fright and showering us with urine and bear muck. Because there were so many branches between our prey and ourselves, our arrows were not always hitting their target. In spite of this, though, some were reaching the mark. The bear was starting to bristle with feathered shafts. He stood up to climb further, and I was able to see his whole body. Grabbing a spear from the ground, I heaved it with all my strength. The spear struck him with a thud. The mui'n turned and pawed at the projectile. The sun broke through the trees at that moment and I could see blood and vomit coming from his mouth. The bear staggered and then plummeted toward the ground, snapping branches, protruding arrow shafts, and then, after bouncing off the tree trunk close to the bottom, he hit the ground with a huge discharge of air and blood from his mouth. The dogs immediately set upon him, with Jilte'g wading into the confusion driving his spear into the animal's heart to make sure he was dead. He then stood over the bear and thanked Gisu'lgw (the Creator) for our success on the hunt with an offering of tobacco. Bending over the body with his knife, he removed the heart and handed it to me.

"Your strength and accuracy proved to be the final blow to finish off our kill, Glooscap," he said.

I took the warm, blood-drenched organ in my hand and ate it slowly. I wanted to inherit the might of this dweller of the forest.

Jilte'g then turned to E's and pointed to the tree. "Gather as many arrows as you can reach without falling and toss them down to us. It will save us having to make more than we have to."

Quickly E's scrambled up the pine and it was not long before arrows started to drop point first into the ground around the base. Apistanéwj was busy collecting and separating them for their owners; he knew the possessor of each by the feathered end.

Matues and Ta's'ji'jg had already started to skin the bear. The dogs sat quietly on their haunches, waiting for the entrails.

Jilte'g inspected the wounds of the dog that had taken the blow from the bear's paw. "This is my best duck dog; I do not want to lose him," he muttered to no one in particular.

Matues stood up from the carcass and came toward me with his hand out. He passed me my spear point, one unbroken arrow, and a few arrowheads.

We were standing in a part of the woods where the sun was fighting its way to the forest floor.

E's came down from the tree and pointed into the deep woods, where the sun was dripping off the leaves like new-fallen rain, highlighting all the colours of the forest. The forest floor burst into a flash of light from what seemed like a bolt of lightning, but it turned out to be only a bright beam of sunlight that had found an opening in the canopy. There in the blast of light stood the lentug with three newly born lentug'ji'j butting each other for their mother's milk. We all looked at each other and smiled. The death of the bear would bring needed food to the village, and our choice at the beginning of the hunt enabled three more lives to begin in the forest.

E's then came around to each of us, handing our arrows back. The dogs were content from their feast and Jilte'g's duck dog looked like it would pull through.

Jilte'g then spoke. "We will stay here for the night. There is fresh water escaping from the rock formation behind us. It pools before disappearing into the ground. Capture what you need for your water sacs and vessels before you wash the blood off your hands from the kill. We need wooden frames built for the dogs to carry the bearskin and meat back to the village. What they cannot lug we will have to transport on our backs."

E's, Matues, Ta's'ji'jg, and I then set upon the body to carve up the meat. We would save the turkey for the trail, but tonight we would have bear meat.

Apistanéwj and Jilte'g busied themselves with making shelter.

Jilte'g came over to us when they had finished and said to E's, "The small cover is for you. We do not know how this meal tonight will affect you. You need to sleep alone."

We all looked up and started to laugh. E's then cut a piece of meat from the neck and tucked it into his pouch.

Matues said, "What are you going to do with that?"

"I'll need this to entice one of the dogs to sleep with me for warmth," he replied.

Apistanéwj warned, "It won't be Na'gweg; that dog has a great memory and he will not spend another night with you!"

That brought more laughter, and the big white dog looked up upon hearing his name and snorted.

By the time the butchering was finished it was nightfall. E's spitted and hung a chunk of meat over the fire. We always lined the fire pit with rocks to generate heat, and the wood that we collected for the fire was laid butt end in. Each of us would shove the wood in front of us farther into the blaze as it burnt down. The bonfire was surrounded by pieces of wood laid like this. Extra pieces were stacked away from the sparks. When one piece was finished, another took its place in line. We built the fire between the lean-tos and throughout the night someone would awaken and push more fuel into the fire.

It was not long before the meat started to drip fat onto the flames, causing flare-ups and flying sparks.

Having had only a couple of strips of turkey meat during the day, we all gorged ourselves on the mui'n. I ate until I thought my stomach was going to burst. As we ate, everyone related their impressions of that day's hunt and the birth of the fawns. Slowly, everyone made their way to where they were going to sleep.

Apistanéwj and I watched as E's enticed one of the Mi'kmaq dogs to follow him with the meat he had kept.

The two of us walked around the fire, shoving the wood into the flames, then retired with the two Eli'tuat dogs. Jilte'g was already in our shelter, lying next to his duck dog. Both were sound asleep.

Tomorrow would bring new adventures; tonight, though, I looked forward to sleep.

During the night I awoke to the sound of the dogs growling. I flung off my robe, walked out of the lean-to, and approached the fire. The dogs were lying in the shelter with their eyes open, not moving but with their teeth bared and snarling. I relieved myself and pushed the ends of the logs into the fire. Sparks flew and the aroma of the wood reached my nostrils. As I stepped away from the fire to adjust my eyes to the darkness, my nostrils picked up a strong, musty smell. Apigjilu (skunk)? Not seeing anything, I went back to my robe and fell asleep.

The next morning we were awakened by Jilte'g cursing. "Where are my spears? Who has taken them?"

"Ta's'ji'jg," he called out, "where have you hidden my spears? I know it was you! You are always playing jokes on me."

"Jilte'g," he replied, "it was not me. I never left the cover of my robe all night."

The young warrior approached Jilte'g and asked where he had left them.

"Right here leaning up against this tree, but now they are gone!"

"You are getting careless in your old age. Look here."

Jilte'g bent down and looked where Ta's'ji'jg was pointing.

"There, these are the paw prints of the trickster, ki'kwa'ju (wolverine). It was a male and he had a gajuewj'j (kitten) with him, teaching the young one the ways of the woods. The old male will show the little one how to take something and hide it, just as they do when they find a kill or when they bring down their own prey," exclaimed Ta's'ji'jg.

"So that was what the dogs were growling at last night," I added, "and I thought it was an apigjilu!"

E's warned, "It is very rare when a dog will knowingly challenge a ki'kwa'ju; they are very efficient killers."

Jilte'g said, "It will not be hard to find my spears. They will have dragged and buried them someplace, then sprayed their musk urine on the hiding place to mark their spot."

He and his dog left to find the weapons. Looking over his shoulder he ordered, "Prepare to leave when I get back and save me whatever you cook from the meal and some tea. I will not be long."

A short time later Jilte'g and the dog returned. We could smell the spears before our leader reappeared.

Ta's'ji'jg looked at Jilte'g and exclaimed, "You said *I* smelled! Well, look who wins the stink contest now!"

While everyone chuckled, Jilte'g grabbed some dirt and vigorously rubbed it on the shafts of his weapons, then looked up and laughed.

That day's trek was uneventful. Jilte'g had taken E's place at the back of the line. The smell of the wolverine's musk was still with him, even with all his efforts to remove it.

The next day we came upon a small pond. E's stopped and motioned for Jilte'g to come forward. E's pointed out to the middle of the pond to a flock of ducks.

Jilte'g snapped his fingers and his dog came forward.

Matues turned to me and whispered, "We have to hide along the shore and let the dog work."

Puzzled by his comment, I followed him, along with Apistanéwj. E's and Ta's'ji'jg hid a short distance away from us.

"Keep the dogs quiet," Matues ordered.

Jilte'g motioned to his dog, which started to run back and forth along the shoreline. This caught the ducks' attention and they started to swim toward the water's edge. As they neared the dog, Jilte'g snapped his fingers again and the dog entered the bush.

Matues motioned for me to pick up a large stick. He grabbed his club. The ducks waddled ashore, following the dog. Leaving our hiding places, we were able to club enough of the birds to make a good meal and add to our dwindling supply of turkey meat.

That evening, as we were eating, I commented that was the strangest thing I had ever seen, a dog luring ducks to their death.

Jilte'g replied, "Our people have trained these dogs for this ability to entice. We acquired the skill to teach our animals by watching the wookwiss (fox) tempting water fowl to shore. The wookwiss are masters at this form of luring."

The Mi'kmaq Village

The sound of a shrill scream piercing the early morning mist roused the people of the hunting party's village. Gaqtugwan Musigisg, their chief, and two warriors rushed to the wikuom, where the shriek had originated. When they reached the lodge, it was total mayhem.

Barking dogs, two screeching women, and a cursing man, along with the cries of children. When Thunder Sky and the two men entered the shelter, they realized they had stumbled into chaos! Inside was a mui'n raised up on its hind legs, fending off baskets, rocks, and dirt thrown at it, while the lone man Negm Guntew (Bloody Rock) was trying to reach his weapons behind the roaring bear.

Thunder Sky and his companions ended the confrontation with three well-placed spears. The beast dropped immediately to the ground, falling upon one of the screaming women, causing her to become even more agitated. Quickly, all involved rolled the bear off the woman, who was now covered in blood and saliva. Once the confusion subsided, the rescuers caught sight of where the animal had come in. The light was streaming in where the bear had shredded the wikuom's birch bark walls to gain entry. The inhabitants had been heating some sismo'gm (maple sugar) that they saved from the previous spring. The sweet smell had lured the starving mui'n to their wikuom. Luckily, no one was seriously hurt, except for one small boy whom the bear stepped on when he came in. The boy had sustained a gash on his leg that the women were now mending. The scar would be a badge of honour for the young child and a point of jealousy among his friends.

The village now had some much-needed food, which caused chuckles. They had a successful hunt without leaving the confines of their shelters! Would they be more successful than their hunting party?

That night the people enjoyed a substantial meal for the first time in many days and everyone fell asleep with swollen bellies.

The next morning the village yet again awoke to screams. However, this time there was no animal intruding.

The people of the village exited their wikuoms to the sight of painted warriors rushing from the forest amid war cries, brandishing spears and clubs. The camp dogs, barking, howling, and gnashing their teeth, bravely charged the intruders, only to be bludgeoned and slashed into submission by the assailants. The outnumbered survivors of the initial onslaught then became victims of the enemies' war dogs, which brutally finished the job. Once the attackers breached the defences of the dogs, they brutally set upon the Mi'kmaq inhabitants.

Glooscap

Jilte'g roused everyone at first light. He already had the fire roaring, heating the cedar tea along with two ducks on a spit.

"We will be able to reach the village well before nightfall. Our trek back will be faster because we do not need the hunter's stealth that we required the past few days," he said.

Each day, Apistanéwj was proving capable of keeping up with the pace that the group set. If he tired, he quickly jumped upon the carrier that we made for the big dogs. The extra weight never seemed to bother the dogs pulling the frame.

We stopped near midday and hastily gulped down some of our turkey and duck meat, washing it down with water from a stream. While we filled up our water vessels, E's waded into the stream and began catching gomgwejg (suckerfishes) with his bare hands. He threw them on shore and yelled, “These are for the dogs!”

In a short while each of the animals had a fish to stave off its hunger.

E’s left the stream, pulled a couple of handfuls of grass from the ground to dry himself, and warned shakily, “That water is cold.”

Jilte’g quickly got our attention and we started out at a brisk pace to get the life-saving bear meat back to the Mi’kmaq camp.

Around midafternoon, Matues, who had been scouting ahead, was rapidly backtracking to our small group.

“Jilte’g, I smell smoke ahead, and it is quite overpowering. It is coming from the direction of the village in the north. It is not yet dry enough in the forest for a fire. The only other thing could be a grass fire from one of the beaver meadows, but there has not been any lightning lately.”

“Glooscap, come with us,” Jilte’g shouted. “The rest of you try to keep up.”

The three of us then started out at a hard run. We ran toward a bald rock rise. Upon arriving there we looked in the direction of the village.

Matues turned to us and said, “That is no forest or grass fire, it is the village!”

We stood there in shock.

The rest of the hunting party caught up with our advance trio. They also stood in mute silence, staring at the columns of smoke.

Jilte’g warned, “We have to be cautious from here on in. Matues, take Ta’s’ji’jg and carefully scout ahead. We have to be alert that we do not surprise a retreating war party.”

Once the two young warriors left to inspect the trail ahead, Jilte'g, Apistanéwj, E's, our five dogs, and I followed vigilantly behind.

Every step we took was in complete silence from the surrounding forest. The only sound was the whoosh of the wind through the pines. Even the birds became quiet, seemingly drawn into the life-and-death situation playing out beneath their forest homes.

Matues and Ta's'ji'jg waited until our trailing group caught up to them. We all crouched down and stared out into the devastation where once existed a bustling encampment. Apistanéwj untied the dogs from their carriers.

Jilte'g motioned for us all to follow. Looking around, I noticed each man had strung an arrow into his bow. Myself, I drew the Eli'tuat axe; my confidence in this weapon was growing each day. As we neared the outskirts of the village, my nostrils filled with the smell of smoke and the stench of roasted flesh.

After entering the burning remains of the site, I eyed two charred bodies tied to a post in a fire pit, burned beyond recognition. It was everything I could do to hold back a gagging reflex. My people very rarely went to war, and when we did, it was with the Inuit. Neither side in those conflicts ever chose to inflict this kind of cruelty.

My companions now started to sing a heartrending death song. My eyes scanned our location. I made out all the bodies of the camp dogs on the village boundary. Scattered around were the contorted and mutilated bodies of the Mi'kmaq warriors and women who died defending their lives and families.

Then someone yelled the word, "Father!" It brought me back from my thoughts. Looking up, I could see Ta's'ji'jg running toward a clearing on the edge of the forest.

"No!" screamed Jilte'g.

I watched in horror as Ta's'ji'jg rushed toward his father, Gagtugwan Musigisig, tied to a tree. Twenty feet short of his father, he screamed in pain. I watched as he fell, shrieking and yelling in agony. Blood spurted from his feet, hands, chest, and neck.

Jilte'g warned the rest of us, "Do not rush to his aid. We must be careful of this Haudenosaunee ruse. They will skin a body and toss the rest of the headless remains into the flames, then stuff the skin with grass. Next, they take the stuffed skin and tie it to a tree with the victim's head impaled on a spear shaft. Then the raiders place spearheads, knives, and sharpened sticks in a semi-circle around the tree. This will trick returning enemies to think the person is still alive. Upon approach, their feet are impaled on the hidden weapons. By not tying the whole body to the tree, the wild animals will not be attracted to the death smell of a rotting carcass."

Jilte'g asked me to follow him and we carefully made our way through the hidden danger. Ta's'ji'jg lay moaning in a pool of blood. I reached down and gently lifted him. Cradling his limp, bleeding body, I followed Jilte'g's lead to safety.

Laying the young warrior on the ground, Apistanéwj approached with a pot of water to wash the wounds. Looking up from the bloodied warrior, he said, "I need bark from the basswood tree for his wounds, tree resin to glue them, and plantain if any can be found. I have some yarrow in my medicine bag. If someone can find a beehive, I can use the honey."

E's, Jilte'g, and Matues left to try to find what he needed in the woods. I went for more water.

The small one worked fervently to stem Ta's'ji'jg's bleeding. E's returned with the bark and Matues was able to obtain pine resin.

Matues started a fire and heated the resin just enough that Apistanéwj could work it over the wounds to seal the skin and halt the bleeding. The resin would be warm when it was applied, soothing the wound while sealing it. The yarrow he had applied before the resin. After sealing the cuts with the pine resin, Apistanéwj laid the bark over the lesions. After cutting pieces of leather from our clothing to wrap around the bark, the task was complete.

"Glooscap, I need some cedar tea made. We have to get him to drink as much as we can force down him to help soothe his pain and heal him from the inside. The boy may soon pass out from the pain and shock."

During all the confusion, we had failed to notice that Jilte'g had not yet returned. I turned to E's and asked, "Have you seen Jilte'g?"

"No," he answered in puzzlement.

The black dog Tepgig then rose with upright ears and looked to the south. There was the scarred one with two women and three children in tow.

"How is Ta's'ji'jg?" he inquired.

Matues answered, "The little one laboured over him painstakingly. I hope that his efforts have not been in vain. Thunder Sky's son has lost a lot of blood, and some of the wounds were deep. His well-being is not good. The spirit world is much closer to him than the real world at this time."

E's interrupted, "Where did you find Musigisg E'pit (Sky Woman) and Saqpigu'niei (I Am Shedding Tears) and the children?"

"I found them in the safe place that our people have always used in the time of danger. The women told me that they had promised the children the night before the attack that they would take them out in the early morning and set snares for rabbits. They had not gone far before they heard war cries and the camp dogs barking. Saqpigu'niei took the children to the safe place. Musigisg E'pit watched the carnage from a well-hidden vantage point and saw most of the warriors slain. The women and a few men who did not die in defence of the village became captives, along with Nukumi, who had gathered all the children in the initial attack and shielded them with her body."

I spoke up. "I will not let Nukumi become a slave of these aggressors. I am going after them, alone or with the warriors that stand here. Either way, it does not matter to me!"

In unison the four of them said, "We will follow you!

"Grandmother did say in time of peril, we should look to you!" Matues added.

"Musigisg E'pit," I said, "who were they and how many are there?"

She answered, "They were Stadaconas, Haudenosaunee, and a couple of Maliseet. I counted maybe fifteen of them after the battle. When they left, they were carrying three of their dead to bury. Of the remaining fifteen I could only notice three men who had suffered wounds."

E's walked up to one of the dogs and clubbed it to death. He turned to me and said, "In times of grief, we slay a dog and eat it. Tomorrow we leave on a Mourning War."

That night Jilte'g came to me and said, "I and the others will follow your lead to bring back our stolen women and children. Nukumi spoke of this! The two women will look after Ta's'ji'jg until he is well enough to travel or until he dies. We will leave them enough mui'n meat for them and the children to survive. If he heals, they will go to the coast, where all our people come together in the summer."

I awoke the next morning to the smell of roasting bear meat and cedar tea. Crawling out of the shelter I had erected for Apistanéwj and myself, my eyes took awhile to adjust to the bright early morning sun. I squatted near the fire and dipped my birch bark drinking vessel into the steaming tea container. Taking my knife, I sliced off a chunk of bear meat from the spit. The juice ran between my fingers and I tried to lick the liquid before it dripped to the ground. The fire was crackling and spitting, fuelled by the fluid dripping from the spit. The pungent odour of the meat and boiling tea flared my nostrils and cleared my early morning head.

I was lost in my thoughts but the sounds of the four remaining dogs raising the alarm of approaching intruders brought me quickly back to the present. I jumped up, rushing into the lean-to for my weapons.

E's met me as I exited and said, "Do not worry, my friend, long before you awoke a runner came into the camp and announced that Migjigi's people were coming from the south. We are safe."

I looked to the south and watched as an old man led a group of about thirty-five people into the burned out village.

Jilte'g approached the old warrior and held out his hands in welcome. They embraced as the women who followed him started to wail and cry at the devastation of what they saw. Many of these visitors would have lost friends and family.

Jilte'g wasted no time in telling the old chief that we were leaving immediately to follow the raiding party. He said, "We need warriors to follow with us!"

Migjigi answered, "I have none to spare. This winter, three of my young men drowned when they ventured onto a lake to chase a deer. The ice gave way and took them. With only nine warriors left and twenty-four women and children, I cannot spare any men. I need all that I have to get my group to the coast."

A warrior stepped out of the group and said, "Turtle does not speak for me! I will go with you."

He was taller than everyone but me. His head was shaved except for a topknot decorated with feathers. The man carried a staff with a bone spike on the end. Surrounding the top third of the staff were bear and cougar fangs embedded into the shaft, point side out. The fangs were forced through a hole and out the other side, then resin had been used to fill in the hole around the teeth to keep them in place. This weapon doubled as a spear and a lethal four-sided club. There was a knife hanging with a leather strap around his neck, another knife sheathed into his knee high right mg'sn (shoe), and a club in his belt, along with two round rocks tethered together with a leather strap. On his back hung the largest bow I had ever seen and a quiver full of arrows. His face had tattoos with black streaks shaped like lightning bolts. The left eye was scarred and closed. His right eye was a crystal blue that seemed to look right through you. However, the strangest thing of all was on his shoulder sat a ga'qaquis (crow), quietly preening itself. When I looked into the bird's eyes, I distinguished an intelligence I had never seen before in an animal. I felt that the bird could understand everything that was transpiring at this time.

"Elue'wiet Ga'qaquis (Crazy Crow), we would be honoured to have such a warrior as you to favour us!" replied Matues.

"Migjigi, we need you to take Thunder Sky's son, Ta's'ji'jg, who is in a bad way, plus two women and three children who were able to survive the battle, to the seaside with you," said Jilte'g.

"I will do that," he replied.

Elue'wiet Ga'qaquis then walked up to me, smiled and said, "You and I, my friend, are going to slay many enemies!"

He then looked down at Apistanéwj and said, "Who is this little man?"

Before I could answer, the crow said, "It is Apistanéwj, the Marten, friend of Glooscap."

I stood and stared at the bird, and Crazy Crow just laughed.

13

THE PLAN

CORN DOG LED HIS GROUP from the Hochelagan camp to his village of Ossernenon, home of the A'no:wara (Turtle) Clan. Here he spent the rest of the late winter and spring petitioning his Clan Mother to appoint him war chief. Ossernenon was a village of twenty kanonhsehs (longhouses), each of them 140 feet long by 20 feet wide. Longhouses on average held fifty residents. There were 941 people in the community, of which 283 were warriors. A wall made of posts embedded in the ground to protect the longhouses and the people inside encircled the village.

Outside the walls, as far as the eye could see, were fields of corn, beans, and squash, which made up most of their diet. Just beyond the fields flowed the Te-non-an-at-che (River Flowing through Mountains) (Mohawk River).

Hunters went out each day searching for game in the surrounding forest and fish from the Te-non-an-at-che to supplement their diet.

Corn Dog

That winter did not take many of our people. Food for once was plentiful. Only a few old people passed away and one woman died giving birth. No children passed on during the cold months. The village entered the spring healthy and strong. A good sign from Hahgwehdiyu (Mohawk Creator), I was sure.

The Algonquin woman Wàbananang stayed in my lodge as my slave, along with her daughter. She never slept in my bed. This woman gave me a certain amount of anxiety. Her beauty was breathtaking, but I knew should any man touch her his life was in danger. I watched with amusement as she and her daughter ran around the stockade each day, singing. Knowing this woman, there was a plan to all this. Escape? Maybe. No, I think she had plans for something else.

Only the Clan Mother of the A'no:wara (Turtle) Clan had the power to put the horns of leadership on the war chief of all the Mohawks. My Clan Mother would set out to Tionnontoguen, the capital, to counsel with her sisters of the Okwàho (Wolf) and Ohkwari' (Bear) Clans, and there a decision would be made on the war chief.

Winpe and I spent this time hunting for the village, making new arrowheads and arrow shafts and feathering them. During these periods, we were also planning our attack to the east to cut off the Bark Eaters from their allies.

My Clan Mother left on a bright spring morning, accompanied by twenty warriors and a pack of dogs. They set out to the next village, Andagaron, a day's walk away. There she will meet up with the Clan Mother of that village and continue on to the capital, Tionnontoguen, where the three of them would come to a judgment. However, after consultation it still came down to the A'no:wara Clan Mother's decision. Even though she could make this selection herself, she always counselled with her sister Clan Mothers.

Her only words to me the day she left were, "Come to Tionnontoguen in seven suns."

The next day I entered our sweat lodge and stayed until my head was clear. Three days later, purified, I made my exit. On the sixth day, Winpe and I left for Tionnontoguen.

We stopped at Andagaron the first night and stayed with a family I knew. They fed us well, and we talked about past hunts and battles. That night, when Winpe and I went to bed, we spread fresh pine needles onto our sleeping platform to keep the lice away.

The next morning, we left in a downpour. It was a warm, welcoming spring rain, enabling Winpe and I to strip down to our breechcloths, go barefoot, and let our bodies soak in the soothing effects of the droplets. We rolled up our clothes and moccasins and encased them in bark to keep them dry. The spring mud under my feet oozed through my toes, providing a pleasant sensation. After being in the sweat lodge, then experiencing this rain, I felt great relief. Another good omen from Hahgwehdiyu?

Arriving at the capital just before sunset, Winpe and I were ushered into the council lodge. There the Clan Mothers sat with the antlers of the war chief.

My Clan Mother of the A'no:wara Clan stood. "We have made our decision. However, it comes with one stipulation," she advised. "You will only be allowed one hundred warriors total from the three villages and ten women for trail-camp duties. How you select them is your choice. We cannot spare any more of our warriors. The villages need warriors to protect us from our enemies that are forever threatening our borders. Your raiding to the west last year may yet cause problems."

She then stepped forward and put the antlers of the war chief on my head.

Stepping out into the open air, I took a deep breath. The smell of a fresh rain and the longhouse fires filled my nostrils and heightened my senses. Then, at the top of my voice, I screamed. "Who will join me to kill our enemies in the east? I leave tomorrow morning for Andagaron and then Ossernenon, where I will select my warriors for the War Path! Who will follow me?"

Men left their longhouses and raised their arms screaming the Mohawk War cry, "Cassee Kouee," at the top of their lungs. I could feel the ground tremble underneath me from the noise. The camp dogs howled in the din. The women came out and sang their songs.

Turning to Winpe, I shouted, "It has begun, yie, yie!"

The total Kanien'kehá:ka Nation from the three villages numbered close to four thousand. Of that, there were maybe eleven hundred warriors. I hoped that my hundred would be the best of the best. Then again, I would have to depend on the luck of the draw. The Clan Mothers had made a decision on the selections from each village. Only half the warriors from each of the three camps would be allowed to go to vie for this honour. Even though it was each individual warrior's decision as to whether he wanted to go on the warpath, the home villages still had to have protection and provisions.

The next morning the men lined up to draw lots. If they drew a dyed black pebble they won the right to follow me to Ossernenon to compete for the honour to make the hundred; otherwise they had to stay in Tionnontoguen to watch over it. The capital, which was the largest in population, would supply me with half the participants. The drawing of lots took up the early morning. Once it was completed, we left for Andagaron. Two hundred and twenty-one warriors left with us before noon. Along with them were about fifty young females who wanted to strive to become one of the ten trail women.

The women selected would be an important addition to the group. They were to be responsible for helping the men with wounds, cuts, and scrapes they acquired on the trail or in battle, prepare meals, and aid the men in their preparation for battle. They would stay hidden during the raid and help with the wounded on the return trip.

Winpe and I set a torrid pace, and we reached the middle village by dusk. When we left Andagaron the next day, we were over four hundred strong. Winpe and I discussed how we should select our raiders. When we reached Ossernenon, our plan was complete. The drawing of lots took place in the last village. We gathered all the lot winners and told them how we wanted to pick our raiders. They all shouted in agreement. Our people loved to compete, and we were giving them the ultimate contest.

Community members that were not striving to obtain a place in the hundred would be there to cheer and wager on the competitors. The next three days would be packed full of action, feasting, storytelling, and dancing. Tonight the celebration would begin.

That night Winpe and I drew into our confidence a group of boys and elders. We told them our plans for the three days and what we needed of them. The first day of the contest would not be starting until the midday sun. This would give them time to prepare for what we wanted. Then they would be able to start working on day two, and then day three.

During the first two days there would be no contestants eliminated. On those days, selections would be determined by skill.

The influx of competitors and visitors for the next three days produced many more mouths to feed. Some of the warriors of our village that were not participating, along with a selection of visiting warriors, were designated to provide game for the upcoming meals. That morning, five different hunting parties of ten or twelve hunters branched out toward the river and forest to seek out fish and animals for the cooking fires.

After the morning meal, I gathered the warriors together to reveal what that day's contest consisted of.

"Each person will have targets to shoot at with bow and arrow. Each man will carry ten arrows in battle conditions, loosing five arrows on the run and five from kneeling or upright positions. We will be using a fallow cornfield to compete. There are six lanes in each field with the same obstacles and targets. Elders will be making the decisions on targets hit. Young boys are controlling the targets. You start at the sound of the drums and will have one hundred drumbeats to complete the course. When the drums stop, you are done. Winpe and I will make known the winners during the evening fires. The drummers will call you to the field at high sun. In the meantime, ready your weapons and good luck. Heh, yi, ah!"

Answered by a roar that made my skin rise, I smiled and left to check that all the preparations were in order where the forest and field came together.

14

THE HUNDRED AND TEN

THE BEATING OF THE drums called everyone to the field. There were 486 warriors trying to win one of the hundred coveted spots. Since there were six lanes, we had chosen six elders the previous day to be guides for each of the six groups. Each of the elders went through the crowd of warriors the night of the feast and touched eighty-one men on the shoulder. These men were to meet their elders the next day after their morning meal. The elders then had them all line up according to height and randomly walked along the line selecting the order of their entrance to the field from one to eighty-one. The first day's order was reversed on the second day of competition.

Standing in front of the six lines of warriors, I explained to them the targets. "You will have five targets to shoot at. The first five shots at each target must be done while running. After you make your first five shots, you will return to the start and go through the targets again, shooting from either a kneeling or standing position. You will start at the beginning of the drums and they will drum one hundred strokes and stop. You are done then. The targets are in the following order: a swinging log, a stationary post, a cornhusk man dropped from a tree on a rope, a full view of a stationary cornhusk man, and lastly, a cornhusk man half hidden behind a tree. All target lines will be marked with a charcoal-painted post driven into the field; you cannot pass the post. The object will be behind the post where the field ends and the forest begins. There will be a total of five elders in the competition row, one at each station to watch to make sure all conditions of the contest are completed according to the rules."

I told the first six men to approach the line. "Once these men start, the next six men must take their place when they enter the field to ready themselves."

Then, turning to the drummers, I shouted, "Begin!"

The sky was a solid blue and the sun relentlessly beat down on the field. There was no wind, and the warriors were drenched in sweat from the heat and the stress of the contest. Young boys and girls were busy filling up bark containers of drinking water for the men. When a drummer tired, another was there to take his place. It was not long before the stench of the contestants burned my nostrils. My head started to throb from the endless roar of the bystanders and the drumming. I turned to look at Winpe. He was standing with his arms crossed, smiling. His thoughts, I knew, were on the outcome of these three days and on the turmoil we should be able to create with the elite force selected from this challenge.

The participants ran through the course with precision, each man fully focused. The watching players cheered on their rivals at the top of their lungs. There were no injuries other than a few sprained ankles, and one young boy who was swinging a log took a flying wood splinter from an arrow deflecting off his forehead. There was lots of blood but no damage. No amount of coaxing could entice him to leave his post. He did not want to show weakness. An elder stopped the bleeding and he continued.

The day's competition ended comfortably before dusk. All then made their way back to the village, where the women had prepared what the hunters had brought in that day.

Winpe and I gathered with the elders who were overseeing the game. They gave us their selections and we made our way to the cooking fires.

"Seventeen men were perfect today," I exclaimed.

There was a roar from the crowd.

Winpe repeated the names given to us by the elders. The seventeen warriors stood to loud cheering and drumming.

"You seventeen have made the roll. You will not have to continue these next two days. You have earned an extra task for this raid, and because of your marksmanship you will also hunt for the group. The next two days are yours to do as you like."

Once everyone's bellies were full, they retired for the evening. The next morning the village awoke to the elders calling everyone to morning meal. While eating we told the contenders that they would need three spears each that day. The day's games would start earlier than yesterday. The remaining competitors needed the extra rest for the gruelling third round.

We gave them a short time to make or borrow the three weapons for the field before the call went out. The first group to start was to consist of only five men to compensate for the seventeen who had made the final unit.

"Today it will be three staggered targets behind each other. One post, one cornhusk man in the open and another partially hidden in bushes, plus you have to throw before you reach a blackened post that is stuck in the ground. However, today you will only get thirty drum beats."

The day was clear again, but hotter, with a slight breeze. The men should find this portion of the challenge different from the previous day. Less time, but accuracy and endurance would still be needed. Throwing accuracy with a spear took talent. I doubted that there would be as many who would qualify today as the first day.

We knew that with short notice the men would have to improvise to make or find three spears. For some, these were not their weapons of choice; for others there would be a feeling of comfort. Still, though, the ones who were familiar with the use of spears would probably only have one or two in their immediate possession. Each man favoured a certain type of wood or shaft size. If he had to borrow or make one hurriedly, there might be a sense of doubt with the weapon in hand. This, Winpe and I knew, ought to bring the best to the top.

As expected, that morning and early afternoon there were many disappointed men. Speed, accuracy, and stamina ruled this day. When it was over, there were eleven more warriors for our raid. The first day gave us our hunters; now we had our scouts, flankers, and rear guards. These eleven were men who were able to make decisions quickly and react immediately.

Tomorrow would be the ultimate test. Stamina and tenacity would prevail, and this was where we would select the ten women.

Before Winpe and I entered our lodge for the night, one of the elders approached us.

"Ò:nenhste Erhar," said the elder, "two of the warriors that you selected on the second day have slain an anèn:taks (porcupine) and left it in the forest."

"Bring them to me!" I replied.

Within a few moments the two warriors were brought to Winpe and I, accompanied by a group of elders.

"The elder Kwa'yenha has told me that you killed an anèn:taks and left it in the forest?"

"Yes, the animal ruined our best hunting dog with a mouth full of quills. We had to put our dog out of its misery!"

"You know it is bad luck to slay an anèn:taks and not eat it. The creator put this animal here to save lost souls. People in the woods who have lost their way can slay these animals, eat them, and survive. You have broken that promise to him by not eating the animal!"

The taller of the two replied, "We ate our dog and had no hunger for the quilled one, so we left him."

I looked each of them in the eyes and said, "Return to your villages. Your actions will bring our raiding party bad luck if you stay with us. I have no recourse except to banish you from the one hundred. You have angered Hahgwehdiyu; he will not take your transgression lightly. Be gone from us!"

Without a word of reply, the two left.

The hunters were again successful this day, and the women prepared an immense feast. That night, just as Winpe and I entered my family longhouse, it started to rain. We sat by the fire as the rain increased in force, dampening the flames. Looking at each other, we smiled. This would definitely make tomorrow's last test interesting. We knew that the seventy-four men and ten women who could defeat this final challenge would be the best of the best.

The next morning, the remainder of the men and close to a hundred women gathered for the final test. A gruelling run through the forests of our lands, plus a double crossing of the Te-non-an-at-che, was the course that the elders, Winpe, and I had set up. The trail was marked out with blazes, with tribal members spaced at intervals to keep the flood of participants from going off course.

The rain had stopped overnight; the air was muggy and the sun bright. Each participant carried a bag of corn and a vial of water. The men had stripped down to only a breechcloth and some were barefoot. Most of the women were clothed similarly, except some wore a small top.

We needed warriors and women who could run all day in all conditions and keep up. Stealth and quickness were the skills needed for this raid to be successful, and a key to everyone's survival. Our desire was to strike quickly, decisively, and destroy all in our path. Fitness was essential for all!

When the first male runner appeared in the clearing to the village at the end of the race, the drums would begin to signify the end was near. When the drumming ended, it would signal that the seventy-fourth runner had crossed the finish and that we had our hundred.

When the first woman was in sight of the village, the women would start singing until the tenth one had crossed.

As I walked through the throng of people to get to the starting position, I neared the Algonquin woman. I told her that she did not have to do this; she was to be part of the raiding party all along. Looking at me with the fire she always had in her eyes, she replied, "I run with my daughter!"

Now I knew why the daughter had run around the village all that winter, but how had they known that there was to be a race? They could not know that. What was this woman up to?

"So be it," I replied.

Reaching the head of the murmuring group of enthused men and women and raising my head and arms to the heavens, I let out a war cry that mimicked the sound of turkey cocks, then, dropping my arms, I signalled the beginning of the gruelling race to select my elite.

Winpe, considered the fastest warrior among all the men of the villages, strongly stated his intentions to run this race to uphold his perceived ability.

The competitors ran between two lines of the villagers as they exited the compound. Once they cleared the front entrance, the people ran after them, yelling their encouragement. It was not long before the runners and spectators became covered with water and mud from splashing through puddles from the previous night's rain. Most of the people then made for a rise that would allow them a clear vantage point to follow the runners' progress on the route to the river and then into the forest. It also gave them a line of sight for when the competitors returned.

A couple of warriors and I climbed a tall spruce tree that contained a sentry lookout post used to protect the village. Here we were able to watch the struggle unfold.

The first hurdle that they had to overcome was the initial crossing of the river Te-non-an-at-che. The entrance to the river ford became a clumped mass of people pushing for position as they entered and then swam to the other side. There were people stationed on the river in canoes and the opposite bank to help anyone in peril. Once the faster swimmers reached the opposite bank, the cluster of bodies began to thin out. The stronger ones were beginning to pull away and set a punishing pace that would be the tone of the day. In the distance, we were able to observe a few women keeping up with several of the faster men.

The warriors that I needed for the coming raid had to be sound of body and able to travel great distances by foot and on water. The women that travelled with us needed the same endurance. They had to be as fit as the men that they travelled with, and they would carry as much importance as my best warriors.

15

WÀBANANANG'S JOURNEY

WÀBANANANG

When Corn Dog gave the signal for the race to begin, Little Wolf and I started out with the leaders. My captor had told me I did not have to run this race since he was taking me anyway. I'd known this all along, but if I went without my daughter Pangì Mahingan, she would be adopted into a Mohawk family and it could be the last that I would ever see of her. All winter I had run with her to strengthen her legs and taught her the tricks of running in a group. During that time I had not realized there was going to be a race; I was preparing her for our future escape. Tall for her age, smart, and the daughter of a great warrior, she caught on quickly with the training. She would be the youngest runner by far, and that should work in her favour. The older women would not even consider her a threat.

Our plan was to let the faster ones and the ones who thought they were fast to lead the way. We would maintain a pace that would not burn our energy reserves, saving our strength for the portion of the race when the course turned for camp. My daughter and I would run an Omàmiwinini race. I cut two small switches, one for each of us. A few brisk slaps with these small, whippy maple branches soon caught the attention of the person ahead of you and distracted them long enough to whoosh by. Pangì Mahingan became adept in this Omàmiwinini art, with my instruction.

The raid that Corn Dog and Winpe were planning was twofold: one of revenge and one of mourning. The revenge part was to slay my husband Mahingan, who had been the cause of the loss of Haudenosaunee warriors in the battle six summers ago. The mourning part was to capture women and children to bring back as captives to become slaves or adoptees into families that had lost members of their families those six summers ago.

I knew I was the bait to snare my husband. Nevertheless, I had plans of my own, which included saving my daughter and my family left behind.

If my daughter earned a spot among the ten, they would have to let her come on the raid. Corn Dog would lose face if he did not allow her, even if she was a child and an Omàmiwinini. He had set the rules. All who earned their spot had the right to go. There were exceptions, like the two foolish warriors who broke a tribal law by killing a kàg and leaving it to rot in the woods.

If I was going to make my escape, I wanted my daughter with me. There would only be one opportunity, and that would be during their attack or an attack on his group. All other times we would be in either a canoe or walking on the trail in the middle of the war party column. Once in enemy territory, the night camps would have guards posted at all times. When we came close to the Magotogoek Sìbì, I would know where I had to go and would be comfortable with the surroundings.

My daughter was now almost seven summers old. My heart ached because we had been here that long. I had been two months pregnant when captured. I had not yet revealed to Mahingan I was with child, waiting until I started to show to surprise him. She was born during a thunderstorm in the month of the Wàbine-Miskwà Tibik-Kìzis (Pink Moon, April), doing it alone without the help of a midwife, no sweet grass to burn, or soothing tea to help with the pain. That previous fall I had collected as much milkweed silk as I could and stored it in a dry space. At least my new child would have a soft absorbent cloth to keep her bum dry in its clothes. She came into the world along with a flash of lightning, a much easier birth than I had expected. After I wrapped her, we lay in the small hutch I had made to give birth. The rain came down in torrents but no water reached us. We fell asleep together there on our first night, her feeding off my breast and I dreaming of my husband Mahingan and my past life.

That day over six summers ago, the day that I hid my son during the Haudenosaunee attack, after making sure he was safe, I made my way back to the village. On my way I heard noises in the woods beside me. Crouching down, I watched as the village came under attack. In the moments of indecision about what to do, an enemy warrior grabbed me from behind. I remember stabbing the man with my knife and then blacking out. When I awoke, the stench of wood and flesh burning numbed my senses, saddening me because I knew that this battle had not ended well for my people. I was bleeding and groggy, but better off than the Haudenosaunee warrior who had tried to end my life. He was lying dead beside me. I started to rise but passed out again. When I came to again it was to the pain of being dragged feet first. A young warrior was pulling me by my legs to the fires. Grabbing a stick, I raised myself up to a sitting position and started beating him in the back of his legs. Dropping me in surprise, he turned toward me, raising his war club to smash me on the head. I jumped to my feet and prepared to defend myself with the stick. Before he reached me, an older warrior with the markings of a leader stepped in between us, and spoke in a tongue I could not understand. The younger warrior slouched and backed away, all the while looking at me with rage.

Then, speaking in our language, he said, "You have the tattoo of a wolf, unlike the other women of your village who only tattoo lines on their faces. You are a leader's wife! You are Mahingan's woman! Come with me." He sneered.

During the journey back to their village, the leader healed my wounds. At the Battle of the Falls, he gave me to the young warrior and I never laid eyes on the leader again. Upon reaching their village, I became a slave for the young warrior's mother. She tried to beat me many times but I always fought back. After three moons, the young warrior traded me to Corn Dog for a deerskin and a quiver of arrows.

Corn Dog, staring at me after the barter, said, "I know of you and who you are; you will be of use to me in the future."

He never physically protected me from harm, but whenever I defended myself that person never bothered me again. After a while they left me alone. I cooked and cared for Corn Dog's needs, and he never took me to his bed while I was there.

I often wonder if he knew I had helped the three Susquehannock boys escape. Was it part of his plan to let Mahingan know I was still alive and that there was now a daughter? He was a devious one, this Corn Dog. Always thinking ahead.

Running with rhythmic strides, our breathing became even and unlaboured. Some of the participants that had started out fast were now tiring, and Pangì Mahingan and I were starting to pass them. By taking my mind off the actual running motion and concentrating on my past, I made the time fly by.

Crossing the river had slowed many down. As we exited the water and climbed the banks, we still encountered a huge group jostling, pushing, and wheezing through the forest. The sounds around us that broke the silence were the continuous pounding of feet, crunching leaves, and sticks breaking from leather moccasins and the few barefooted runners. The tempo of the surrounding runners' breath as they tried to take in enough air to keep their bodies fed with the Great Spirit's nourishment were coming in loud gulps. Overhead, the tendesì (blue jays) and àndeg (crows) voiced displeasure with the intrusion into their areas.

Some of the runners ahead would push aside branches that then sprung back and slapped the following person in the face or shoulders, causing them to stumble and, if the branch was big enough, to fall, causing others behind to slow or stagger and trip.

Pangì Mahingan was not tall enough for this ploy to work on her. I always kept a close eye on the person ahead and was able to avoid the dupe by reacting quickly. My right forearm had taken a couple of good swats and was bloody and welted. This helped take my thoughts off the oncoming pain that the rest of my body was starting to experience from the run. Glancing at my daughter, I watched as she ran with a smile, singing songs that I had taught her to help control her breath, to pass the time, and to take her mind off the pain.

When we had crossed the river, we had taken off our footwear and tied it around our heads with leather to keep it dry. Some runners had not, and when they exited, their moccasins were full of water, causing some to fly off the their feet, sending them scurrying to seize their wayward shoes amongst the churning feet of the other runners.

The day before we had set out on our run, my daughter and I had put mullein leaves in our moccasins to help pad them.

The route that the elders had chosen for the race was not overly strenuous. They were looking for skilled runners with stamina and agility. There were a lot of deadfalls and rocks to scramble around and avoid, but very little climbing.

Every once in a while my daughter would look up and say, "How am I doing?"

My answer was always, "We are getting nearer to the end!"

By midmorning, we made the turn. There were many behind us. I reasoned that only about a third of the group was in front of us. Of the ones ahead, very few were women. Leading everyone was Winpe, always wanting to prove his prowess as the dominant one! Now the time had arrived for us to proceed with what we had trained for.

Looking at Little Wolf I shouted, "Kijìkà (Go)!"

We then sprang forward, catching those ahead of us off guard with our burst of speed.

Thoughts again came to my head of the man I almost slew who tried to come to me in the night. Of the Stadacona warriors who had identified me as an Algonquin and also suffered the wrath of my skinning knife. Again, Corn Dog kept me safe with his words. Never because he cared for me, only because he had revenge on his mind and I was an essential part of the coming plan.

He was showing me that my life belonged to him and that when the time drew closer he would control how I die, not someone else.

An old Haudenosaunee woman had approached me after the first incident with the man in the night and cackled with a toothless grin, "Corn Dog wants you and your man roasting together in the fires; he has much to avenge!"

Now, as Pangì Mahingan and I sped up, we laid our small switches on two young women running ahead of us. The sudden shock of the stinging switches caused them to break stride, enabling us to pass. I turned to look back at them; they wore a look of shock, and then they started to laugh and point at us. My daughter, hearing the women laugh, started to giggle, making the laughter contagious. The other runners within hearing as well started to chuckle too.

For Pangì Mahingan, with her height and long legs, running came naturally. For this race I had bound my breasts tightly with a piece of leather that I had taken from a discarded pair of leggings. I noticed that others stared at me in wonderment when I ran by them with no bouncing. Even some of the warriors noticed, pointed, and smiled.

Finally, we came to the river again, in a deeper spot. Tying our moccasins around our necks and then tucking them in our shirts behind our heads to keep them dry, we entered the river. Little Wolf hung on to my leather top and kicked her feet to stay afloat while I slowly waded through the water, not fighting the river but becoming one with it. Then I started to swim with Little Wolf hanging on. This was where we gained on all the competitors. Others fought the river while we let the watercourse's strength guide us to the opposite shore. Praying to Michabo, the Creator of water, to guide us, we reached the opposite shore and crawled up the bank. Putting on our moccasins, we ran as fast as we could, crossing the end near the front of the racers.

The old women at the finish were laughing. Corn Dog met Winpe at the finish and both glared at me. Now I had them thinking.

Corn Dog

Once the moving mass of individuals disappeared from my sight, I and the other warriors lowered ourselves from the lookout.

Entering the village, I approached a longhouse that had a fire going by the front door. Hanging over the flames was a steaming bark container with an old man dipping a bone spoon into it and transferring the misty broth to his toothless mouth.

Sitting beside him, I reached into my jacket and took out my own spoon. We sat there taking turns filling our utensil. Not a word was spoken until he looked at me with broth dripping off his chin. "Your enemies are stronger than you may think; they have mysteries that our people have never encountered. Beware!"

With that, he passed gas, stood up, and disappeared into the dwelling.

I sat there and continued helping myself to the meal. A spotted dog approached the fire and tried to stick his head into the pot. A quick motion of my hand drove him back. He stood there watching to see if I would leave. After a while he gave up, went to lie nearby in the sun, and soon went to sleep. Sitting there, I watched as the flies circled the soup and the dog. Lost in thought, I fell asleep.

Boom, boom, boom beat the drums. *Aye, aye, aye.* I woke with a start. The drums were beating. Was my mind playing tricks on me? The women were singing? No, there could not be any women that close to the men in this race! Winpe and the men and women who were striving to join my war band were entering the village. As I started to stand up, the previously sleeping dog, in his anxiety to approach the noise, ran through my feet, causing me to drop to one knee. From there the only view I had was of the tangle of legs and feet of the village occupants and the onslaught of hyperactive dogs eagerly scurrying to where the gasping and sweaty race participants would finish. As I rose to join the melee, my face and mouth were splatted with mud flung in the air by the feet and paws of the anxious mob.

After wiping my face and spitting out small bits of dirt, I was able to find a high spot to see the finish. In the first five or six finishers I could see Winpe, but to my astonishment the Algonquin woman and her daughter were right there with them.

Approaching Winpe, I asked, "How can this be? This woman and her young daughter running a race like this and finishing so well?"

Winpe gazed at the woman, turned to me, and said, "She is an Otkon Yakon:kwe (Spirit Woman)!"

I thought back to what the old man had said. *"Your enemies are stronger than you may think; they have mysteries that our people have never encountered."*

Wàbananang

After Pangì Mahingan and I had finished the race, we sat down and watched the others finish.

Once everyone was done, Corn Dog called together the warriors and women who had succeeded in earning a spot and said, "We will leave for Sharató:ken (Saratoga Springs) in the morning to take in the strength and healing qualities of this sacred place. Then we will proceed to the Caniaderi Guarûnte (Lake Champlain). There we will pick up our canoes that our people will have made for us."

Unlike where the Omàmiwinini live, the Haudenosaunee do not have an abundance of birch trees in their homeland. They make canoes by peeling the bark off large elm trees. It takes five or six days to build a boat like this, but the result produces a strong boat that seems to serve them well.

During the evening, the drums started and the people danced and sang songs about past battles. Everyone ate their fill and then near the end of the night the women brought out clay pots. Filling them with a mixture of sand and corn kernels, they hung them over the fires. Our people, the Omàmiwinini, had never done anything like this. After a while, I could hear a sound like when a bone is popped open coming from the pots. Once the sound stopped, the women lifted the pots with a pair of sticks so they would not burn themselves. Then, turning the container upside down, they spilled the contents on the ground. Standing nearby, my nostrils caught the pleasant smell of the corn that now transformed into what looked like white fluffy flowers. I hastily grabbed some. I shared with Pangì Mahingan, and we ate and smiled at each other. It was good. For the rest of the night the village women kept making this new food until all had had their fill.

That morning, while the mist still surrounded the village, Corn Dog and Winpe gathered the one hundred and eleven who had earned their spot on this journey. Single file, we walked silently into the fog trailed by a dozen war dogs, disappearing from sight and into the legends of the people.

16

SPRING HARVEST AND THE DECISION

MAHINGAN

"Anokì, Anokì," I screamed.

Very few of our people were strong swimmers. Most were just able to keep themselves above water and get to shore in times of peril and not much more, myself included. In spite of this, I now found myself running to the riverbank with a pounding in my head and drenched from nervous sweat. Just before I leapt into the water, I could hear to my right a resounding splash that covered my already sodden body with river water. Turning toward the sound, I was able to glimpse the head of Ishkodewan moving frantically to the bobbing figure of my son, swimming into the gushing torrent of white water. As powerful as this wild beast was on land, the dominance of the river could easily defeat him.

For what seemed like an eternity, I stood and watched the big wolf gain on my rapidly vanishing son. It was as if I were in a trance. I could not move, nor speak. Battling through the powerful current, the huge animal never faltered; defeating the force of the mighty river, he grasped the boy by the scruff of his neck in his huge mouth and turned toward shore. Anokì was gagging and spitting water. The wolf snapped his huge head to his left side and the boy grabbed onto to the scruff of the wolf's neck, pulling himself up onto the animal's broad back. With renewed vigor, the beast forced his way through the flow and clambered up the riverbank. Anokì dropped down from his safe perch to the grassy ground and lay on his back. Ishkodewan stood over the boy and violently shook the water from his fur, covering my twice-soaked frame. The wolf then lay beside my son and started licking him. Leaving my dream-like state, I kneeled down, embraced both the animal and my son, and with tears in my eyes thanked Kitchi Manitou for this wondrous life-saving event and Nokomis for leading me to this big wolf when he was a pup.

There was not a word spoken by anyone until Anokì raised his hand up, opened his fist, and excitedly exclaimed, "See, Father, I got the frog I was after!"

Everyone started to laugh and Nigig's two daughters came and grabbed the boy to dry him and find him warm clothes.

I reached into my leather bag, retrieved a piece of dried meat I kept for an emergency, and gave it to the wolf, who gulped it down in one bite. Grabbing the animal by the neck, I hugged him as hard as I could while he gave me huge lick with his rough tongue.

Standing up, I caught the eye of Mitigomij. He said, "Well, that certainly broke the stillness of the day." Then he smiled and walked away.

Looking to the edge of the forest, I could see the massive black cat lying there with his huge tail twitching, knowing all the time that between the wolf, the cat, and Mitigomij, Anokì had protection from all sides.

That night around the fire I watched as Anokì sat and ate his supper, sharing it with Ishkodewan. The wolf sat patiently waiting for the boy to feed him small scraps of meat.

The boy was a fast learner, even though he sometimes reverted to an inquisitive child at times, as he had today. Mitigomij was teaching him the way of the hunter and the boy caught on quickly. He was able to snare small game, and the time was approaching when he would become strong enough to draw back a bow sufficiently to bring down a deer, or an enemy if need be. He had been taught long ago never to pass between the fire and an elder or a visitor, never to speak when others were speaking, and finally never to make fun of a disfigured or crippled person. Being brought up with Mitigomij and his handicap, I do not think that it ever entered Anokì's or any of the other children's minds that his uncle was different. Then there was Kànikwe's heavily scarred head; here again, the young children never stared at his disfigurement. They accepted him for who he was: a strong warrior they looked up to. Many times Kànikwe has told his story around the fire, recounting the battle long ago with the Haudenosaunee and the reason he had no hair.

Because of the near drowning of Anokì, we made the decision to camp below the rapids for the night. Before I slept, I formed a plan to bring my family back together. With my son spared death today, I took it as a sign that I now must trek to the lands beyond, find my wife and daughter, and re-unite my family. Tomorrow we would continue to the falls, where our people would gather to spear and net fish, feast, and talk about the future.

I would not stay with my group after the spearing of the ogà, name, and namebin below the Asticou (boiling rapids) at Asinabka; I had a quest to start and a sense of urgency about it.

The next day dawned with a glorious sunrise, revealing the immense blue sky and the river sparkling and calm. We ate a hurried meal, loaded the canoes, and glided into the current, heading toward our anticipated meeting with other family groups.

My wounds from the Battle of the Falls sometimes caused stiffness in the cold, wet weather. Nevertheless, today, with the warm sun shining down, the scars of the battle felt like they were healing just a bit more. As I paddled, my thoughts slipped back to the aftermath of the conflict. Our Shaman had to use several stitches to close up the wounds on my right arm and left shoulder. He then used a poultice of yarrow leaves to help heal the damage. The healing process took many painful days. Now all that shows are scars that the sun cannot colour. After tending to the bloody wound he used onagàgizidànibag (plantain) to help reduce the swelling of my left shin. He mashed the leaves of the plant, and after mixing with water, he applied a poultice to the shin, wrapping it with moss and tying it with leather. After the swelling subsided, a huge discolouring of the area appeared, which became tender to the touch. To help cure this, I would hold juniper branches above the fire, heating them and then wrapping them around the bruised area. After a moon, my wounds for the most part healed and I was able to walk without a limp. Still, even to this day the shin will bother me at times.

The noise of the sacred rapids awakened our hearing before we caught sight of them. As our canoes neared, the river current grew stronger and the colour of the water started to whiten and become foamy in spots. Closer yet, we could feel dampness in the air from the spray caused by the power of the falls. The two women and No Hair directed our group toward the shoreline. Once we reached the beach, two old friends appeared from the forest and aided our landing upon the rocky shore: Pangì Shìshìb (Little Duck), the leader of Agwanìwon and Kìnà Odenan's old family unit, and Minowez-I (War Dance). Two friends who had answered my call for help those many years ago.

Once the boats were on shore, more people came from the woodland and assisted us with our possessions. The constant chatter of the women and the laughter of the men caused our dogs and the big wolf to start barking, and that brought their dogs out to the waters' edge on the run. After a lot of growling, snarling, and posturing, the big pack of dogs seemed to merge into one contented mass. The resident pack quickly realized that there was an alpha wolf dog, and none of them wanted any part of that!

Anokì's feet barely touched the ground as he jumped from the canoe.

"Stay away from the falls and the frogs," I yelled after him.

"Yes, Father," he replied as he ran toward the other children with the big wolf at his side.

I watched as Anokì grabbed Ishkodewan around the animal's neck. The wolf never lost a step dragging the boy along with the small dog nipping at the boy's heels, trying to pull off his moccasins, while Anokì squealed in delight the whole time. Then the wolf stopped and rolled with the boy on him and the small dog caught up in the turmoil. That was the cue the other children needed, and soon it was just a massive ball of children and dogs wrestling, laughing, and barking, adding to the voices of the already excited adults who were rapidly catching up on news; the sounds of a happy village.

I watched as Agwanìwon and Kìnà Odenan carried the deerskin from their canoe. They were preparing to tan the hide by scraping all the meat from the skin. Once they finished that job, they would rub the deer's brain into the hide to help cure it. They would then take the hide to the river to wash and to help soften it. After that, they would stake it on the ground until it dried. Once dried they would again scrape the hide clean of any meat they had missed, again working the brain into the skin. Once completed, they would chew on the pelt to soften it to make shoes, leggings, and shirts from the deer's contribution to our well-being.

Kànikwe came ashore along with the others of the band and began to set up camp among the old wàginogàn that we used every spring and fall. It only took a few small repairs to make them livable. Some of the people would still sleep under their canoes or just by the fires. The spring will do that to the people. Forced to crowd together all winter for warmth, now all they wanted was a bit of solitude at night.

The family leaders came together to plan the next few days and to make sure there were out guards away from the camp for protection. Mitigomij, of course, took on this job, gathering the young warriors, among them the three Susquehannock youths, Abgarijo, Oneega, and Sischijro.

"Mahingan," exclaimed Pangì Shìshìb, "we have a surprise for you and your people in the morning before we spear the ogà."

"My friend," I answered, "I have seen the stones and sticks that are piled in the big clearing. I know what the morning will bring!"

That evening our friends fed us, and in no time at all the food containers were wiped clean. Everyone's bellies were bloated from eating too much. As we lazed around the fires and lean-tos, warriors searched in their pouches for nasemà (tobacco) to share. After they lit the pipes, the stories started to flow about winter hardships and successes, deaths, and births.

That morning I awoke to the loud sound of *keck, keck*. I opened my eyes and watched what seemed to be an early morning soft snowfall covering the landscape around my head and my beaver blanket.

I soon realized that it was not snow that was falling on the camp. "Omìmì (pigeon)!" I muttered to myself.

As I looked up into the early morning sky, the birds blackened the heavens so thoroughly that it seemed like it was still nightfall. They had left their perches to find food for the young ones in the nests. As I looked up, I watched as the hawks and eagles attacked the seemingly endless flock. The raptors dove into the mass and always left with a bird clutched in their talons.

Many a time I have watched these omìmì blacken the sky for days as they flew by during migration. This flock was nesting nearby, and there would be as many as the insects on the ground. When the birds hatched and before they left the nest, our people would take blunt arrows to shoot into the bottom of the nest and knock the birds out onto the ground. Other times we would cut long saplings and poke the nests from their perches. Their roosts would have from twenty to fifty nests in each tree. Their diet consisted of mostly nuts, acorns, beechnuts, and chestnuts. In the summer they foraged on berries, worms, caterpillars, and snails. The young nestlings were good eating. Today, though, we would go after the adults.

Everyone rushed to the piles of rocks and sticks. The birds were flying very low and each person snatched something from the pile to hurl into the air. Birds immediately started falling. The young children raced around, gathering the fallen stones and sticks, putting them in piles within reach of the adults. During this time, if the child came across a fluttering bird on the ground, he would snap its neck to put it out of its misery. There were so many of these birds that all morning we threw at them until our arms tired.

The women and children spent the rest of the day pulling feathers from the birds, cutting them into strips and hanging them to dry. After two or three days, they would pack the dried meat in birch bark containers, along with dry grass for storage. The women saved the fat from the birds to mix with berries later in the summer.

Minoweziwin told me that the birds had been nesting now for almost three weeks and that the young fledglings would soon be big enough to go after once our families were finished at the falls.

While the preparation of the omìmì continued, the men started searching for straight saplings that we could cut and make into fishing spears. The bones of the deer that had been slain recently would now be used to make spear ends. The older boys took on the task of barbing the bones and cutting strips of the deer hide to use to help fasten the finished bone onto the saplings the men brought in. Once the men had gathered enough spear shafts, we sat down and notched the ends for the barbed bone. Sliding the bone into the notch, we heated up some pine gum using just enough to be able to fill the gaps around the bone. As the gum started to harden, we took wetted strips of deerskin and wrapped them around the end of the spear. We tied the skin on as tight as we could and then, once it dried, it would tighten even more.

While the men toiled at making spears, the women were working on the fishing nets. During the running of the fish, our people would go out onto the rivers and drop nets, spearing the fish from the canoes and from along the shore. The job of the small boys walking the shoreline was to gather the fish speared from land and take them to the women and girls to clean, dry, and smoke. The boys also made sure there was enough wood for the smoking fires. The men spearing and netting from the canoes used birch bark containers to store the fish until they came back to shore, where they would take the catch to the women.

We worked all that afternoon until dark. More family units would be coming to the camp in the next few days for the running of the pickerel at the falls. When they arrived, we would have enough spears made for everyone and then the harvesting would start. The Flower Moon would bring up the water temperature, signalling the fish that it was now time to run the rapids and proceed to their spawning beds.

Tonight we would feast on omìmì roasted over the fires, our bellies full again for a second evening. It was so different from when we suffered through the Wolf and Snow Moons of the winter, eating maybe every second day if we were lucky. The spring weather led to the Algonquin families coming together, along with new life sprouting from the ground, rivers, skies, and the emergence of baby animals. When the family units converged, there was always the sound of babies laughing and crying, new life as well for our people. The winter moons, though, took our old and weak, some from the lack of food, others from accidents or in some cases our enemies. The cold, icy fingers of Kitchi Manitou would take others when they were not careful on the hunt.

Spring, though, always brought promise along with the renewal of the land. With a bit of luck our numbers would have grown from the previous fall, with the newborns outnumbering deaths from the past winter. Our allies to the west, the Ouendat, and our enemies to the south, the Haudenosaunee, had the climate, the land, and the ability to grow their own food, a gift from Kitchi Manitou. My people only survived by hunting, gathering, and trading for food. Our friends the Ouendat lived in large villages and there was a constant strain on them to feed all their people. Fields of corn, squash, and beans surround their villages. Even though there was protection in numbers, I sometimes thought that our way of life was much more relaxed. We did not have the constant worry for rain to provide moisture to grow the three sisters. Digging in the soil with pointed sticks to plant seeds, then making sure the weeds do not take over, and the hungry animals do not devour the plants once they start to sprout, was not the Omàmiwinini way.

The Omàmiwinini were happy to hunt, gather, trade, and war. This tilling of the soil looked like too much time and bother. Our women were very successful at gathering berries, fruit, and roots to eat. We could live off the land. Forcing the earth to provide seems unreasonable. Our brothers to the west liked to trade for our furs, and we were happy to receive their corn, beans, and squash in return. Even though the winter season shrunk our bellies, our lives were still good. Our people did not grow as tall and heavy as our brothers the Ouendat, but our warriors were just as fierce and our skills as fine as all others and superior in most ways. We knew how to endure and were able to work with what the Great Spirit had given us!

Mitigomij approached and said, "Brother, the fish will come tomorrow once the sun has reached the midday sky."

I nodded. The time was nearing for me to tell him I knew of his abilities and magic. I would require his warrior skills and the power of the big cat for what I had planned in the coming days.

That night during my sleep, a dream came to me. In it was my wife Wàbananang holding out her hands to me. As I looked at her, a young girl walked from the bright light that shone on my wife.

"This is Pangì Mahingan, your daughter," a voice said.

Then the light dimmed and Wàbananang's final words as she disappeared into the darkness were, "We will find you when you come for us."

I awoke to the sounds of new voices in camp. Most of our immediate family units had arrived. My head, though, was still full of the dream. Now I had a vision to support what I was planning. A good omen to lead me to my wife and child. I would need warriors to follow me! The call would go out for volunteers after the spring fishing was over. For the Omàmiwinini warriors, taking up the war club and accompanying me would be their decision and no one else's.

First things first — the fish were running.

17

THE WARRIOR THEY CALL CRAZY CROW

GLOOSCAP

When we left, Migjigi and his people had promised to care for the two women and the three children who survived the massacre. His group made up a carrier with two poles and a moose skin stretched between them. Here they laid Ta's'ji'jg. Migjigi's warriors took turns pulling it on the trail. One of the women walked beside Ta's'ji'jg to tend to his needs.

E's, Jilte'g, Matues, Apistanéwj, Elue'wiet Ga'qaquis (Crazy Crow), the two big dogs and I, Glooscap, struck out after the raiders.

Jilte'g and I walked side by side. E's had taken Tepgig and was leading the small column. Crazy Crow guarded the rear. The others were following behind us.

"Jilte'g," I said, "tell me about this warrior you call Elue'wiet Ga'qaquis!"

"Crazy Crow," he replied. "Now there is a great warrior and his story I will tell you to pass this time today.

Crazy Crow's Story

Our people found him when he was very small. This was maybe twenty-five summers ago. A group of our people had been hunting near the river that the Wolastoqiyik (Maliseet) called Wolastoq (Beautiful River in the Maliseet language, now known as the St. John River). The Mi'kmaq group was throwing fish nets from the shore when they noticed what looked like an empty canoe coming down the river, carried by the current. On the bow sat a big black ga'qaquis (crow). The crow acted as if he was guarding something. One of our warriors who was a strong swimmer grasped the opportunity to obtain a valuable boat to help with our nets. He swam out and pushed the boat back to shore. The crow never moved. Two of his fellow warriors grabbed the bow of the canoe and pulled it up on the shoreline. One of the men looked into the vessel and said, "A baby!" Everyone ran over to the canoe and looked in. Nukumi, who had travelled with the hunting party that day, grabbed the baby and lifted it out of the boat; as she did this the crow flew off and sat in a tree.

"The little one is a boy," she said.

Nukumi kept the child fed during the rest of the hunting trip and took him to her lodge. We thought that maybe he was from either the Pestomuhkati (translates as "pollock-spearer," also known as the Passamaquoddy tribe of Maine and New Brunswick) or Wolastoqiyik

Nations, but no one ever found out or cared. Always, though, he had a crow around him, on his shoulder, following him on the ground, or sitting in a tree watching over him. Nukumi named him Ga'qaquis.

As a young child, Ga'qaquis was able to supply the home pot with rabbits, squirrel, and other small animals. When he was only nine summers, he killed his first deer, gutting it and bringing it back to the village by himself over the course of three days, not wanting any help.

By the time he was fourteen summers old, he had developed into a strong warrior and hunter, taller than the rest of the boys his age. He made friends easily but seemed more comfortable when he was on his own. Ga'qaquis would disappear for days on end, coming back with either game slung over his shoulder or a scalp hanging from his belt. He made a staff that doubled as a spear. On this staff, every time he slew an enemy, he embedded a bear or cougar tooth into the stick. It soon became a formidable weapon. Just looking at it would make you shiver. Beside his bow, arrows, and knives he had made an unusual weapon. He had taken a couple of stone plummets off one of our nets that we used for fishing. Taking a length of woven rope about three feet long, he tied the plummets at each end. Now the boy we called Crow had a weapon that he would twirl around his head and throw at the feet of an escaping deer, rabbit, or other small game, bringing them down, which enabled him to slay the animal without any further pursuit through the forest. He was also quite adept at using these stones to bring down fleeing enemies.

During the summer of his fourteenth year, Crow slew his first tia'm. After the feast, one of the elders stood up and said, "Your warrior name now will be Elue'wiet Ga'qaquis (Crazy Crow). I have decided on this name for you because nothing stops you from obtaining what you have set out to do. You seem like a man possessed at times with a spirit, there is always a crow near you, and only a crazy man would befriend a crow. Our people think that at times you are crazy. It is a good crazy! Our people are proud that you are a Mi'kmaq and our Elue'wiet Ga'qaquis!"

For the next three days the people feasted and danced. They knew that there was a future warrior among them.

After he received his warrior name, he took a sharp bone and had a fellow warrior carve lightning blots into his forehead and on each side of his face. Crazy Crow then took charcoal from a dead fire pit and rubbed it into his wounds. That was how he tattooed his face.

As he grew, Crazy Crow always was the first to volunteer for any hunting or raiding party, continually the first in battle. The Haudenosaunee and our other enemies grew to fear the warrior with the topknot and the toothed club with the spear point. He was easy to pick out in battle because he was always in the centre of the melee.

How he lost his eye is a story that all Mi'kmaq people know and tell. Crazy Crow and two other warriors were hunting one fall. By this time he was a feared warrior, strong, tall, and ruthless in battle. A leader among our people! The three hunters had just slain a tia'm far from our village.

As they were cutting the animal up to transport back, a small raiding party of nine Haudenosaunee who were also far from their homes surprised them. In the ensuing clash, one of the Mi'kmaq warriors died. The other was knocked senseless and captured, leaving Crazy Crow to fight alone. Crazy Crow stood his ground. Unable to use his bow, he grasped the big staff covered with animal teeth. His first victim he impaled on the spear end of his weapon, pulling the point from the enemy warrior's body as he turned to meet another adversary rushing him. Catching the man behind the legs with the staff, he took the feet out from under him, flipping him on his back. Dropping to his knees, Crazy Crow reached for the knife strapped to his leg and jammed it into the Haudenosaunee's heart. His body now spattered with blood, he rose to meet the third attacker, swinging his staff and catching the man full in the face with the lethal animal fangs. The force of the blow broke the attacker's neck and he crumbled into a quivering ball at the Mi'Kmaq warrior's feet. At that moment, the force of an arrow that entered his left cheek and exited his eye stunned Crazy Crow. While he grabbed the shaft and pulled it from his eye socket, four warriors tackled and brought him to the ground.

The Haudenosaunee warriors knew whom they had captured and quickly made a small fire. They did not want this man to die; this enemy was a true prize who would suffer for days before burning at the stake. Heating a pointed stick from the fire, they used it to close the wound on Crazy Crow's face. Crazy Crow's surviving companion, upon regaining consciousness, could smell the burning flesh from their captors cauterizing the wound. Not a word escaped from the lips of Crazy Crow.

Usually the Haudenosaunee use their teeth to pull out captives' fingernails and then force their hands into a bed of coals. This action stopped the bleeding and prevented infection. They pulled the nails from their captives to prevent them from untying their bindings during the night. Either the Haudenosaunee overlooked this because of a lack of time or they had other things on their minds. They seemed too consumed by cutting off the fingers and ears of the dead Mi'kmaq warrior. After finishing with him, they dug graves for their three fallen warriors. They placed them in the sitting position, laying the dead men's weapons and some food alongside them for their journey to the afterlife. They laid rocks on the graves to keep the wild animals from digging them up. The Mi'kmaq warrior they left for the wild beasts.

Crazy Crow's friend had suffered a broken wrist during the battle. The enemy splinted his wrist and then tied both his and Crazy Crow's hands behind their backs and a noosed rope around their necks to be led on the run to the Haudenosaunees' homes. There they would have unmentionable tortures inflicted on them until they died. Crazy Crow and his companion knew this, and they would have done the same to the Haudenosaunee warriors if their circumstances were reversed. Their foes did not want them to die or lose strength before they administered the pain and suffering in their village. The longer they could make their captives suffer, the more enjoyment it would bring to the Haudenosaunee people. For Crazy Crow and his friend, not crying out during the ordeal would prove their bravery and strength. It was all a macabre game.

Once at the village, the mothers and wives of the men killed in the battle would have the final decision about their fate.

They ran through the forest for two days, rarely stopping during daylight for food or water. At night they tied up the two captives and then trussed them to a tree. The Haudenosaunee covered their own bodies with grease to ward off the insects. The captives, though, suffered the continuous swarms of insects that devoured them while they were bound. Death surely would be more desirable than this.

On the morning of the third day, they reached the village. One of the warriors had run ahead to announce their arrival. As they dragged the captives through the community, women and children threw stones at them. The dead men's wives, mothers, and sisters were crying and hitting the two of them with sticks.

When they reached the end of the rows of longhouses, they looked back and saw the people lining up for the gauntlet. Crazy Crow's companion started to sing his death song. The enemy looked at Crazy Crow for his reaction. He remained silent for a long time, then "AWK, AWK, AWK!" He sounded the crows' distress call. Soon the trees filled with crows.

The people of the village looked up in astonishment at the gathering spectacle.

Crazy Crow and his friend had food and water given to them as they stood awaiting the coming nightmare.

Crazy Crow knew they would not die in the gauntlet; their deaths would not come that easy. Their ending would be to suffer and die in the fires. Even there he knew the

Haudenosaunee would keep them alive as long as possible to test their bravery. At the end, if they were considered strong and brave warriors, the Haudenosaunee would cut their hearts from their ravaged bodies and eat them.

They stripped their captives' bodies and painted them black. Now Crazy Crow knew for sure death was in store for them. The dead warrior's female relatives had made the decision. Painting them red destined them to captivity and spared their lives. Even half red and half black meant there was a chance of survival.

They picked Crazy Crow's friend to go first. A large warrior at the start of the line had a club made from a huge tree knot and hit the Mi'kmaq runner square in the stomach, causing the wind to explode from his mouth, staggering him but not dropping him. As he stumbled forward, sticks, stones, clubs, and bare fists rained down on him. Warriors turned their spears around and jabbed him in the ribs, causing immense discomfort. After much torment, bloodied and dazed from a gash on his forehead, he reached the end, where two warriors grabbed and held him up to watch Crazy Crow's suffering.

Crazy Crow was shoved to the front of the line, only one eye open and the other seeping blood and pus through the dressing. He was a pitiful sight. When they cut his ties, immediately he made a rapid crow fight call: "CawCawCawCaw!" Instantly the roosting crows swooped down and started to attack the two lines of people. While they were occupied with the attacking crows, Crazy Crow grabbed the club from the first warrior's hands, and before he even knew what was happening Crazy Crow was by him. He was fifteen or twenty steps into the gauntlet before the Haudenosaunee even knew what was unfolding. A warrior with a spear tried to stop him, but Crazy Crow made him reel with a blow to the head. With a stunned look, the man dropped to his knees, grasping his head with blood running through his fingers. By then Crazy Crow was on the dead run, swinging the club and slashing with the spear. The Haudenosaunee, meanwhile, were being attacked by the crows and barely realized what was happening with their prisoner. They did not stop the one-man onslaught leaving a trail of bruised and bewildered enemies behind him. When Crazy Crow reached the end, he rushed the two warriors holding his friend. Swinging the club, he knocked the first man senseless and then drove the spear into the other man's chest. He grabbed his companion and they ran into the forest, led by a single crow.

For the rest of the day, led by the crow, they ran, never faltering, even though they had suffered serious injuries. The crow led them to a beehive where they hastily covered themselves with mud from a swampy area. With the mud keeping the stinging bees at bay they were able to grab enough of the honey to treat their wounds with some left over to hastily gulp down to ward off their hunger. Crazy Crow's friend had an ugly gouge on his forehead. Crazy Crow took the honey and slathered the wound, and then he took the resin from a stogon (balsam) tree and smeared it on the cut. The resin would close the wound, allowing the honey to heal it.

Resuming their run, the two men followed the crow over rocks, into small creeks, and through the forest, always trying not to leave any sign that they had been there.

That night when they stopped, Crazy Crow produced a knife. Finding some straight saplings, he snapped three off near the bottom. Taking the knife, he sharpened the ends to a fine point. Not wanting to start a fire, he would have to forego hardening the points.

Covering themselves again with mud to keep away the ravenous night bugs, they went to sleep. Before daylight, the crow woke them. Crazy Crow silently motioned to his companion to follow the crow and that he would come later. The crow had told him there were three warriors running in the early morning light on their trail. He handed his fellow warrior one of the makeshift spears, and his friend left with the crow as his guide. Crazy Crow prepared his trap for the pursuing warriors.

The first one came out of the forest into the small clearing, straight for the fire Crazy Crow had made. Crazy Crow waited until the man had almost reached the fire then rushed out of the shadows, impaling the surprised pursuer with the sapling spear. The man dropped to the ground, squirming around the shaft like an eel. Crazy Crow swiftly dropped to his knees and repeatedly stabbed the victim. Grabbing the dead man's club, he readied himself for the remaining trackers. They were not long in coming. The early morning sunlight caught their glistening, sweat-covered bodies as they left the protection of the forest. Crazy Crow could see the fear in their eyes as they glimpsed their fallen companion. With his knife in one hand and the club in the other, he waited for their onslaught. Just as they reached him, one of the assailant's mouths spouted blood as a sharpened sapling exited his throat. Crazy Crow then caught the remaining

Haudenosaunee full in the chest with the club, hearing the man's breastbone crack with the force of the swing. Gasping for air, the man stood as Crazy Crow slit his throat in one motion with the knife. In a matter of minutes, death had come suddenly to these three warriors.

Crazy Crow turned to the forest as his friend walked into the clearing.

"I thought I asked you to wait for me up the trail?"

His friend replied, "The crow led me in a circle!"

Crazy Crow smiled and said, "We have to leave here quickly. Gather what you need from the dead, scalps included, and then we must hurry. I have a feeling there are more following. These men probably were their fastest runners. Not very good fighters, though."

Crazy Crow and his friend, led by the crow, outran their pursuers. They ran through a fire-cleared area before they reached their lands and stood on a rocky ledge. From there they could see five chasers enter the scorched clearing. Crazy Crow and his companion stood there and gave the sound of a crow's "look here" call: "Caw-aw, caw-aw, caw-aw."

The Haudenosaunee looked up, raised their weapons in a salute, and turned back. Before they returned to their village the next day, they had been able to track and slay a deer. They did not want to come back empty-handed from the hunting trip.

"That, my friend Glooscap, is how the great Elue'wiet Ga'qaquis lost his eye, and is also how I, Jilte'g, came by the scar on my forehead!"

"Jilte'g, that is an amazing story," I exclaimed.

"I owe that man my life," he answered.

"Jilte'g!" It was E's and the dog Tepgig running toward us from where they had been scouting ahead. "There is a valley below where I could see the treetops from my vantage point. The jays and crows are causing a disturbance. I think we may have caught up to the raiders," he exclaimed.

"Elue'wiet Ga'qaquis," Jilte'g shouted out.

"Yes, my friend," he replied.

"Send your crow friend down to the valley to see what is causing the birds down there to be scattering."

"E's, take me to where you have seen this disturbance," said Elue'wiet Ga'qaquis.

Just as they started to leave, a sudden bolt of lightning streaked across the sky, followed by a deafening boom of thunder, causing our eardrums to ring. Then the skies opened up with a torrent of rain, sending everyone running for cover.

18

THE TIME HAS COME

MAHINGAN

We spent the week spearing and netting fish. It was a good harvest. Everyone worked at something. The children transported the catches to the women, the older girls helped the women clean and dry the fish, the older boys helped with the nets. The dogs werc getting their fill from the fish guts, although most of these innards were going into the pot at night. When we became bored with fish for a meal, the pigeon meat would reappear. Twice during the past week, Mitigomij's young warriors brought in a deer and a few rabbits. With all these people, there were many mouths to feed. The community was not long beside the fires at night before finding their beds. The days were long and busy.

Near the end of the first week, some of the elders had hunted a flock of geese up the river away from the falls, and that night we eagerly looked forward to a meal of nika.

After about ten days, when we were nearing the end of the harvest, a small group of four Ouendat braves landed above the falls.

We went out and met them with welcome hands. The Ouendat (Hurons) were our most loyal allies.

The tallest of the group spoke. "I am known in our language as Tsou'tagi (Beaver). These are my friends, Achie (White Ash), Öndawa (Black Ash), and Önenha' (Corn). My father is the one you gave the Algonquin name Ozàwà Onik (Yellow Arm). He fought with you at the Battle of the Falls against the Haudenosaunee over six summers ago."

"Tsou'tagi, I remember well your father's bravery," I replied.

Looking at his friends, I saw they were all tall and sinewy. The two brothers, Achie and Öndawa, had the familiar Ouendat scalp lock, were bronzed from the sun and dappled with black body tattoos. Their fourth friend, Önenha', had not yet shaved his head in their style; instead, he had long hair with turkey feathers braided in, a few arm tattoos, and a scar on his chin that was as red as a ripened anìbimin (cranberry). Tsou'tagi shaved his head like the brothers. There were no tattoos on his body, but there were several lines etched into his forehead and cheeks.

"Mahingan, my father said that if we wanted adventure this summer, we may find it with you. That's why we are here. At this time, hunting or warring, we are here to be at your side."

With a smile, I replied, "Welcome my friends. I may have what you are looking for!"

After a few more days of harvesting fish, the people decided that they had all they needed, leaving the rest to spawn. We all enjoyed eating fish broth loaded with the eggs that women saved from the gutting process.

Some of the women would make strings of fish heads and throw them into the water tied to the end of a stake or tree branch on shore. They did this early in the harvest because the heads needed to lie in the water for six to seven days. When taken out the women cut off the noses for the pot and the rest of the head given to the dogs. The Haudenosaunee would have used these heads to fertilize their corn, planting a fish head with a corn seed. We just ate them.

On the night of the final day of harvesting, we held a great feast. The fires burned high and the drums played long, the people stripped down and enjoyed the freedom of wearing no clothing for the first time since the fall snows. There was a lot to eat and our stomachs were bloated from all the food.

The family units would stay for three more days. The first day they would rest and the second day they would go into the forest with blunt arrows and long poles to poke and shoot the bottom of the omìmì nests to knock out the nestlings. These young omìmì were a delicacy for my people.

The next morning I called together all the men and asked for volunteers to go with me on my quest for my wife and daughter. Algonquins never had to go on the warpath if asked; it was their own free decision to go. If they thought they were following a brave and capable leader, many would follow him. If the warrior asking for men was not a revered warrior, few would risk their lives for him.

It being early in the spring, I knew that few of the married men wanted to leave their families since many of the women were close to birthing. This I expected.

The four Ouendat warriors stepped forth immediately, followed by the three Susquehannock boys. My brother Kàg, the twins, and my brother-in-law Mònz quickly came to the front. My sister Wàbìsì was with child; Kinebigokesì made the choice to stay and help her deliver her first child. The two of them would travel with the others to the summer camp. Never ones to avoid a good fight, the two warrior women Agwanìwon and Kìnà Odenan, along with their friend Kànikwe, also stepped forward.

Lastly, the Wàbanaki family that spent the winter with us stepped ahead, and the father, Nigig, said, "It is time we went home, Mahingan, to our tribe for the summer."

Before he could volunteer, I asked Odìngwey, the young Ouendat who had suffered a wound at the fight for the elk, to watch over my sister and sister-in-law. I knew that his wound was still bothering him, and by me personally asking him for this favour, he would not lose face among the other warriors.

"I will be honoured to do this for you, Mahingan!" he replied.

I was relieved that Nigig and his family had made the decision to come. The four women from his family would be a valuable addition to this small band on the trail. I also thought the twins and Nigig's two daughters shared a mutual interest! And Anokì would have some younger company.

Mitigomij was standing to the side. Everyone knew because of his limitations, long-distance raids were a good reason for him not to come.

Walking up to him, I whispered in his ear, "I know your powers and your secrets."

I saw a faint smile appear.

He whispered back, "Then I will accompany you. When on land I will find my own way."

Seventeen warriors, four women, and Anokì — a small group, but very capable. If the Susquehanna brothers were correct and Corn Dog was raiding our eastern allies before us, we would have an advantage in knowing his whereabouts. Getting to the Wàbanaki and Mi'kmaq first would strengthen all concerned and give us time to lay a trap for him and rescue my wife and daughter. Although small in numbers, our group would be able to travel fast.

That night we loaded six canoes for our journey. Each canoe would carry one dog: my two, the wolf, and his constant companion the Pìsà Animosh, who were both Anokì's guardians.

My brother's black panther, as always, would patrol the shore.

That night the village held a feast in our honour. Pangì Shìshìb and Minowez-I came to me during the evening, and Pangì Shìshìb said, "Once the rest of the family units arrive at the summer camp and all are settled in, myself and Minowez-I will ensure the village is well protected with scouts on a constant patrol. Then he and I will gather a group of young warriors to come look for you. At the most, we should not be any more then twenty suns behind you. Hopefully it will not be too late for the help you may need!"

"I will look for you. Knowing that you are coming will ease my heart, my friends!" I replied.

The three of us embraced, sat down by the fire, and filled our bellies.

19

IT STARTS

THE RAID BY THE STADACONAS and the ten Haudenosaunee warriors that Corn Dog had left with his allies turned out to be quite successful. The small Mi'kmaq village proved to be an easy conquest. The raiding party was composed of an equal number of Stadaconas and Haudenosaunee, plus three Maliseet warriors that the Stadaconas had forced to lead the raiders to the village. The aggressors had struck early in the morning, catching the village groggy from sleep. The defenders had put up a spirited defence, men and women, but the leader of the assailants, Onekwenhsa Okàra (Blood Eye), and his followers were brutal in their ferocity. They hacked and slashed their way through a small group of men that rushed to the defence of the village. One older woman had gathered a group of children around her like a turkey hen protecting her brood.

Defiantly, she stood her ground with a rock in one hand and a stick in the other, daring his men to try to do harm to her charges. Her bravery saved herself and the children from harm, but not from capture.

Onekwenhsa Okàra personally slew the chief. He then skinned him and tied him to a tree, arranging the trap of arrow and spearheads set into the ground to damage the feet of any unsuspecting Mi'kmaq that became intent on untying the seemingly alive victim.

The battle was quick and decisive. One Stadacona died during the initial onslaught, taking an arrow in the throat; two suffered superficial wounds and would live. The three Maliseet warriors they left on the battlefield. The attackers carried the fallen warrior from the burning village with the intent of burying him before nightfall.

The invaders, besides reaping the benefits of the meagre stores of food and furs of their conquered foes, had also captured the old woman and the six children she was harbouring, two other women, and two men who would supply entertainment once they returned home. The younger women and children should prove useful to their home village, while the old woman, if she survived the passage back, might prove useful as a slave.

They stopped to bury the fallen warrior as the sun started to descend. Blood Eye took this moment and approached the old woman.

"What is your name?" he asked.

"Nukumi," she replied.

"You were a brave woman today protecting the children. I could have easily clubbed you to death, but I admire your daring! The future may not hold the same kindness that was shown to you today."

"Your destiny was decided the moment you and your ravenous dogs of war wiped out my village," she snarled. "You think you are safe? Smell the air around you. It smells like death. Death is stalking you right now! My son Crazy Crow by now has met Glooscap. With the Tall One's help, Crazy Crow will have your scalp before you reach your hidden canoes and escape on the river!"

Nukumi watched as the colour left her adversary's face. More than any living Mi'kmaq, his people feared this one the Mi'kmaq called Elue'wiet Ga'qaquis. His people and the Haudenosaunee called him Tsyòkawe Ronkwe (Crow Man), as brave and brutal an enemy as they had ever encountered. As much as he wanted to meet this feared warrior on the battlefield, now was not the time. The advantage now rested with his pursuers; the Stadaconas did not have the advantage of familiarity of their surroundings.

Nukumi watched as Blood Eye turned to his men, who were occupying themselves with jabbing their spears into the chest of Gesga't Ji'nm (Lost Man), one of the two captured Mi'kmaq warriors. Gesga't Ji'nm sang his death song, which irritated his torturers. They could not get him to cry out in pain; he just kept singing his song. Gesga't Ji'nm's body was covered with puncture wounds from the spear points and his hands dripped blood from where they had pulled out his nails. The singing of his death song stirred the crows and jays into leaving their forest perches, cawing and screeching their displeasure at this encroachment on their homes.

Nukumi sat and smiled. The birds were sending out a message.

Blood Eye snapped at his warriors, “Hurry! We have to distance ourselves from this land. Any captives who cannot keep up, put them under your clubs and leave them for the wolves!”

As his men gathered up the male captives, Blood Eye reached for his war club; he was pondering ending the old woman’s life when a huge bolt of lightning lit up the day sky, followed by earth-shattering thunder. Then the rain and wind came, drenching them in seconds. They rushed for cover. He watched Nukumi as she gathered the children and two young women, shoving them all under a huge overhanging pine tree. Just as she disappeared under the tree, she looked back at him, laughing and smiling in an eerie manner.

Mahingan

The next day my group of Omàmiwinini warriors and allies left at sunrise. The waters were calm and the smell of new life was in the air with the budding of the trees. Our friends that had not come for the harvesting of the fish would now be taking the sap from the trees to share with others. Food was always a community effort to be shared. Elders and orphans were never shunted aside, either families took them in or Two-Spirited people cared for them. My people have always been this way: share and we become strong. Hoarding among us does not promote unity of the community, and it is a sign of weakness and greed. There was no such thing as theft among us; if someone was in need all they had to do was ask and they received what they needed. Food, tools, weapons, shelter, and all other needs we gave in a cooperative spirit, always for the betterment of the community.

Our journey to the Magotogoek Sìbì was uneventful. Agwanìwon, Kìnà Odenan, and Kànikwe kept us in fresh game. The two young girls and Anokì became adept at fishing from the canoes during the day. It took us eleven suns to reach the big river, although we lost almost two days when a big storm kept us on land. After the storm, the biting insects came at us in droves. The dogs and my wolf continually snapped at them and shook their bodies to rid themselves of the pests. We, on the other hand, were able to coat ourselves with protection and swallow the ones that entered our mouths. Digesting these flying biters did not give us much sustenance; mostly we just spit them out. We always looked forward to the heat of the day and a bit of wind, because this seemed to drive the hordes ashore.

Once on the big river we had to be careful. The Hochelagans lived near the mouth of the Kitcisìpi Sìbì and the Magotogoek Sìbì. Once we neared their lands, we went ashore for the rest of the day. There was a huge set of rapids that we had to portage around at dusk, then creep by their village on the opposite shore during the dead of night with only the light of the moon to guide us.

Once past this danger, we were able to make good time with the current during the day. We were now aware that another danger might present itself. Haudenosaunee! The big river was their domain when they came north from their lands up the Magwàizibò Sìbì. We made it past this river with no incidents.

Nigig's village was south of the lands of the Mi'kmaq and Wolastoqiyik. He was enjoying the time his family was spending with our group. His family had been gone from their village now almost three years. They had ventured north on a trading trip to the Mi'kmaq and then accompanied them to our lands, wintering with us while the Mi'kmaq returned. The four women in his group now had urged that, whatever happened on this trip, they wanted to stay with us. Nigig thought it was because his daughters had decided the twins were in their future.

I smiled at him and said, "Nigig, you are welcome to stay as long as you want. You and your family are appreciated by all, not just the twins."

"Thank you, Mahingan," he replied.

We made the decision to go ashore, hide the canoes, and continue on foot, not wanting to risk being sighted passing the Stadacona village. The river narrowed there, and everyone that passed through did so with the knowledge that the inhabitants would see them.

When we went ashore, to keep Mitigomij's secret as long as possible, I said that he would continue solo in his canoe, meeting us each evening to camp, when in reality he and the panther would be ahead of us, with Mitigomij shape-shifting to travel as the Trickster Hare.

After three days, we came upon a ridge looking into a small valley. As we stood overlooking the trees below, we watched as a mixture of crows and jays began taking to the air, voicing their displeasure at something that disturbed them. As the birds rose to flight, Mitigomij appeared from below. He was just opening his mouth as a bolt of lightning flashed across the sky, followed by earsplitting roll of thunder and by a sudden cloudburst that sent us all for cover. Mitigomij followed me to an outcrop of rocks that was large enough for the two of us to stay dry. I watched as Anokì followed Ishkodewan and the small dog to a low-hanging spruce, where the three of them crawled under out of the weather.

"Brother, there is a problem below!" Mitigomij advised.

"What is the problem below, my brother?" I replied to his hurried warning.

"A party of Stadaconas and Haudenosaunee, maybe twenty in total, and they have captives. They were torturing one of the men just before the storm came upon us. His singing disturbed the birds and they took flight, sending out a forest warning," he replied.

"Yes, we noticed their alarm from here. They have a few more warriors than us; however, we will have the advantage of surprise."

"Ah, my brother, there is more. He held up a crow feather for me to see. Our old friend Crazy Crow is on the other side with his Mi'kmaq family. This feather means they are preparing to attack. Whoever strikes first between our two groups will send the enemy on a line of retreat to the other. We have to attack now, to aid the Mi'kmaq in their plan!"

Crazy Crow was a Mi'kmaq warrior who Mitigomij had competed against a few times in games between our tribes. Both were revered by their people as fierce warriors and competitors in the games. Crazy Crow and my brother had become fast friends, creating a lifelong bond. Though they had never fought beside each other, their friendship was unquestionable.

As Mitigomij disappeared down the slope, I could see the big cat leave his hiding place to follow his friend. What shape my brother took from here was beyond my guess. I did know, though, he would be with us when needed.

Turning to my followers, I warned them to be prepared; death awaited us down there if we were not careful. As I explained to the men and the warrior women what lay ahead, they reached into their bags and produced bits of charcoal to smear black on their bodies and coloured powders that they mixed with water to mark their faces.

I called the Warrior Women and my brother Kàg forward. "Agwaniwon and Kìnà Odenan, the two of you take Kànikwe and the three Susquehana brothers to the left. I will lead the Ouendat warriors up the middle, and Kàg, you take the rest up the right side. Nigig's family and Anokì can follow at a distance behind. I will leave the dogs as protectors with them, and they all can handle weapons if an enemy breaks our line. Ishkodewan will accompany me."

We silently walked through the forest. Whenever we brushed up against a leaf, it dumped its store of water on our bodies, causing our war paint to run in spots. Above our heads, the sun tried to shine through the treetops, creating a sparkling effect as the light reflected off the droplets that the soft wind was moving from the trees. Overhead I caught the glimpse of a solitary crow circling in the sky. It seemed to be intently watching something travelling below. Every once in a while the bird tilted its wings, as if pointing at something.

My ears were attuned to the sounds of the forest. On both sides I watched as our warriors crept forward, patiently waiting for the sounds from either Mitigomij or the Mi'kmaqs that should direct us to our quarry.

Wàbananang

Once Corn Dog and his men left the village, they kept a hurried pace through the forests of their lands. Pangì Mahingan and I were able to keep up with very little effort. We had proven our skills, much to the distaste of Corn Dog. The man was becoming suspicious!

Corn Dog was taking the men to Sharató:ken (Saratoga Springs). Here they would take in the spiritual healing powers of the hot springs. All the tribes in the area used these healing springs because they thought that this was where the Great Spirit lived. The place was also a neutral area for all the tribes. All who came to the sacred springs could travel and rest unmolested.

Once we arrived, Corn Dog sent warriors out to hunt for game. Upon entry to the springs, we found a group of Muhhekunneuw (Mohicans) who lived in the area using the springs. Even though they were enemies, the area was sacred and the two groups of men sat and shared food and news. The women used this time to enjoy the springs.

I could feel the healing powers of the spring the moment I sat down. The warmth of the waters made me drowsy and I turned to see my daughter fast asleep with just her head above the warm waters.

That night we enjoyed a peaceful rest, even though the Haudenosaunee were among enemies. The next day the men left all their clothes in a pile. We also removed our clothes, and gathering the men's coverings, we searched out several anthills. Here we laid the clothes out on the hills for the ants to feast on the lice and nits, eradicating the pests from our clothes. The men, meanwhile, were taking in the warmth and healing of the springs while shaving their heads, leaving only a centre cut of hair. This would eliminate the head lice that became prevalent from the close winter quarters of their longhouses.

The women continually used bone combs on each other's hair to pull out the little bloodsuckers. The Haudenosaunee were able to keep most of the bugs from infesting them by using pine needles in their bedding. It was not a flawless prevention but it certainly aided in the fight.

My people did not have as much infestation as the Haudenosaunee because we did not live fifty or sixty people to a lodge in the winter months, which gave the bugs ample breeding opportunities. Our warriors, unlike Corn Dog's men, did not have to shave their heads to rid themselves of the problem.

After spending three days at the springs, our group left. The Muhhekunneuw had left the previous day, happy that they were able to avoid a confrontation because of the sacred grounds.

It took us a day at a quick pace to reach the canoes. A group of men from Corn Dog's village had spent the early part of the spring preparing them for this group. The land of the Haudenosaunee does not have the birch trees that are prevalent in the land of the Omàmiwinini. They have to cut down huge elm trees then burn out the inside by putting tree rosin on them. Keeping a careful eye on the log while it burned, they would scrape away at it with clamshells. The whole process would take a moon. There were six canoes waiting for us when we arrived, with paddles for everyone. With the boats holding eighteen to twenty paddlers each, it only took us seven suns to make the big river. The only things that slowed us down were the few portages and the constant repairing of the boats.

Corn Dog did not stop at the Hochelagan village. His agreement was with the Stadaconas, and he knew that if the Hochelagans caught sight of an Omàmiwinini woman in their midst it would create a problem that he did not have time to solve.

The Haudenosaunee travelled swiftly with so many paddlers and we reached the Stadacona village in six suns. The only holdup was half a day ashore, staying out of a steady rainfall. The night they stayed in the Stadacona village, Pangì Mahingan and I had to stay with the boats with four warriors. Corn Dog told me he did not want another incident like the last one.

The next morning Corn Dog and his warriors came back to the boats. He was in an angry mood. The old chief only gave him fifteen warriors. The old man told him it had been a rough winter with nearly twenty elders and children dying from starvation. He needed men to go out and hunt to restore his people's health. The lack of Stadacona warriors maddened the Haudenosaunee war chief, but there was other news that caused him great anger. The old chief had given permission for some of his warriors and the ten men he left behind last year to take up the war club against the Mi'kmaq. This foolish action would alert and put his enemies on their guard. Entering the Mi'kmaq territory in secrecy now became that much more difficult. The enemy would be on edge and prepared.

Myself, I was beginning to wonder if there would be a chance for our escape. Corn Dog would not take the women into battle, which would be our chance for freedom. The Omàmiwinini Nation had allies to the south in the Wàbanaki Nation. That was where we would head. Mahingan and I had travelled there many years ago, and I could still find my way to their main village using landmarks and stars.

Snarling, Corn Dog said to his friend Winpe, "Have them load the boats; we leave immediately!"

The Stadacona men piled into their own vessels, and the eight canoes hit the water.

Little did I know that as we made our way downstream and as the sun made the noon sky, we were passing my husband Mahingan and his men, plus a group of Mi'kmaq and the Stadacona raiding party who were on the south shore of the river. For some reason I looked back toward that shore, and away in the far distance just barely in my eyesight I glimpsed the distant horizon and thought I had seen a blackening of the sky by a flock of birds. I could not be sure, though, since our boats whisked through the water, driven by the current that was hurrying us on our way. We were hugging the south shoreline when a bolt of lightning streaked across the sky, and then there was an ominous boom. Muscles strained as we quickened our paddle strokes, making for shore. Once we beached the canoes, they were overturned. Then warriors and women scrambled for shelter under the boats and to the nearby forest as the skies opened up with a driving rain. In the frenzy, I snatched a bow, a spear, a quiver of arrows, and a sack of corn. I grabbed my daughter's hand and we disappeared into the forest under the cover of a curtain of rain. We had to put as much distance as we could between the shore and us, hoping the storm kept Corn Dog unaware that we had vanished. I turned to Pangì Mahingan and said, "Run as you have never run before, my daughter!"

I handed her the spear, slung the bag of corn, arrows, and bow across my shoulders, and we ran for our lives and freedom.

20

THE CLEANSING RAIN

MIGJIGI

Migjigi and his group of Mi'kmaq, plus the survivors of the massacre, reached the shores of the sea without any incident. They were able to hunt on the way, building their strength up as they travelled. The young warrior Ta's'ji'jg was improving as each day passed. The women hovered over him like a turkey hen. It would not be long before he was able to walk again. The wounds never became infected and his appetite in no way faltered, helping him to regain his health.

Upon arriving, they discovered a group of about one hundred and fifty of their people, among them about thirty warriors. One person stood out. A boy, maybe fourteen summers old, with hair the colour of the sun and strange furs on his body. He was taller than most of the Mi'kmaq people gathered there.

Walking up to an old Innu friend who had brought a group of his people to trade and spend the summer, Migjigi asked, “Who is the boy?”

“He is an Eli’tuat,” was the reply.

His friend then told the story. “We reached the seas six suns ago, and as we came out of the forest on stood on a hill overlooking the shore, we noticed an Eli’tuat ship in the distance. I recognized it as a similar vessel from a previous visit seven summers ago. During that occasion, they tried to take several of our women who were digging clams on the beach. The ship, though, was quite a distance from shore and motionless. Diverting our eyes from the sea, we noticed a group of Mi’kmaq approaching from the east, walking on the beach. From our vantage point, we could see the small river running to the sea where we always camped. Here a huge sand dune that some trees had taken root on blocked the view of the river mouth from the nearing Mi’kmaq on the beach. As we looked down to where the river met the salt water, we noticed two boats. The Eli’tuat had come ashore for fresh water and there were several of them filling large wooden containers on the boats. Further along the shore, away from the dune, this young man was digging clams. The Mi’kmaq were going to stumble onto the Bearded Ones without advance notice for either of them. I quickly sent one of my men down to the beach to warn our friends and tell them we would attack once they gave the signal. The Eli’tuat had not brought any dogs ashore with them to warn of intruders, nor had they posted any sentries.

“Attacking from two sides, we forced the strangers to their vessels under a volley of arrows and spears. Only a few of them reached the boats without an arrow protruding from their bodies. One man had taken a spear in the throat and his companions struggled to drag him to the safety of their vessels. Even though many of them had wounds, they were able to get the oars into the water and leave the shore out of our arrow range, leaving one boat behind.

"Just as the Eli'tuat left our reach, I heard a yell and looked around to see the boy charging me with a stick he had picked up from the beach. Sidestepping his charge and turning my spear around, I struck the charging man-child square on the forehead, dropping him in his tracks with a resounding thud. The other warriors stood around staring in awe. I instructed two of my men to take him to our women and have them watch over him until he regained consciousness. Someone this young and this brave would not see the fire stake. He would have a future with us."

"Makadewà Nigig, it is good to see you again," said Migjigi. "I am happy that this time some of our people did not fall in battle with these Eli'tuat, as in previous encounters! I also see that you have taken some weapons from the boat they left behind."

Migjigi then told his friend the story of the attack on the village of Ta's'ji'jg and the death of his father.

"Migjigi, I have a feeling there may be more trouble coming. Our enemies will think we are weak and return in greater numbers. We must be wary and have out guards at all times this season!"

"I agree, Makadewà Nigig."

...

Glooscap

The rains came down steadily until midday. The ground had not yet dried from the spring melt, and the added barrage of moisture from the skies created a quagmire in spots. For the most part, my Mi'kmaq companions and I had been able to stay dry. Apistanéwj had surrounded himself with the two dogs, staying warm and dry. Arising from our sheltered spots, we soon discovered that staying dry might not be an easy chore. The droplets that caught on the leaves of the surrounding forest were now making their way off these small catch-basins that had briefly impeded their travel. Seemingly, they were making one last stop on their way to the forest floor — our bodies. We removed our shirts and rolled them up to keep them dry. The sunlight beamed through cracks of the forest's guardian trees and glistened off the shirtless warriors.

Crazy Crow approached our small group with his ga'qaguis sitting on his shoulder. "My friend has informed me that those we seek are below. They are preparing to leave now that the rain has ceased."

Jilte'g quickly replied, "We attack them now before they gain higher ground on us!"

"Oh, but there is more my friend," he replied. "The crow tells me that there are warriors on the far ridge. He whispered to me that they were Omàmiwinini and some Ouendat that he could see. Allies to our Nation! There is a powerful friend with them. He is the warrior Mitigomij, a friend from long ago. I will send my bird to the air again with a crow feather in his mouth. Mitigomij will know its meaning and know I am close by. This day will be ours!"

Nodding at my small friend and his two dogs, I grabbed the Eli'tuat axe and shield. We followed our friends into battle.

Blood Eye and his warriors crept from the sparse shelter they had sought during the sudden and prolonged cloudburst. He hastened his men to break camp, and just as they were gathering their weapons, he heard a crow. Looking up, he saw a huge man swinging a weapon he had never seen in his lifetime. The last thing he remembered was feeling the weight of the weapon on his neck, the crunch of his spine, and blackness.

Glooscap

I swung the big axe with all my might at the man in front of me as he bent over picking up a spear. For a moment our eyes met, him motionless and struck in a pose of horror, myself with my arms straight up in the air, starting the descent of the axe. The weight and momentum of the weapon carried me forward as the sharpened blade cleanly severed the man's head, causing both the warrior's body and skull to drop at my feet simultaneously with a resounding thump.

Turning, I caught a glimpse of Crazy Crow swinging the staff he carried. The jutting animal fangs that he had on the weapon had become red from the blood of his victims. As I prepared myself to continue, I watched as he took a bone-crunching swing at a Haudenosaunee combatant, the fangs of the weapon entering and embedding in the man's upper torso. Not wasting any time disengaging the weapon, Crazy Crow reached for his two knives and waded into the melee, slashing and slicing at all who approached him.

Frantically, I searched the battlefield for my small friend and the two dogs. Upon seeing them, my heart almost came to my throat. Apistanéwj and the dogs were taking on three warriors who had cornered him. The little one and the dogs had made their way to Grandmother and the children and were defending against all comers. One of the attackers had one of Apistanéwj's arrows in his shoulder and two dogs on his legs ripping his thighs. Apistanéwj stood in front of Nukumi with his war club raised. As I approached, an enemy warrior moved toward me from my left. I swung my shield upwards and felt his chin give way as my shield struck his face. Just as I neared my friends, there was the horrendous scream of a wild animal. Then, from the forest, a huge, snarling black cat grasped hold of the man nearest Grandmother and the two of them rolled in a tight, bloody ball. Next, a crack like a falling tree branch exploded in my ear and a Stadacona warrior dropped to his knees with a huge hole in the back of his skull. At that moment out of the darkness of the forest, before I could even imagine moving, a muscled warrior limped out with a war club and brained the man struggling with the two dogs. I stood awestruck as Crazy Crow strode by. He winked at me and embraced this warrior. "Mitigomij, my old friend! I see you still are keeping company with that wild cat. He has not eaten you yet?"

...

Mahingan

As we crept through the forest, my wolf started to growl. I whispered to the Ouendat men, "The time is near!"

Then I heard the sound of a crow's fight call, followed by the forest echoes of men yelling. Led by the big wolf, we charged into the noise of battle. Immediately our small group came head-to-head with three young Haudenosaunee warriors. They were frantic and tore into us like wild animals. I caught the sound to my left of the sickening thud of bones breaking. Following the reverberation of the noise, the Ouendat warrior Öndawa crashed at my feet. Raising the hand with my war club in it, I turned to face a scowling man just inches short of myself, wearing a hat of feathers. He was preparing to take a swing at me with his club. I raised my weapon to block his attempt, which the man's powerful swing knocked out of my grasp. With my club dangling on my wrist by the leather thong, I had no time to regrip the handle. With my other hand, I took a jab at him with my spear, using an upward motion that caught him in the armpit. The spear broke the skin with a spurt of blood but did not slow down my adversary.

I swung my right arm upward, hoping to flip my club onto the palm of my hand. During this motion to retrieve my only defence, I watched in dismay as my foe swung his weapon at my head. In that instant, before the crushing blow, the man disappeared from my sight in a blur. Looking to my right I realized the enemy was now in a death struggle with Ishkodewan. The big wolf had the man by the neck, dragging and shaking him as if he were a small rabbit. The warrior did not utter a sound as the grip on his throat suffocated him. I took my spear and drove it into his chest. Calling off my wolf, I bent down and thanked him for his timely appearance.

As I rose, I watched the three remaining Ouendat warriors unmercifully clubbing and hacking to death another of our foes. In the woods there were small, scattered duels going on between attackers and defenders. I approached a small clearing and found Mitigomij embraced by Crazy Crow. With them was a giant of a man, a little person, and two dogs unlike any I have ever seen before. My wolf growled a warning at them, but I raised a hand to him. In the hands of the tall man I noticed a strange weapon covered with blood and a different kind of shield from our own.

Crazy Crow stepped forward to embrace me, saying, "My friend, it is so good to see you again! Please meet my new companion Glooscap and his warrior friend Apistanéwj. They have travelled to the Land of the Mi'kmaq with the guidance of Nukumi, my mother, who says these two very different-sized warriors have special powers yet to be discovered. Myself, they have impressed me with their bravery. Although the little one seems the spunkier of the two!"

Everyone broke out into laughter, relieving the stress of the battle and close brushes with death.

As with every battle, there are the losses to mourn. Because we were able to ambush our foes, we kept our losses to a minimum. The three Susquehanna boys, Abgarijo, Oneega, and Sischijro, had all suffered wounds. Oneega's was the most serious, an arrow in his left shoulder. Nukumi, with the help of Nigig's wife, was working on his wound, trying to remove the arrowhead and applying healing herbs and salves. We had lost two warriors, the Ouendat Öndawa fatally wounded, along with one of the Mi'kmaq warriors, Matues.

The Haudenosaunee and Stadacona had suffered more losses than us: six dead and maybe as many wounded. We had captured two of the wounded men, and the Ouendat men were presently taking liberties with them by the fires. The captured men were singing their death songs in preparation for their demise.

No Hair and the two warrior women had taken to the forest to chase down the escaping remnants of this war party. Knowing those three, they would never give up until they chased some of the fleeing warriors down.

Tonight we would bury our dead, rest, and plan our next moves. I began telling Jilte'g what the Susquehanna brothers had relayed to me about Corn Dog's plans when Crazy Crow interrupted.

"My friend the ga'ququis has brought back disturbing news."

21

THE CLASH OF NATIONS

JILTE'G AND I BOTH stared at Crazy Crow.

"The crow says that a woman and young girl are running toward us in the forest. A large force of Haudenosaunee is pursuing them. Two or three times as many men as we have! And more that stayed behind with their boats."

With my heart in my throat, I asked, "How close are they?"

"Not far, but she is veering off to the south. She seems to know where they are going. They are probably Maliseet women."

"Crazy Crow, they are not Maliseet. I think they are my wife and daughter," I replied.

"Your wife!" he blurted.

Quickly I told him the story of her capture close to seven years ago.

Jilte'g broke in and said, "We do not have enough men to take on this force."

"I can get men," Crazy Crow said. "There is an old shaman I know in the Maliseet village close to here. If I send the ga'qaquis, he will know enough to follow with a force. I always told him that if a crow came to him, it was from me. He was to gather as many men as he could and follow the bird because I was in need. He will come with help."

Crazy Crow whispered to the crow and sent him off.

Just as the bird left, No Hair and the Warrior Women returned with no prisoners, but they were carrying bloody ears.

Crazy Crow looked at Kànikwe and saw the scalp hanging from his war club.

"They call you No Hair, I am told! Whose famous scalp is that on your club?"

"It is mine," he replied. "I took it back from the warrior who had ripped it off me in the first place."

The Mi'kmaq warrior looked at Kànikwe and roared out a huge laugh. "This man and his female companions will come and sit with me! Come, everyone around the fire, it is a full moon tonight and there is no time to waste. If we are to save this woman and child, this is what has to happen."

Wàbananang

We had been running for most of the day, stopping only twice to drink from streams and to take a handful of corn. The dry corn swelled our bellies with the addition of water, staving off our hunger.

"Pangì Mahingan, my daughter, how are you doing?"

"Fine, Mother," she replied. "You can set the pace faster; I can keep up!"

So far we had been able to keep ahead of the pursuers I knew were behind us. If caught, I was sure it will be the fires for me. My daughter might still figure into Corn Dog and Winpe's plans, saving her life if caught.

"Mother, look, an àndeg (crow). It is flying so low!"

The bird, shockingly, landed right on my shoulder. I turned and looked into the bird's eyes, and then it raised its head, kept nodding it, and flew off. I watched as it circled then came back.

"Mother, it wants us to follow! Let's do it!"

Thinking it a sign, we followed the bird through the densest part of the woods, hoping beyond hope that someone was watching over us.

Mahingan

Crazy Crow had divided our force. It was a gamble. To the young Mi'kmaq, E's, he gave the task of leading Kàg and myself to a sheltered ravine in the deep woods. Here, he said, one of his feathered friends would be leading Wàbananang and my daughter to us.

Nigig's family, Nukumi, and the Mi'kmaq captives we had rescued were left with the three wounded brothers and the two Mi'kmaq men that were barely hanging on to life from being tortured.

Crazy Crow had taken Glooscap, Apistanéwj, Mitigomij, and the two big dogs. As hc left with this group, he turned and said, "With these warriors I can take on anyone!"

The other eleven warriors split in two groups. Jilte'g took the three Ouendat warriors and Nigig. Mònz, the twins, No Hair, and the two Warrior Women were left together.

Seventeen against forty or more elite Haudenosaunee warriors. Very poor chances if the Maliseet warriors did not get to us in time.

The plan was to get my wife and daughter to the protection of the ravine. Crazy Crow and his group would stay between the oncoming Haudenosaunee and us, with the other two groups staying to the sides, hidden and trying to pick off the enemy from their concealment.

Corn Dog

"Winpe, this woman and her daughter are well conditioned. We need to try to get ahead of her and double back. I am taking six of our best runners and we are going to circle and come back to her. She must not outrun us. You keep pressing from the rear. I have had enough of this woman. She will feel the flames of the stake once we capture her!"

Mahingan

E's led the wolf, myself, and Kàg to the ravine. We sat down and waited, watching the sky for the big crow Crazy Crow had sent. I was just dozing off when Ishkodewan started to growl. Quickly standing, I looked to the sky. There was the bird, and then I could hear hurried footsteps. Out into the small clearing ran a woman and a young girl. They stopped suddenly with fear in their eyes. The woman drew an arrow into her bow.

I yelled, "Wàbananang!"

Dropping the bow, she cried, "Mahingan!" and wrapped her arms around me, sobbing. "I love you!" she said. Then, turning, she held out her hand and said, "This is your daughter, Pangì Mahingan."

Just as I bent down to reach her, I felt an enormous pain below my left shoulder blade. Looking down at the front of my shoulder, I saw an arrowhead protruding through from where it had entered my back. Still with presence of mind, I was able to guide my family to a jumble of huge rocks near the small stream that ran through the ravine. We had barely reached the cover when another arrow hit me and tore through my right leg. Stumbling, I fell behind a huge rock for shelter. Looking up, I watched as my wife loosed two arrows in quick succession. E's and Kàg were beside us. Kàg, though, had an arrow protruding just below his ribcage on the side of his heart.

The pain was excruciating. I grabbed the arrow in my shoulder and pulled it through. Then I did the same with my leg. The blood spurted out, but with the help of my daughter I was able to jam clumps of moss into the holes and stem the flow. Reaching for my arrows and bow, I thanked my father under my breath for teaching me to pull back a bow with either of my hands. After holding the bow and loosing one arrow, I realized that I did not have the strength in my left shoulder to do this. I used my feet for a bow brace and loosed an arrow at a shadowy figure in the tree line. I was losing strength and could taste blood in my mouth.

"Brothers," I could hear Mitigomij yell, "we cannot reach you from here. You have to hold out."

"Mitigomij, Kàg, and I have taken arrows. You have to get Wàbananang and my daughter out!"

"I have spent what seems a lifetime without you, my love; I will not leave again of my own free will," my wife whispered to me. "Mitigomij, it is I, Wàbananang. Send the Black One down for my daughter. She has to live!"

Then a shout came from the tree line. "Mahingan, it is I, Ò:nenhste Erhar. I have come for you today, for you, your brothers, and all who are with you. Today you die."

I had no energy to answer him; I could feel my strength slowly disappearing. One of the Haudenosaunee charged from the trees, straight for our hiding place. The two others followed him. E's drew his bow and Kàg gripped his war club. Then, over the enemies' war cry, I heard the distinctive crack of a slingshot. Looking back out from around our cover, I watched as one of the rushing men's heads cracked open like a duck's egg. Down he went, skidding to an abrupt stop.

I could hear the twang of my wife's bow as she shot three arrows in quick reply. Then I heard a deep, ominous growl. Looking behind, I stared into the eyes of Makadewà Wàban.

I pointed at my daughter. "Take her." Then to my daughter, "Do not be afraid. Go with him."

The big cat grabbed her behind the neck, holding her shirt in his mouth. With one powerful leap, he was gone.

One of the charging warriors saw this happen and chased the two of them into the darkness of the forest.

"Ishkodewan, go," I said.

The big wolf chased after the unsuspecting man, and as he disappeared into the gloom there was a bloodcurdling scream and then the sound of a wolf howling after it has made a kill.

Mitigomij

Mitigomij and his three companions were trying to keep the enemy warriors below them pinned down. Mitigomij stopped one in his tracks with the slingshot. He started to reload when the forest behind him and his companions erupted in screams.

The four of them turned to await their fates. Warriors started streaming out in ones and twos. The little one stood and fired his bow as quickly as any seasoned warrior. The two big dogs beside him were ready to pounce and defend the small one with their lives.

Crazy Crow, with a big smile on his face, was picking off Haudenosaunee warriors as if it was just ordinary target practice.

Then, out of the trees strode a warrior as fierce as any of them had ever seen, tall and straight, with chiselled features and the lithe body of the finest Haudenosaunee warriors.

"Winpe!" the man's voice boomed. "It has been a long time, my friend, and today we finish this!"

With giant strides, the man Mitigomij knew as Glooscap set upon this warrior.

The first warrior looked out on the land
that was his Home.
He saw the hills
And the stars
And he was happy.
For giving him his home, the first warrior
told the Great Spirit
That he would fight and win many battles
in His honour.
But the Great Spirit said, "No, do not
fight for me.
Fight for your tribe,
Fight for the family born to you,
Fight for the brothers you find."
"Fight for them," the Great Spirit said,
"for *they* are your Home."

AFTERWORD

The character of Glooscap is a very important part of the Mi'kmaq culture. His introduction in this book is a significant new character. Glooscap came from the "Land of Granite" so I introduced him from present-day Newfoundland as an ordinary man. As the story progressed, if the reader knew who Glooscap was in popular lore, they would realize that the little person, the dogs, and grandmother were integral parts of his coming life as Glooscap. In addition, Winpe in the final scene fills out the legendary characters that are part of Glooscap's life and lore.

The Vikings, though, they never could set down permanent roots in this part of the world, would give the Natives of this era a small hint of what was yet to come.

When Natives tell stories of the exploits of their fellow warriors, they are spreading the tales of great warriors and leaders. The ultimate accolade a warrior could receive is that his peers tell the story of how he became a warrior.

Glooscap, told by E's the story of how Scar (Jilte'g) gained the trust and respect of his people in his becoming a warrior, now realized why the Mi'kmaq people respected and followed Jilte'g.

Later, Glooscap is told the story of Crazy Crow by Jilte'g. Crazy Crow's bravery was so extreme it gained the respect of his enemies, and the saving of another warrior's life by putting his own life at risk during this adventure was the supreme test of a warrior.

When warriors go on the warpath they will only follow men who will bring them back alive. On a hunt, again they will only follow men who they are confident will bring them success during the hunt. If they do not trust the leader to do these things, they will not follow him.

In this novel, set during the 1300s, Percé Rock has three arches. The erosion of the ocean eliminated one of the arches, and that is what we see today.

The Vikings' use of a floating board was a pelorus, an ancient sea compass. During cloudy days, they used a sunstone made from Icelandic spar (crystal) to navigate.

Wolverines were eradicated in New Brunswick after the arrival of the Europeans.

Porcupines are not native to Newfoundland, and thus Glooscap would be seeing one for the first time on his hunt with the Mi'kmaq warriors.

ALGONQUIN GLOSSARY

For an Algonquin talking dictionary, please go to *www.hilaroad.com/camp/nation/speak.html.*

Àbita	Half
Achgook	Snake
Àgimag	Snowshoes
Agwanìwon	Shawl Woman
Amik	Beaver
Àmò-sizibàkwad	Honey
Àndeg	Crow
Anìbìsh	Tea
Anìbimin	Cranberries
Animosh	Dog
Anokì	Hunt
Asab	Net

Asinabka	Place of glare rock (Chaudière Falls)
Asin	Stone
Asticou	Boiling rapids (also Chaudière Falls)
Awsìnz	Animal
Àwadòsiwag	Minnow
Azàd	Aspen
Gichi-Anami'e-Bizhiw	The Fabulous Night Panther
Guhn	Snow
Haudenosaunee	Iroquois
Ininàtig	Maple
Ishkodewan	Blaze
Kabàsigan	Stew
Kàg	Porcupine
Kànikwe	No Hair
Kekek	Hawk
Kìgònz	Fish
Kije-Manidò	the Great Spirit
Kijik	Cedar
Kijìkà	to go
Kìnà Odenan	Sharp Tongue
Kìnà	Sharp
Kinebigokesì	Cricket
Kishkàbikedjiwan	Waterfall
Kitcisìpi Sìbì	Ottawa River
Kitcisìpiriniwak	People of the Great River

Kòn Tibik-Kìzis	Snow Moon, February
ʹLenepi	Delaware
Magotogoek Sìbì	Path That Walks (St. Lawrence River)
Magwàizibò Sìbì	Iroquois River (Richelieu River)
Mahingan	Wolf
Makadewà	Black
Makwa	Bear
Maliseet	Malècite
Mandàmin	Corn
Manidò	Spirit
Meʹhiken	Mahican
Michabo	The Great Hare, Trickster God, inventor of fishing
Mìgàdinàn	War
Migiskan	Hook
Minoweziwin	War Dance
Mishi-pijiw	Panther
Mitig	Tree
Mitigomij	Red Oak
Mònz	Moose
Name	Sturgeon
Namebin	Sucker
Nasemà	Tobacco
Nìj	Two
Nigig	Otter
Nika	Goose

Nokomis	Mother Earth
Odàbànàk	Toboggan
Odawàjameg	Salmon
Odenan	Tongue
Odìngwey	Face
Odjìbik	Root
Odjìshiziwin	Scar
Ogà	Pickerel, Walleye
Omàmiwinini	Algonquin
Omìmì	Pigeon
Onagàgizidànibag	Plantain
Onigam	Portage
Ouendat	Huron
Pakìgino-makizinan	Moccasins
Pangì	Little
Pênâ-kuk	Pennacook
Pibòn	Winter
Pikwàkogwewesì	Jay
Pimizì	Eel
Pine	Partridge
Pìsà	Small
Shangweshì	Mink
Shàwanong	South
Shìshìb	Duck
Shìbàskobidjige	Set a net under ice
Tendesì	Blue jay
Wàban	Dawn
Wàbanaki	Abenaki

Wàbananang	Morning star
Wàbek	Bear
Wàbidì	Elk
Wàbine-Miskwà Tibik-Kìzis	Pink Moon, April
Wàbìsì	Swan
Wàbòz	Rabbit
Wàginogàn	Lodge, home
Wàwàshkeshi	Deer
Wàwonesì	Whip-poor-will
Wegimindj	Mother
Wìgwàs chìmàn	Birch bark canoe
Wolastoqiyik	Maliseet

ALGONQUIN PRONUNCIATION GUIDE

From *www.native-languages.org/algonquin_guide.htm.*

VOWELS

Character:	**How To Say It:**
a	Like the *a* in *what.*
à	Like the *a* in *father.*
e	Like the *a* in *gate* or the *e* in *red.*
è	Like *a* in *pay.*
i	Like the *i* in *pit.*
ì	Like the *ee* in *seed.*
o	Like the *u* in *put.*
ò	Like the *o* in *lone.*

DIPHTHONGS

Character:	**How To Say It:**
aw	Like *ow* in *cow.*
ay	Like *eye.*
ew	This sound does not really exist in English. It sounds a little like saying the "AO" from "AOL" quickly.
ey	Like the *ay* in *hay.*
iw	Like a child saying *ew!*
ow	Like the *ow* in *show.*

CONSONANTS

Character:	**How To Say It:**
b	Like *b* in *bill.*
ch	Like *ch* in *chair.*
d	Like *d* in *die.*
dj	Like *j* in *jar.*
g	Like *g* in *gate.*
h	Like *h* in *hay*, or like the glottal stop in the middle of *uh-oh.*
j	Like the *ge* sound at the end of *mirage.*
k	Like *k* in *key* or *ski.*
m	Like *m* in *moon.*
n	Like *n* in *night.*
p	Like *p* in *pin* or *spin.*

s	Like *s* in *see.*
sh	Like *sh* in *shy.*
t	Like *t* in *take.*
w	Like *w* in *way.*
y	Like *y* in *yes.*
z	Like *z* in *zoo.*

HURON GLOSSARY

Achie	White ash
Öndawa	Black ash
Önenha	Corn
Tsou'tagi	Beaver

MI'KMAQ GLOSSARY

For the Mi'kmaq talking dictionary, please go to *www.mikmaqonline.org.*

Apigjilu	Skunk
Apistanéwj	Marten
Apji'jgmuj	Black duck
Apli'kmuj	Rabbit
Apsalqigwat	Have small eyes
Ap'tapegijit	Turkey
Atu'tuej	Squirrel
Bootup	Whale
E's	Clam
Eli'tuat	Men with Beards
Elue'wiet	Crazy
E'pit	Woman

Ga'qaquis	Crow
Gaqtugwan	Thunder
Gajuewj'j	Kitten
Puglatm'j	A little person
Gesga't	Lost
Gespe'g	Lands End
Gespe'gewa'gi	People of the Last Land
Gisu'lgw	Creator
Gitpu	Eagle
Giwnig	Otter
Glmuej	Mosquitoes
Gomgwejg	Sucker fishes (plural)
Guntew	Rock
Gtantegewinu	Hunter
Imu'j	Dog
Jenu	Giant
Jilte'g	Scar
Ji'nm	Man
Jipji'j	Bird
Ki'kwa'ju	Wolverine
L'nu'k	The People
Lentug	Deer
Lentug'ji'j	Fawn
Magisgonat	Big nose
Matnaggewinu	Warrior
Matues	Porcupine
Matuesuei	Porcupine meat
Megwe'g	Red

Mg'sn	Shoe
Migjigi	Turtle
Mui'n	Bear
Musigisg	Sky
Na'gweg	Day
Natigòsteg	Forward Land (Anticosti Island)
Negm	Bloody
Nukumi	Grandmother
Penamuikús	Birds lay eggs, April moon
Sabawaelnu	Half Way People
Saqpigu'niei	I am shedding tears
Siggw	Spring
Stogon	Balsam tree
Ta's'ji'jg	Little bit
Tagawan	Salmon
Tepgig	Night
Tia'm	Moose
Tmawei	Tobacco
Wikuoms	Wigwams

MI'KMAQ PRONUNCIATION GUIDE

From *www.native-languages.org/mikmaq_guide.htm.*

VOWELS

Character:	**How To Say It:**
a	Like the *a* in *father*.
á	Like *a* only held longer.
e	Like the *e* sound in Spanish. In English, the Micmac pronunciation sounds like a cross between the vowel sounds in *met* and *mate*.
é	Like *e* only held longer.
i	Midway between the vowel sounds in *hit* and *heat*.
í	Like the *i* in *police*, only held longer.

ɨ	Schwa sound like the *e* in *roses*.
o	Like the *o* in *note*.
ó	Like *o* only held longer.
u	Like the *u* in *tune*.
ú	Like *u* only held longer.

DIPHTHONGS

Character:	**How To Say It:**
aw	Like *ow* in *cow*.
ay	Like *eye*.
ew	Sound does not really exist in English. It sounds a little like saying the "AO" from "AOL" quickly.
ey	Like *ay* in *hay*.
iw	Like a child saying *ew!*

CONSONANTS

Character:	**How To Say It:**
j	Like *ch* in *char* or *j* in *jar*.
k	Like *k* in *skate* or *g* in *gate*.
kw	Usually it is pronounced like *qu* in *queen*, but at the end of a word, it is pronounced more like a *k* with a puff of air after it.
l	Like *l* in *light*.

m	Like *m* in *moon*.
n	Like *n* in *night*.
p	Like *p* in *spill* or *b* in *bill*.
q	Guttural sound that does not exist in English. Like *ch* in German *ach* or *g* in Spanish *saguaro*.
qw	Guttural sound that does not exist in English. Usually it is pronounced q and a w together, but at the end of a word, it is pronounced more like a *q* with a puff of air after it.
s	Like *s* in *Sue* or *z* in *zoo*.
t	Like *t* in *sty* or *d* in *die*.
w	Like *w* in English *way*.
y	Like *y* in English *yes*.

MOHAWK GLOSSARY

For the Mohawk talking dictionary, please go to *www. ohwejagehka/mohawk.*

Algonquin	Bark Eaters
A'no:wara	Turtle
Andagaron	The middle Mohawk village of the three main ones
Anèn:taks	Porcupine
Atiron	Raccoon
Caniaderi Guarûnte	Door of the Country (Lake Champlain)
Ennisko:wa	Much lateness moon, March
Erhar	Dog
Hahgwehdiyu	Mohawk Creator
Kahònsti	Black

Kaniatarowanenneh	Big Waterway (St. Lawrence River)
Kanien'kehá:ka	People of the Flint, Mohawk
Kanonhsehs	longhouse
Karònya	Sky
Kayènkwire	Arrow
Kionhekwa	Three Sisters
Kohsera'kène	Winter
Kwa'yenha	Rabbit
Ò:nenhste	Corn
Ohiari:wa moon	Ripening time moon, June
Ohkwari'	Bear
Ohnehta'kowa	Pine tree
Ohsahèta	Beans
Ohskennonton	Deer
Okàra	Eye
Okwàho	Wolf
Onekwenhsa	Blood
Onekwenhtara	Red
Onon'onhsera	Squash
Ononta'kehàka	Onondaga Nation
Ossernenon	One of three main Mohawk villages
Otkon	Spirit
Ronkwe	Man
Sharató:ken	Saratoga Springs
Shotinontowane'hàka	Seneca Nation
Ska'nyonhsa	Moose

Sorak	Duck
Tionnontoguen	Mohawk capital of the three villages
Tsi'tenha	Bird
Tsihsterkeri	Owl
Tsyatak	Seven
Tsyòkawe	Crow
Wahkwari'tahònsti	Black bear
Yakon:kwe	Woman
Yonen'tòren	White cedar tree

MOHAWK PRONUNCIATION GUIDE

From *www.native-languages.org/mohawk_guide.htm.*

VOWELS

Character:	**How To Say It:**
a	Like the *a* in *father*.
a:	Like the *a* in *father*, only held longer.
e	Like the *e* in *get* or the *a* in *gate*.
e:	Like the *a* in *gate*, only held longer.
I	Like the *i* in *police*.
i:	Like the *i* in *police*, only held longer.
o	Like the *o* in *note*.
o:	Like the *o* in *note*, only held longer.

CONSONANTS

Character:	**How To Say It:**
h	Like *h* in *hay.*
k	Like *g* in *gate*, soft *k* in *skate*, or hard *k* in *Kate.*
kw	Like the *gw* in *Gwen* or the *qu* in *queen.*
r	Like *r* in *right* in some dialects, but like *l* in *light* in others.
n	Like *n* in *night.*
s	Like *s* in *sell.* Before *y* or *i*, the Mohawk pronunciation sounds more like the *sh* in *shell.*
t	Like *d* in *die*, soft *t* in *sty*, or hard *t* in *tie.*
ts	Like *ts* in *tsunami.* Before *y* or *i* the Mohawk pronunciation sounds more like the *j* in *jar*, and before *hy* or *hi* it is pronounced more like the *ch* in *char.*
w	Like *w* in *way.*
wh	Some Mohawk speakers pronounce this sound with the voiceless "breathy w" that many British speakers use in words like "which," but others pronounce it like the *f* in English *fair.*
y	Like *y* in *yes.*
‘	A pause sound, like the one in the middle of the word "uh-oh."

OLD NORSE GLOSSARY

Björn	Bear
Blakkr	Black
Bleikr	White
Lax	Salmon
Njörðr	The God of sea and wind
Óðinn	Odin
Rakkis	Dogs
Rheindyri	Caribou
Rôdr	Row
Sigla	Set sail
Skræling	Native
Suður	South
Sverð	Sword
Taufr	Red ocher

þræls	Slaves
Ullr	The God of skill and the hunt

SUSQUEHANNOCK GLOSSARY

Abgarijo	Dog
Oneega	Water
Sischijro	Eat

BIBLIOGRAPHY AND SOURCES

BOOKS AND ARTICLES

Berleth, Richard. *Bloody Mohawk*. Delmar, NY: Black Dome Press, 2009.

Costain, Thomas B. *The White and the Gold: The French Regime in Canada*. Toronto: Doubleday, 2012.

Drake, Samuel G. *The Book of the Indians of North America*. Boston: Antiquarian Bookstore, 1833.

King, Thomas. *The Inconvenient Indian: A Curious Account of Native People in North America*. Toronto: Doubleday, 2013.

Long, John. *Voyages and Travels of an Indian Interpreter and Trader*. New York: Cosimo Classics, 2007.

Nerburn Kent. Compiled and Edited. *The Wisdom of the Native Americans*. Novato, CA: New World Library, 1999.

Newman, Peter C. *Caesars of the Wilderness*. Toronto: Penguin Books, 1988.

_____. *Company of Adventurers*, Vol. 1. Toronto: Penguin Books, 1985.

Shimer, Porter. *Healing Secrets of the Native Americans*. New York: Black Dog & Leventhal, 2004.

"Through Native Eyes." *Readers Digest*, 1996.

MUSEUMS

New York State Museum (Albany, New York)
Fort William Henry Museum (Lake George, New York)

WEBSITES

www.accessgenealogy.com
www.firstpeople.us
www.freelang.net
www.heritage.nf.ca
www.historymusuem.ca
www.history-world.org
www.indigenouspeople.net
www.mikmaqonline.org
www.native-languages.org
www.songofthepaddle.co.uk
www.thealgonquinway.ca
www.thenibble.com
www.woodenboat.com
www.viking.no

THE FIRST ALGONQUIN QUEST NOVEL

I Am Algonquin

An exciting journey seen through the eyes of the Algonquin people.

This book paints a vivid picture of the original peoples of North America before the arrival of Europeans. The novel follows the story of Mahingan and his family as they live the traditional Algonquin way of life in what is now Ontario in the early 14th century. Along the way we learn about the search for moose and the dramatic rare woodland buffalo hunt, conflicts with other Native nations, and the dangers of wolves and wolverines. We also witness the violent game of lacrosse, the terror of a forest fire, and the rituals that allow Algonquin boys to be declared full-grown men.

But warfare is also part of their lives, and signs point to a defining conflict between Mahingan's nation, its allies the Omàmiwinini (Algonquin), Ouendat (Huron), and the Nippissing against the Haudenosaunee (Iroquois). The battle's aftermath may open the door to future journeys by Mahingan and his followers.

A 2013 CanLit for the Classroom selection.